The Amazing HARVEY

ALSO BY DON PASSMAN

All You Need to Know About the Music Business

The Visionary

Mirage

The Amazing HARVEY

DON PASSMAN

MINOTAUR BOOKS
A THOMAS DUNNE BOOK ≈ NEW YORK

This is a work of fiction. All of the characters, organizations, and events portrayed in this novel are either products of the author's imagination or are used fictitiously.

A THOMAS DUNNE BOOK FOR MINOTAUR BOOKS.
An imprint of St. Martin's Publishing Group.

www.thomasdunnebooks.com
www.minotaurbooks.com

Designed by Steven Seighman

Library of Congress Cataloging-in-Publication Data

Passman, Donald S.
The amazing Harvey : a mystery / Don Passman. — First edition.
p. cm.
"A Thomas Dunne Book."
ISBN 978-1-250-04187-6 (hardcover)
ISBN 978-1-4668-3914-4 (e-book)
1. Magicians—Fiction. 2. Murder—Investigation—Fiction.
I. Title.
PS3566.A774A83 2014
813'.54—dc23

2013033838

Minotaur books may be purchased for educational, business, or promotional use. For information on bulk purchases, please contact Macmillan Corporate and Premium Sales Department at 1-800-221-7945, extension 5442, or write specialmarkets@macmillan.com.

First Edition: February 2014

10 9 8 7 6 5 4 3 2 1

In loving memory of my Mom, Bea;
Thanks for always taking me to the magic store.

CHAPTER ONE

When I drove my battered green Toyota into a parking space marked SUBSTITUTE TEACHER, the woman getting out of the next car raised her eyebrows. It was probably my black jacket with sequins on the lapel. Could've been my red tie with the yellow shooting stars. Maybe the white cockatiel perched on my shoulder.

I felt the woman's eyes on me as I turned off the ignition. My car shuddered as the engine shut down. I leaned over to the passenger seat and pawed through the mess of papers, crinkling the fast-food wrappers as I threw them on the floorboard. *Ah.* There it is. I grabbed that day's teaching assignment, sat up, and opened the car door. As I climbed out, my bird, Lisa, dug her claws into my shoulder.

I smiled at the woman who was still standing there and said, "Good morning."

Guess she didn't hear me.

As I walked toward the school building, I took Lisa off my shoulder and slid her into the secret pouch of my jacket. My jacket has a secret pouch because it's the same outfit I wear onstage when I do magic. That's my real job: magic. Substitute teaching just pays the bills until I make it as a magician. Well, it pays most of the bills anyway.

See, the real dough for magicians is in Las Vegas. David Copperfield, Lance Burton, Siegfried and Roy in their day. Guys with their own theaters built for them. That's where I'm headed. I've already designed the tricks that'll get me there, and as soon as I have enough money to build them, I'll get a Vegas gig. Maybe just a small one to start. Hey, I'll even work in one of those casinos with a red-and-yellow sign that says 99¢ SHRIMP COCKTAIL. Whatever it takes to get in the game.

In the distance, a class bell rang. *Ooops.* As I picked up my pace, Lisa shifted around in her pocket.

When I neared the redbrick building, I heard the slamming of two car doors. Glancing over at the street, which was maybe fifty yards away, I saw two men dressed in white shirts and black ties, walking away from a parked gray car. Although they weren't looking at me, it felt like they had me in their sights. Something dangled from one of their shirt pockets. Too far away to tell what it was.

I smiled at them. They looked down at the sidewalk, like they didn't see me.

I hurried up the steps to the school building, opened the door, and hustled down the empty hallway of Walter Reade Junior High. The only sound was the slapping of my leather soles. Breathing heavily, I stopped at the administration office, then looked behind me down the hall. No sign of those men from the street.

I opened the office door and went inside. Behind a long counter, three people were standing in a cluster, holding Styrofoam coffee cups and chattering away. A horse-jawed man glanced my way. His eyes widened as he took in my outfit. He tapped a short woman on the shoulder, who nudged a heavyset matron with gray hair pulled into a tight bun. The volume of their conversation dropped, and they gave me those quick glances that you get after someone whispers, "Wait a couple of seconds, then sneak a peek over your shoulder."

The bun-haired matron broke from the huddle and strode my way. She stopped about a foot behind the counter. "May I help you?"

"I'm Harvey Kendall. Subbing eighth-grade English for"—I pulled the coffee-stained assignment sheet out of my jacket—"Mrs. Duggan."

The woman stepped a little closer to the counter. She picked up a clipboard with several pages clamped to it, lifted the half-glasses that were dangling on a silver chain around her neck and set them on the end of her nose. After flipping through a few pages, she looked up. "You're late, Mr. Kendall."

I smiled at her. Truth is, I usually get to class a little late. I think it's better to come in after the kids are already sitting down. That, and the fact that I can't seem to estimate time very well.

The matron placed the clipboard on the counter. "Room two eleven. Second floor."

I spun around and started off.

She called after me. "Mr. Kendall?"

I turned back.

"Do you think that's appropriate clothing for a teacher?"

I turned my palms up. "It'll have to do. My chicken suit is at the cleaners."

I hurried out of the office, climbed the stairs to the second floor, and looked at the numbers painted on the doors. *There.* Two eleven.

Through the closed door, I heard kids talking in the classroom. I looked at my reflection in the door's glass panel and tried to poke down the wildest strands of my curly black hair. Didn't really help. No matter what I do, my hair always looks like the springs of an exploded mattress.

I straightened up, smoothed my coat, and yanked the door open. That shut up the kids. As I walked to the teacher's desk, their eyes followed me. I didn't need much peripheral vision to see a few mouths open.

I turned to face them and said, "Good morning!"

A few of them squinted at me. A couple were stifling grins.

I grabbed a piece of chalk and wrote *MR. KENDALL* on the blackboard. When I finished, I turned around and dusted my hands, so they could see they were empty, and said, "Everybody needs to behave in my classroom. If not, I'll know about it, even if I'm not looking."

In the back, a freckled boy leaned over to whisper something to a blond girl in the next row. He saw me looking at him and straightened up.

I said, "How do I know what's going on behind my back? A little birdie tells me." I whisked a red silk scarf out of my breast pocket and waved it up and down, like I was on a ship about to pull out of the harbor. While the kids' eyes were on the handkerchief, I sneaked my other hand into the coat, grabbed Lisa around her wings, and brought her up behind the scarf. When I let go of her, she flapped her wings and came out of my hands like she was materializing right there.

A couple of kids started clapping. Then everybody did. One boy stuck the tips of his pinkies in his mouth and whistled.

I let Lisa step off my hand and onto my shoulder. She sidestepped toward my neck, then bit my earlobe just like I trained her. I looked surprised and said, "Ow!"

The kids laughed, then sat back in their seats.

I clapped my hands. "So. I understand you're reading *Huck Finn*. Who wants to tell me?—"

The classroom door flung open. The heavyset schoolmarm from the administration office hustled in so fast that the glasses around her neck bounced against her large chest. She stopped a few feet away from me, panting, and looked at the bird on my shoulder. The bird looked at her. The class sat up straight.

The woman curled her lip. "Mr. Kendall?"

"Yes."

Her face was beaded with perspiration. "Could you step outside for a moment?"

"What's the problem?"

She took a crumpled Kleenex from her skirt pocket and dabbed her forehead. "It's a private matter."

Lisa cocked her head, like she was wondering, What's up with the old lady?

A boy in the back said, "Let him stay."

A girl said, "Yeah."

The woman glared at the room, swiveling her head like she was fanning the area with a machine gun. The kids looked down at their desks. The only sound was the squeak of a student's chair.

The woman said, "Please step into the hall."

I whispered, "I only dress like this on the first day. It's just to put the kids at ease."

"Outside, please."

I looked at the kids and shrugged. Most of their eyebrows were raised, like they were saying *Awwww*. I walked toward the door, rubbing the bird's chest with my index finger, as the woman told the class, "Keep quiet and study on your own. Another teacher will be here shortly."

Just outside the door, I saw the two white-shirted men from the street. One of them started toward me.

Now I could see what was dangling from his shirt pocket.

A leather holder with a gold badge.

CHAPTER TWO

The man with the badge looked like he was in his late fifties and stood at least four inches over my five foot ten. He was bald on top, except for a gray patch of frontal hair that looked like a hairy island in a sea of skin. Behind him was a skinny guy with a pencil mustache, carrying a worn leather briefcase.

The badge man stuck out his hand. "Hi. I'm Sergeant Morton, Los Angeles Sheriff's Department. No relation to the salt." He chuckled. The skinny guy smiled like he'd heard that joke a few thousand times.

I shook Morton's hand. "Harvey Kendall."

Morton gave me a quick nod. He gestured toward the skinny guy and said, "This is my partner, Lieutenant Dupont." Dupont stared at me.

Morton turned back to face me. "Nice bird. What's his name?"

"Lisa."

The policeman scratched the back of his neck. "You're twenty-nine years old?"

"Yes . . ."

And you live on Moorpark in North Hollywood?"

"What's this about?"

"Is that you?"

"Yes, yes." I glanced back at the classroom. "What do you want?"

Morton threw his head toward the hallway behind him, in a "Let's go that way" gesture. He said, "The school's been nice enough to let us use one of their offices. We can talk more privately there." Morton turned and walked away. Dupont stepped around behind me.

As I followed Morton down the stairs, the back of my neck prickled with the feeling that Dupont was staying very close. I picked up my pace.

We walked down the main hall, where Morton opened a door and gestured for me to go inside. I glanced back at Dupont, then went into a small office with bare white walls. The only furnishings were a gray metal desk with a high-backed leather chair, and two metal guest chairs.

Morton said, "Have a seat." He gestured for me to take one of the guest chairs. I went around the desk and pulled out the high-backed chair. As I sat, Lisa dug her claws into my shoulder.

Morton lowered himself into a guest chair. Dupont set his briefcase on the floor and stood behind Morton, staring at me.

Morton said, "Were you arrested for a DUI in Virginia a few years back?"

I jolted. Lisa fluttered her wings, slapping my neck. I said, "That was just some college stupidity. The charges were dismissed."

"We know. No problem there."

I leaned back a little. "What do you want?"

"Mr. Kendall, do you remember that they took a sample of your DNA when they arrested you in Virginia?"

I certainly did. They wanted to take my blood with a needle

and I freaked out so badly that I had to be restrained by two officers. I couldn't help it. I have this horrible phobia of needles, because I was really sick when I was a kid and I got a lot of painful injections. The few times I needed shots as an adult, they had to first give me something close to a horse tranquilizer. Remembering it, I felt my pulse beat in my neck.

I swallowed drily. "What's this about?"

"We'd like to ask you a few questions."

"I've got students waiting for me."

"Won't take long." He kept smiling at me. His grin was starting to feel like saltwater taffy, the way it starts out sweet in your mouth but then you keep chewing and pretty soon you think your teeth are going to rot.

I said, "What's this all about?"

"You thirsty? Want something to drink?"

"I guess. . . ."

Morton turned to Dupont. "Grab us a coupla Cokes, okay?" He turned back to me. "Coke all right?"

"Just water."

Dupont left, closing the door behind him.

The room went quiet.

The air felt thick.

Morton massaged his temples with his fingertips. "How'd you get interested in magic?"

"How do you know about my magic?"

He chuckled. "I used my detecting skills. First clue was your outfit." Morton leaned back, tipping his chair onto its back legs. "And to be honest, I've done a little nosing around. I love magic. How'd you get started?"

"Sorry, but what's that got to do with my DNA?"

Morton leaned forward, clunking the chair legs against the floor. He held up his palms in a gesture of Hey, didn't mean any harm. Morton said, "Just making some friendly conversation."

I stood up. "I need to get back to my class."

Dupont came through the door with two Coke cans and a bottle of water. He gave Morton a can and handed me the icy plastic water bottle. I twisted off the top and gulped down a mouthful, feeling my Adam's apple bob as I swallowed. I sucked in more water, squeezing the bottle hard enough to make the plastic crackle. I felt a chest freeze from the ice water.

Morton popped the top on a Coke can, took a sip, and let out a sigh like it was a good year for that batch of syrup. He said, "Please sit down, Mr. Kendall. I promise this won't take long."

I slowly sat, keeping my eyes on him. Dupont stood against the wall behind Morton.

Morton said, "You know someone named Sherry Allen?"

Both men watched me intensely.

I scrunched my forehead. "Who?"

"Sherry Allen."

"No."

Morton leaned forward. "Woman in her early twenties. From Van Nuys?"

"No."

"Single mom, with an eighteen-month-old son. She worked with autistic kids."

I shook my head.

Morton said, "Maybe you know her under another name." He reached back over his shoulder with an open hand, moving his fingers in a request for Dupont to hand him something. Dupont opened the battered briefcase, took out a photo, and placed it in Morton's waving fingers.

Morton stood up and handed me a picture of a young woman with electric blue eyes and long blond hair that brushed across her bare shoulders. She was smiling sensually at the camera, biting her bottom lip like she was keeping a delicious secret.

I shook my head. "I've never seen her. Why do you keep asking?"

"She was raped and murdered."

"What?" The picture suddenly felt grimy in my fingers. I handed it back to Morton. He didn't take it.

I dropped the picture on the desk. "Why are you showing me this?"

Morton still had that jovial expression. "We found DNA at the murder scene. When we ran it through the databases, we got a match." His smile dimmed a titch. "It matched the DNA they took from you in Virginia."

CHAPTER THREE

I stared at Morton.

He stared at me.

I leaned forward in the desk chair and said, "Is this a joke?"

"No sir."

The bird on my shoulder cocked her head.

I said, "Did some of my buddies at the Castle put you up to this?"

"The castle?"

"The Magic Castle. It's a private club for magicians."

"It's not a joke, Mr. Kendall. Your DNA matched the DNA at the crime scene." Morton looked hard into me. "Miss Allen was tied up on her bed, beaten, and strangled. Do you tie people up in your magic act?"

I glanced down at the desk, then looked at Morton. "Only myself sometimes. You know, escape routines."

"How did your DNA wind up at her murder scene?"

I shook my head. "That's impossible."

"It's a fact."

"There's been some kind of mistake."

"Not likely. But if there was, help us clear it up."

The bird moved closer to my neck. "Are you accusing me of murder?"

"Should we be?"

I forced a laugh. "Do I look like a killer?"

Morton raised his eyebrows, as if asking, Well . . . ?

I shook my head. "I never met that woman. I don't know anything about this."

Morton kept staring at me. "Do you mind if we take your picture? For our records?"

I felt my chest tighten.

Murder? Me?

Ridiculous. This is some colossal screwup. Why don't they see that?

Morton said, "Mr. Kendall?"

"Huh?"

"Your picture?"

"Oh. Yeah, okay. I guess."

Dupont took a small camera out of the briefcase, came around in front of the desk, and clicked off a few shots.

When Dupont stepped back against the wall, Morton said, "Where were you on February twenty-second? Around ten P.M.?"

I felt myself leaning back in the chair. "I don't know. What day of the week was that?"

"Wednesday."

"I'm at the Magic Castle almost every night. I was probably there."

"That's the magicians' club you mentioned?"

"Yes."

Morton picked up his Coke, drank the rest of it, and crushed the can with one hand. "Can anybody verify that?"

"I have some friends there. I'll ask if they remember." I drained the water bottle and set it on the desk.

Dupont opened the briefcase and took out a brown paper bag. He came over to the desk, carefully lifted my water bottle by the neck, and dropped the bottle in the bag.

Whoa. These guys just took my fingerprints.

I shifted in my seat as I watched him put the bag into the briefcase.

Morton stood up. "Thank you, Mr. Kendall. That's all we'll need. For today anyway."

I stood up quickly, causing Lisa to dig in her claws.

Dupont, clutching the battered briefcase that held my picture and fingerprints, opened the door.

Morton said, "Don't leave town, Mr. Kendall."

CHAPTER FOUR

After taking the photo and fingerprints, Morton and Dupont left me sitting in the empty office. My heart thudded in my ears.

My hand trembled as I stroked the feathers on Lisa's chest with my index finger.

Murder?

Me?

Why did their stealing my fingerprints feel like they'd stripped me naked?

I looked at the blank wall for a clock.

Is someone coming back to this office? I need some time to get myself together.

Out in the hall, a school bell rang.

Shit. I missed my entire class. Through the closed door, I heard the erruption of footsteps, students chattering, lockers banging.

I need to get out before someone walks in.

As I stood up, I could feel my pulse thumping in my neck. I dug into my pants pocket, took out one of the vintage Walking

Liberty fifty-cent pieces that I always carry, and ran it over the backs of my knuckles. That usually calms me down.

Not working.

Maybe I should try the anti–stage fright routine that I use before big shows. I closed my eyes, took a deep breath, and let it out slowly.

Then another.

Still a little jagged.

A few more.

Better.

Sort of.

Gotta get outta here.

I straightened up. Should I hide Lisa? Nah. I'll get enough stares because of the outfit.

Rubbing the bird's chest, I opened the door and headed for my car, ignoring the looks from passersby.

What the hell was that about? Why me? Obviously some massive mistake. Probably a computer error or something.

I didn't do anything.

They'll have to figure that out.

Right?

Absolutely.

Won't they?

I spent the rest of the morning buying birdseed, cleaning Lisa's cage, and calling around for substitute teaching work.

No one needed a substitute.

Is that because of the cops?

Don't get paranoid. It's not unusual that there's no work. A lot of teachers have specific substitutes they like, so us floaters can go several days without assignments. Besides, knowing the school board's efficiency system, the people who hire substitutes won't know about the cops for a year or two.

Right after lunch, my cell phone rang. When I answered, it, my mother said, "You need to come over. Right now."

Whoa. Mom never sounds like that. "What is it?"

"Not on the phone."

I walked up the concrete pathway to Mom's tiny one-story ranch house on McCormick Street in Van Nuys, past a line of plaster baby ducks who were following their plaster mother across the lawn. The ducks' white paint was peeling off in large splotches, which wasn't so surprising, since the ducks had been left by the home's previous owner some thirty-odd years ago.

I opened the unlocked front door, with Lisa balanced on my shoulder. Mom's three foster kids, Ed, Max, and Skye, ran toward me, yelling, "Uncle Harvey!" Skye hugged my leg as I picked up the six-year-old boys. Max said, "Show us a trick!"

I said, "Where's Mom?"

"Where do you think she is?"

That meant the backyard garden.

Max said, "Show us a trick."

I shook my head. "Mom said she had to see me right away."

"C'mon. One trick. Pleeeeease."

"Yeah, pleeeease."

I looked toward the back of the house. "Okay, okay. Real quick."

I set down the kids and put the bird on Max's head. That always made them giggle. They squeezed in close to me, eyes wide.

What's a fast one? I never go for vanishing a coin and pulling it out of a kid's ear. It's incredibly trite, though for some bizarre reason it's amazed children for hundreds of years.

Ah. Got it.

I reached into my pocket and took out two foam-rubber rabbits, each about the size of a quarter. I had Ed squeeze the rabbits in his fist. After a few magic words, I told him to open his hand. Out popped the two rabbits plus ten little ones. The kids oohed.

Ed said, "Good one!"

I thought, When you're older, you'll have a whole different take on that trick.

Max said, "Do another one."

"I gotta see Mom."

I took Lisa off Max's head, put her on my shoulder, and walked through the living room, past the Wall of Photos. There was a large picture of me in the center, surrounded by twenty-plus pictures of the foster kids who'd lived with Mom after Dad died. I hurried through the den, past a cluster of handmade clay planters that overflowed with strands of ivy. The planters were remnants of Mom's pot-throwing era. Hanging on the wall was a tie-dyed piece of cloth, which was a remnant of Mom's pot-smoking era. Her current passion sat by the window—an easel with a half-finished painting. On a small table next to the easel were brushes on their heads in a jar of cloudy turpentine, along with a wooden palette with multicolor splotches that smelled like oil paint. The painting showed a man walking on a country path with what was probably supposed to be his dog, though it looked more like a weasel.

In the backyard, I saw Mom on her hands and knees, wearing jeans and a loose paisley blouse that was supposed to hide the thickness around her middle. Her long gray hair was tied in a ponytail that trailed over her spine, with rubber bands clipping it every few inches, so that it looked like a string of gray mini–hot dogs. She was tickling a plant with a paintbrush.

When she saw me, she dropped the brush and squinted at me through her purple-framed rectangular glasses. I heard her knees crack as she stood.

Mom wasn't smiling.

I said, "What were you doing with the brush?"

She pushed a few wisps of gray hair off her forehead. "Pollinating the vegetables. It's been a bad year for insects, so I'm playing Ms. Bee and moving pollen from the males to the females. If the females don't get pollen, I don't get zucchinis."

"I love it when you talk dirty."

She didn't laugh.

Uh-oh. "Mom, what's wrong?"

She bent down, grabbed the paintbrush, and stuck it in her back pocket.

Mom dusted her hands on her jeans and lowered her voice. "Inside."

Mom sat me at the kitchen table and hustled the kids into the den. She gave me a piece of toast with peanut butter on top, cut into four triangles. My favorite breakfast when I was little. Lisa perked up on my shoulder.

Mom stuck a teakettle under the faucet and turned on the tap. The water hissed against the metal pot.

I took a bite of the toast. Why does food always taste better at Mom's?

She put the kettle on the stove, then came back to the table but didn't sit.

Through the sticky peanut butter, I said, "What's the emergency?"

She stood there, staring at me while I chewed.

"Mom?" I took another bite.

"The cops came by this morning."

Suddenly, the peanut butter clotted in my mouth. I set down the half-eaten piece of toast. "I'm really sorry."

She crossed her arms over her chest. "What is this about?"

"It's obviously a mistake. What did they say to you?"

"They said they were talking to you about a girl who was killed. They asked where you were on some date in February. They wanted to know all about your childhood. I didn't tell them anything."

I swallowed the gritty bits of toast. "They shouldn't have bothered you."

Mom sat down and pulled her chair close to the table, squeaking the legs against the linoleum. She whispered, "I got busted when I was about your age."

"You did? For what?"

"It's not important. Just like it's not important what you did."

"I didn't do anything."

The teakettle shrieked on the stove.

Mom got up and grabbed the kettle. It whimpered as she took it off the burner. She poured the boiling water into a cup, dropped in a tea bag, and came back to the table, working the bag's string up and down. Mom sat and said, "I've contacted Michael Nadler, the criminal lawyer."

I pushed away the plate of toast. "That guy who's always talking to reporters on TV?"

"When you have a problem, you go for the best."

"Mom—"

"Remember when your father needed his angioplasty? We flew to Houston because that's where the best surgeon was. You need the best lawyer."

"Nadler's a publicity hound."

"He got that former Miss America off a cocaine charge, and you know she was guilty as hell."

"But I'm *not* guilty. I can clear this up without a high-priced lawyer."

"Don't be naïve. The government crushes little people like us."

I shook my head. "Nadler would cost a fortune."

She stood up, trying to tower over me. She was too short, even when I was sitting.

Mom said, "This is not open for discussion. You have an appointment with him this afternoon at five o'clock. Here's his card." She pulled a wrinkled business card out of her jeans pocket and held it out.

I didn't take the card. "I can't afford this guy."

"I'll help."

"*You* can't afford this guy."

She wagged her finger at me. "You're seeing him at five o'clock."

"Absolutely not."

That afternoon at five, I rode an elevator up to the Beverly Hills offices of attorney Michael Nadler. This is ridiculous, I thought. Why should I hire an expensive lawyer when I'm innocent? It's obviously some mistake with the DNA. The cops will figure that out on their own. Otherwise, I can get a public defender for free. I'm sure my income is way below whatever the poverty line is.

The elevator doors dinged open. I stepped into a waiting room that was decorated with ultramodern black-and-white furniture. There were three signed Roy Lichtenstein prints hanging on the blond wood walls. The largest was a cartoon soldier, done with big dots to look like newsprint. The soldier was crouching low, running forward with a bayonet, waving for unseen troops to follow him. The balloon over his head said, "This way, boys. For family and country!"

I walked up to the receptionist, who sat ramrod-straight in a dress so crisp that it looked like she ironed it during her breaks. The woman looked at me. "Yes?"

"I'm Harvey Kendall. To see Michael Nadler?"

She looked at her computer, picked up the phone, dialed, whispered into the mouthpiece, then told me to take a seat.

I sat on a white couch, feeling like I was staining the fabric.

After a few minutes, I poked through the magazines on the glass coffee table. *Time, Newsweek, Forbes.* No *Guns & Ammo*? I settled on a month-old issue of *Time.*

A few minutes later, I looked at my watch. Pretty rude to keep me waiting like this. I mean, when you've got a client accused of murder, doesn't that rank some priority? I knew this guy was too big to give a shit about someone like me. Waste of time and money.

About three magazines later, the receptionist said, "Mr. Nadler will see you now. Through the door to my left."

Her left . . . my right . . . Got it.

I stood up, took out a fifty-cent piece, and rolled the coin over my knuckles as I walked. Ooops. Almost dropped it.

The receptionist pushed a button by her desk. The door buzzed. I opened it and saw an older lady in an equally well-pressed suit. Probably last year's model.

She said, "This way, Mr. Randall."

"Kendall."

The woman smiled, like that was one of the better jokes she'd heard in a long time, then turned and started down the hall.

I followed her toward Nadler's throne room.

CHAPTER FIVE

When I walked into Nadler's office, he wasn't there. It was a large corner office, with views spreading all the way from L.A.'s downtown skyscrapers to the ocean. His desk, made of glass and chrome, stood on a platform about six inches higher than the rest of the office. The guest chairs were black leather poofy things. One wall had a giant painting that looked like a drop cloth but probably cost more than Mom's house. Floor-to-ceiling bookshelves held neatly arranged leather books, accented with silver-framed pictures of Nadler: Nadler golfing with President Bush, Nadler boarding a private jet, Nadler sunning himself on a yacht, Nadler with his arm around his recent client, Miss Cocaine America.

A door on the other side of the office opened. Nadler came out of his private bathroom, with the sound of a flushing toilet behind him. The man looked like he was in his late forties and stood maybe five foot six. He was dark-complected, with a splotch of pigmentless white skin on his neck, and wore a pin-stripe navy suit with a burgundy silk handkerchief folded neatly in the breast pocket. I had this incredible urge to grab the handkerchief and make it vanish.

He came over and stuck out his hand. "Michael Nadler." His grip was firm, and he looked into my eyes with an intense gaze that made me feel like I was the only thing in his life that mattered.

Hmm. The guy's way more magnetic than I expected. Maybe that's why the juries love him.

Nadler broke the connection, stepped up on the pedestal, and sat behind his desk. He waved in the direction of the guest chairs and said, "Have a seat."

I sank into one of the poofy black leather things. Nadler looked down at me. "I've done some checking with my connections in the police department. Frankly, you've got a serious problem. Now the first thing—"

His phone rang.

Nadler said, "Excuse me. They'd only put this through if it was urgent." He picked up the phone and listened. His face brightened. "Yes, Senator." Nadler swiveled his desk chair toward the window and started mumbling into the phone.

After a few minutes of watching the back of his chair, I got up and walked around the office. I touched the cold chrome floor lamp and saw my fingerprint on the polished surface. Just like the cops got on the water bottle. *I'm an idiot,* falling for that.

I went to the bookshelf and studied the framed photos. I'd noticed that Nadler was wearing a wedding ring. Didn't see any pictures of a wife or kids. Unless he was married to Nelson Mandela.

I picked up a leather-bound volume that had gold lettering on the spine: *Michael Nadler, Press Clippings, 2008.* I opened it up. Newspaper articles mounted on parchment paper. I thumbed through the pages, then put it back in line with the other volumes.

Nadler was still mumbling into the phone. I went over to his desk, where there was a sword-shaped letter opener stuck in a glass globe, as if it were waiting for King Arthur to pull it free. I stepped onto the raised platform, took out the sword, and waved it over my open palm like a wand. I closed my fist and waved the sword again.

Nadler swiveled around in his chair and hung up the phone. When he noticed the sword in my hand, he scowled. I put Excalibur back in its rock. He made a microscopic adjustment of the sword holder's location on his desk, then gestured for me to sit. In other words, Get off my platform.

I stepped off the raised area and kept standing.

Nadler said, "Sorry about the phone call. It really was an emergency."

I nodded.

He said, "So. As I was saying. I've spoken to my friends with the police. The DNA match is a serious issue. The cops have definitely focused on you."

"If they're focused on me, why haven't I been arrested?"

"They don't consider you a flight risk. Besides, they're still building their case. As the cops say, when they arrest someone, they want them to stay arrested."

I shifted my weight to the other foot.

Nadler took a yellow page of scribbled notes from the stack on his desk and looked at it. "The victim's name was Sherry Allen. Is there anything to connect you to her?"

"No. I never met her. Mr. Nadler, what's the charge for this?"

"They'll likely go for second-degree murder. Maybe first."

"Not the criminal charges. How much are your fees?"

Nadler dropped the page and looked at me with his mouth open. From his expression, you'd think I'd asked if he liked having sex with goats.

He said, "Excuse me?"

"What do you charge?"

"Your mother's already taken care of that."

"How much is she paying you?"

He blinked a few times. "She asked me not to discuss it with you."

I stepped back onto his pedestal. I said, "Aren't I the client, here?"

"Well . . . yes."

"Then tell me."

He steepled his fingers. His chair squeaked as he rocked back.

Nadler leaned forward and put his hands on the desk. "All right. I'm giving her a discount from my normal rates. One hundred thousand."

Did the floor just buckle? "One . . . hundred . . . *thousand*?"

"My usual minimum is one fifty."

I shook my head. "My mother hasn't got that kind of money."

"I'm satisfied she can take care of it."

"Well, I'm not. I think I need to shop around a bit."

The veins in his temples pulsed. Nadler stood up. "Mr. Kendall, I don't accept every case that walks in the door. Your mother pleaded with me, and I finally said I would take a meeting with you. Believe me, it's just fine if you'd like to go elsewhere." He made a shooing gesture with the back of his hand. "You go 'shop around' all you want. However, there's no guarantee I'll have time for your case when you're done."

I turned to leave.

Nadler said, "Here's some free advice. Hurry up with that shopping. You're facing serious charges and your case does not look good."

CHAPTER SIX

I'd been out of Nadler's office less than fifteen minutes when my cell phone rang. The caller ID said MOM.

I sighed and pushed ANSWER. I didn't need the phone anywhere near my ear to hear her. "Do you know how hard I had to beg Nadler to take your case? Do you know what it took to get you in the same day?"

"I really appreciate it, but this guy was arrogant to the tenth power. Besides, I'd be number nine thousand two hundred and twenty-six on his list. Look, this is just some stupid mistake. I'll get a public defender."

"Talk about low priority. Those people have fifty thousand cases and couldn't care less about you. They'll push you to take jail time just so they don't have to be bothered. Harvey, you can't screw around with something like this. Now go back to Nadler and apologize."

"Mom? Hello? Can you hear me?"

"I hear you perfectly. Answer me."

"Mom? Mom?" I hung up.

That night, I drove up the long driveway to the Magic Castle. The private club is on a hill above Hollywood, in a two-story Victorian mansion with turrets, gargoyles, Gothic dormers, and stained-glass windows. I slammed on my brakes to avoid hitting a car that stopped suddenly in front of me. Shit. Three cars in front of me. I never have to wait for parking.

C'mon. Move it.

Why is my stomach twisting like a balloon animal?

When those idiots finally got out of the way, I pulled up to the front door and stopped beside the trickling fountain, which is guarded by two stone lions. I climbed out of the car and threw my keys at the parking attendant so hard that he had to dodge them. I said, "Sorry, Jimmy."

"No sweat, Cy Young."

I went inside the front door to a small wood-paneled reception room, dimly lit by an overhead Tiffany chandelier. Two of the walls had floor-to-ceiling dark wood shelves, filled with old books. Tillie, behind the desk, was telling a middle-aged couple to go over to the bookshelf, look at the gold owl sitting there, and say "Open Sesame."

The woman screwed up her face, then looked at the man. The two of them walked to the bookshelf, stared at the blinking lights in the owl's eyes, and said, "Open Sesame." The bookshelf lurched to the side, sliding open to let them into the club. The man shook his head with an expression that said, What in tarnation will they think of next?

As soon as they were gone, Tillie looked at me. "What's eating you tonight?"

"You got a schedule of the magicians who were here in February?"

"Maybe. What's eating you?"

I started chewing on a cuticle and looked down at the carpet. "Nothing. You got that schedule?"

She shook her head, as if to say, If you don't want to talk about it, then it's not my problem. Tillie opened a drawer, rummaged around, then opened another drawer. She shut the drawers, grabbed a file box under the reception desk, and flipped through the folders. "Aha." She took out a schedule and handed it over. "One last chance to tell me what's bugging you."

"Nothing. I'm hunky-dory."

"And I'm Marilyn Monroe."

I stuffed the flyer in my pocket and opened the other wall's bookshelf, which is really an exit but we regulars use it when there aren't newbies in the lobby. I walked through the noisy bar area into the men's room. Mounted on the wall was a large metal box labeled THE GREAT AMERICAN ALIBI MACHINE. For fifty cents, you can play the sounds of a busy office, an auto-repair shop, or an airport, while you call someone to say you're stuck. I wondered if I'd need an industrial version of that machine.

While I stood at the urinal, a devil's face appeared behind a two-way mirror on the wall above it. He said, "Wow. I'll bet *you* never hurt the one you love."

Usually, that made me smile.

I washed my hands, splashed cold water on my face, then went back to the bar area, which was formerly the living room of the mansion. The large room was paneled in dark wood, with tufted red velvet furniture, a grandfather clock with a serpentine pendulum, and an oil painting with mechanical eyes that looked back and forth. A dark wooden staircase led to the second floor, flanked by newel posts that were carved to look like wooden lions standing on their hind legs.

I spotted my pal David Hu sitting at the long bar. He was a skinny Asian-American with a whispy mustache, and we'd known each other since junior high. By day, David was a white-shirt investment banker. By night, he was David the Dragon, a thoroughly mediocre magician.

I walked over to him and stood there. He didn't notice me because he was hunched over his usual whiskey. I clapped him on the shoulder. David looked up and grinned, flashing the clear plastic braces he'd recently strapped to his teeth. "Hey, Harvey." Judging by his breath, this wasn't the night's first whiskey.

I sat on the adjacent stool, right next to the gag stool that slowly sinks if you give the bartender a nod. David said, "You're not gonna believe the guy who walked into my office today."

I raised my eyebrows in a "Go on" expression.

"He's the son of a billionaire client, so we had to take him seriously. Anyway, this guy gets four of us in the boardroom and makes us sign a three-page confidentiality agreement before he springs his brilliant idea."

"Yeah?"

David leaned toward me. I leaned in. *Definitely* not his first whiskey of the night.

David said, "So I'm gonna breach that confidentiality agreement and tell you what he wants to do. Can you keep this to yourself?"

I held up my hand in a solemn oath. "Your secret is safe with a magician."

David whispered, "He wants to manufacture cat food."

"That's it?"

"He's got an angle."

"Which is?"

"A flavor that's never been done before. It's so obvious when you think of it, but no one's done it."

"What?"

He leaned in closer. "Rat flavor."

David started guffawing.

I said, "You're joking, right?"

"Yes, I'm joking. One of the guys circulated a memo like it was real. Got us all going."

Shaking my head, I said, "Must be a riot around your shop."

David took a pack of cards from his jacket, opened the box, and pulled out the deck. He took the ten of clubs off the top and said, "What do you think of this?"

David stuck the ten halfway into the deck, covered the deck with his other hand as he pushed the card all the way in, then moved the deck a few inches to the side. He flipped over the top card, which was the ten of clubs.

I said, "Do it again."

He repeated the move.

"Good. But I can see your hand jerk when you do the pass. You might want to video yourself."

He nodded, took a sip of his whiskey, and repeated the move. Then again. David looked at me. "Is that better?"

"Yeah." Not really.

He kept making the same move while he talked about Harry Dexter, a twenty-two-year-old magician who said he could recreate Dai Vernon's single-hand ball vanish. Not very likely.

I took the Castle's February schedule out of my pocket, smoothed it on the bar, and cleared my throat. "Say, David."

"Hmmm." He didn't look up from practicing his move.

I pointed to February twenty-second on the schedule. "Remember we saw Andy Valentine here on February twenty-second?"

Still making his move, he glanced at the schedule. "Kinda. Why?"

"I need you to remember."

"Huh?"

"I need you to remember."

He kept practicing.

I touched his arm and said, "It's important."

David put down the cards. "What's the big deal?"

Jordan, the bartender, came up. He set down my usual fizzy water and lime. Jordan said, "Harvey, you know where I can buy a used fifty-cent shell?"

"I think Mark's got one, but it's the old Franklin fifty-cent piece."

He shook his head. "Thanks anyway."

The bartender walked off. David had gone back to the cards.

I said, "So, David, you do remember about the twenty-second, right?"

He kept making the move with his cards. "You going to tell me what this is about, or do we play twenty questions?"

I stuck a plastic straw in the water and sucked down half the glass. Does the lime always make it so acidic? "Well, I got asked some questions by the cops."

"Cool, dude." He grinned, flipped over the ten of clubs on top.

"No. Really."

He made the move again. "Why would cops question you?"

I sucked down more bubbly water. "Something about a murder."

David laughed. "Yeah. And I got questioned about an assault with a Pyrex dildo." He stuck the ten of clubs in the middle of the deck.

"I'm serious."

David stopped, holding the deck in midair. "For real?"

I nodded. "It's just some evidence mix-up. I'm sure it'll get straightened out."

"Yeah, probably." He started to work the deck again.

"You think I, uh, need a lawyer?"

He set down the deck. "Are you a suspect, or just a witness?"

"Well, I guess you might say I'm a little bit of a suspect."

David looked at me. "You're a murder suspect and you're asking if you need a lawyer?"

"It's just a mistake."

"I think I heard a guy say that in a death-row interview."

I drank more of the fizzy water and could feel the bubbles in my chest. "Won't it be enough if you tell them I was with you on the twenty-second? You'll do that, right?"

"Sure, fine. But get a lawyer."

I sighed. "Maybe I'll get a public defender."

He turned toward me on the stool. "Can you afford to hire a private lawyer?"

"Well . . . not really. I mean, my mom offered to help, so maybe."

"Trust me on this one. Get the best lawyer you can."

"But it's just a mistake."

He put the tip of his index finger against his lips and narrowed his eyes, mocking deep thought. "Let's see. Spend a few grand on legal fees? Or become Charlie Manson's bitch up at Corcoran?"

I sucked on the straw. The glass emptied with a slurping sound. "You know anybody who wouldn't be too expensive?"

"Everyone I know is expensive. But they're the wrong guys anyway, unless you're planning the hostile takeover of a public company." David put the cards back in the box and stuffed the pack in his jacket. "I'll make some calls tomorrow." He turned back to the bar and motioned for another glass of whiskey.

I said, "So you remember I was here on the twenty-second, right?"

"How many ways do you want me to say yes?"

The bartender swooped up David's glass.

He swiveled on the stool to face me. "What about Hannah Fisher?"

"Who?"

"Hannah. From high school?"

"I'm not sure. . . ."

"She was number one in our class. She weighed three hundred pounds."

Of course! Fat Hannah. She had frizzy blond hair that made her look like Bozo the Clown on cortisone. Worse yet, she was always making eyes at me. That put a whole new spin on the concept of having a "crush."

David said, "Hannah went to Harvard Law School. I think she's a criminal lawyer now. Maybe she'd give you a friend's discount."

Fat Hannah?

Late that night, when I walked into my apartment, my bird, Lisa, was walking along the back of the couch like a cat. When she saw me, her eyes went red with excitement. She fluttered toward me, flapping her clipped wings as she fell onto the couch cushions. I went over, let her step on my finger, then put her on my shoulder while I dumped some birdseed in her trough. When I put her in the cage, she dug into the dish, splattering seeds through the bars.

How can these cops come crashing into my life like this? They make a mistake and a little guy like me has to pay a fortune to straighten it out? Shit.

I yawned, even though I was pretty wired up. No chance of sleep anytime soon.

I picked up my pile of mail and flipped through. A couple more red "Overdue" bills. What kind of sadist prints cutesy little "Did You Forget?" notes with the drawing of a finger tied with a bowknot? I opened a desk drawer, stuffed the bills inside, and slammed it shut.

I closed my eyes and pushed on my temples with the tips of my index fingers. How am I going to pay a lawyer? Even a cheap one? I've been falling behind my goal of two magic gigs a month. For a while, I was getting three or four. Okay, so they weren't the most glamorous gigs. I mean, I even worked a plumbing convention where I made a toilet-tank ball float in the air. Still, the money was decent, and it kept away the string-around-the-finger notes. Now I can't even get those shitty gigs, and I have to deal with tens of thousands in legal fees?

I sat down at my desk, shoved the switch on the computer, and listened to it whir to life. When the programs loaded, I Googled Sherry Allen and Van Nuys, where the cop said she lived.

Could I have ever met her? The picture Morton showed me didn't look familiar. Wouldn't I remember her?

The Google search came up with gibberish.

I shut down the computer and leaned back in my chair, cracking my spine. I know I've never met this Sherry Allen. I'm positive.

I got up and went over to Lisa's cage. She was scratching the side of her head with one claw, like a dog scratching its ear. I threw the flowered cloth over her cage, blew out a breath, and headed for bed.

Maybe I should track down Fat Hannah.

Guess it can't hurt.

CHAPTER SEVEN

Next morning, I found Hannah Fisher, attorney, on the Internet. I called her office, got voice mail, but didn't leave a message. Why ruin the surprise?

I jumped in my Toyota and drove toward her office address on Magnolia, just off Lankershim in North Hollywood. As I went down Lankershim, banners hanging from the lampposts told me I was in the NoHo Arts District. The graffitied stucco buildings, cracked parking lots, and open trash bins looked a lot more on the No than the Ho side. Well, actually, the neighborhood seemed to have its share of Ho.

I turned onto Magnolia and saw Hannah's office, a two-story Spanish building with fake log-ends sticking out of the front wall, just below the red-tiled roofline. Guess that's supposed to give it an Early California Settler vibe. I parked in the asphalt lot next to the building and went inside. The hallway smelled like some guy had eaten a plateful of asparagus before relieving himself in a corner.

I found Hannah's name on the directory and walked toward her office. On the way, I passed doors marked *Madame Louisa,*

Psychic Advisor, and *Richard Gomez, Tailor to the Stars.* The last door said *H. Fisher, Attorney at Law.* I stopped in front.

Are you supposed to knock on offices?

I don't think so. . . .

I knocked lightly as I opened the door and stepped inside. A trim woman in a black business suit was pacing on the worn carpet while she spoke on the phone. Her shoulder-length black hair swished as she strode back and forth. Two phone lines blinked, like they were waving their arms for attention. Although her electric green eyes darted around the room, she didn't seem to notice me.

The woman spoke into the phone, "This is a good kid, Glen. The judge is going to give him community service anyway." She kept pacing, stopping short when she got to the end of the phone cord. Behind her, I noticed a desk covered with stacks of paper, a computer monitor, and an open briefcase. There were more stacks of paper on chair seats, on top of a wooden filing cabinet, and on the floor along an entire wall.

The woman said, "Thanks, I owe you." She hung up, started to punch another line, then looked up, as if I'd just come in. When she faced me, I saw that her nose came to a sharp point, as if it had been pinched.

She said, "Yes?"

"I'm looking for Hannah."

"And you are?"

"Harvey Kendall. I knew her in high school."

She squinted at me. "Harvey?"

I blinked. "Hannah?"

She smiled.

Did her eyes always have a sexy twinkle? I wondered.

I said, "Sorry. I didn't recognize you. You look . . ."

"Brunette and a hundred and eighty-three pounds lighter."

"Um, yeah."

She stuck her hand out. "How have you been?"

"Good." I shook her hand. She gave me a firm pump and release.

I said, "Well, maybe not so good."

Hannah twisted her mouth to the side, as if to say, Hmm.

I'd never noticed that dimple before. Was it there when her face was all puffed out?

She said, "Have a seat." Hannah took a stack of papers off a chair, looked around for a place to put them, then set them crosswise on top of another pile on the floor.

As I sat down, Hannah punched the other two phone lines and told them she'd call back. Then she half-sat on the edge of her desk and said, "So, what's up?"

I forced a little chuckle. "Well, there's been this stupid mistake with the cops, and some of my friends think I need a lawyer."

"What kind of mistake?"

Her phone rang. She reached around and flipped a toggle switch on the side. The phone shut up, though the line kept blinking.

I told her about the cops questioning me and how they said they found my DNA at a crime scene.

She said, "Your friends are right. You need a lawyer, even if it's just a mistake. I can recommend some good people."

"Recommend? Aren't you a lawyer?"

"I'm really busy. Besides, I can't represent someone when there's another relationship."

"What relationship? I haven't seen you in ten years."

She smiled. "Then let's leave it that I'm too busy."

"Look, Hannah, I'd really feel more comfortable with a friend helping me." *Especially a friend who might give me a discount.*

Hannah shook her head. "Murders take too much time. The cases are real—"

"Killers?"

She gave me a stiff grin. "I'm sorry. I just can't. It's nothing personal."

How do I bring her around? To get an audience involved in a trick, you first have to hook them. Get them going the way you want, then pull the switcheroo. I said, "I'm a magician now."

She cocked her head. "Really? I remember you doing magic in the high school talent show."

"Yeah. I dropped my floating chrome ball. I can still see it clunking against the wooden stage and rolling into the audience. I've never been so humiliated."

Hannah laughed. "I don't remember that. I was in the show, too. I played guitar and got so nervous that my leg started shaking."

I remembered that. She was so huge that the guitar looked like a ukelele.

I said, "If you take my case, I'll get you into the Magic Castle whenever you want to go."

"Harvey . . ."

I stood up. "What'll it take? I'll do magic at your birthday party. I'll cut your lawn on weekends."

She smirked at me.

I got on one knee, clasped my hands in a begging gesture, then produced a red silk handkerchief from between my hands. I held the silk out for her. "If you take me on, there's more where this one came from."

Hannah laughed. She didn't take the handkerchief.

She said, "Were you this weird in high school?"

"No. I'm less weird now."

She shook her head, let out a sigh. "Tell you what. I'll look at your case tomorrow. No promises."

I grabbed her hand. "Thank you, thank you."

She pulled her hand back. "I said, 'No promises.'"

"Of course." I got up off my knee. "Say, what do you charge?"

"I didn't say I was doing this."

"I know. I mean, hypothetically. Isn't that what you lawyers say?"

"Hypothetically, I would charge you a friend's rate. Ten thousand. I know that sounds like a lot, but it isn't."

Next to Nadler, it sounds like Kmart. "Fine. Done."

"Not done. I'm only going to take a look. Come back tomorrow at two fifteen. I'll call the cops and get a copy of your file."

"Thank you, thank you." I turned to hustle out before she changed her mind.

Behind me, I heard her call, "No promises."

Without turning around, I waved my arm over my head.

When I got back to my apartment, my mother was standing in front of the door with her fists on her hips. She said, "Why didn't you call me back about Nadler?"

"I had bad cell phone reception." At least, I'm sure the reception would have been bad if I'd turned the phone on.

"For eighteen hours?"

I took my keys out of my pocket. "Sorry. I found another lawyer."

Her eyes burned into me. "I went to a lot of effort to get Nadler."

"I appreciate it, but I hated the sonofabitch. Besides, I can't let you spend that kind of dough."

"That's my business."

I toyed with my keys, jingling them. "You can't afford it."

"I've got savings for emergencies."

"No. You've got savings to live on. Besides, I found someone who's just as good and way cheaper."

Mom gave a sarcastic "Ha." "And just who do you think is as good as Michael Nadler?"

"Hannah Fisher."

She wrinkled her forehead. "Who?"

"She's a Harvard lawyer. She'll make me a priority."

"Yeah, probably because she's got nothing else to do. How did you find her? Yellow Pages?"

"I knew her in high school."

"High school? You want to use someone *your* age?"

"I'm twenty-nine, you know."

She shook her head. "You need a lawyer with years of experience."

"I didn't do anything wrong. The cops will see that. Mom, I'm using Hannah. That's final." Assuming she'll take my case.

Mom let out a breath. "Let's put it this way. I'm happy to pay for Nadler. But if you want to go off on some tangent, you can pay for that yourself."

"Fine."

Yikes!

CHAPTER EIGHT

Next morning, I phoned in to ask about substitute teacher work. When the nasal woman told me there was nothing available, I said, "How's it possible that every teacher in Los Angeles is healthy today?"

"Mr. Kendall, I don't make the rules."

That afternoon, at two fifteen sharp, I grabbed the handle of Hannah's office door and twisted it hard.

Locked.

I looked at my watch. I actually managed to show up on time. Where the hell is she? We had an appointment.

I leaned against the door, looking down the hall. A middle-aged woman came out of an office wearing a flowered dress with little gold disks sewn onto the fabric. She walked over and handed me her card. "Hello, I'm Madame Louisa."

I glanced at the card. Ah, yes. The Psychic Advisor. "Harvey Kendall."

"If you're a friend of Hannah's, I'll give you a free fifteen-minute session."

"Not today, thanks. You know where Hannah is?"

"She's gone every day from a little before one until about now."

"Where's she go?"

Madame Louisa shrugged.

Some psychic.

I heard the sound of the building door opening and looked over to see Hannah hustling down the hall, swinging a shiny black leather briefcase. When Louisa saw her, she backed up and disappeared into her office.

Hannah said, "Sorry I'm late."

"I hear you're out every day around this time. Where do you go?"

She glared at me. "Not relevant."

I put up my hands in surrender. "Sorry. Objection sustained."

She unlocked her office. I followed her inside. Hannah hit a wall switch and the fluorescent lights flickered on with a low buzz. The answering machine blinked angrily.

Hannah said, "Sit." She waved at the guest chair, where the stack of papers had grown larger since yesterday. I put them on the floor and sat down.

Hannah opened her briefcase, pulled out a few sheets, and picked up a yellow pad. She stuck a ballpoint pen sideways in her mouth, rolled her desk chair around in front of mine, and sat facing me. As she crossed her legs, her skirt rose up her thigh.

Hannah took the pen out of her mouth. "Okay," she said, brushing a strand of hair from her eyes. "Let's talk about your case. First, what's Michael Nadler got to do with this?"

I slid back in my seat. "What do you mean?"

"I spoke to the cops. They said Nadler was asking about your case. What's his involvement?"

"Nothing. My mother wanted him to represent me. I wanted you."

She narrowed her eyes. "Did you meet with him?"

"Yes."

"And?"

"I thought he was an arrogant sonofabitch."

Hannah's face relaxed. "Good for you. Nadler is a scum-sucking publicity hound who puts his own interests in front of his clients'."

I smiled. "You don't have to hold back your true feelings."

"Sorry. That wasn't very professional."

Memo to self: Do not piss off Hannah.

She scribbled something on the yellow pad and said, "Tell me what you know about this."

"I never met Sherry Allen. I certainly didn't kill her."

"Uh-huh." Her tone sounded like that was irrelevant. Without looking up from her notes, she said, "They found your semen in the dead girl."

I felt my breath catch. "Semen?!"

She looked up at me. "Yes."

I realized my mouth was open. "Semen? That's absurd."

"It's a perfect DNA match. Any idea how it could have happened?"

I ran my fingers through my hair. "It didn't happen. It's ridiculous. It's . . . impossible."

"At the moment, it's a fact."

I stood up and started pacing, shaking my head. "It has to be a lab mistake."

"Possible. Not likely. If you slept with her, that would explain the semen. It doesn't mean you killed her."

"I didn't sleep with her. I never met her." *In reality,* the only woman in my life for the last six months is my bird, Lisa.

Hannah said, "Do you have an identical twin? That could explain the DNA."

"No. Only one of me."

"Is there anything that could connect you to this girl?"

"No."

She looked at me. "You sure?"

"Yes."

"Maybe you knew her under another name?"

"You sound like the cops."

"Good."

I made a sweeping flat-hand gesture with both hands, like the umpires use when someone's safe on base, and shook my head in an absolutely not. "I don't know her. I mean, I didn't know her. Whatever you're supposed to say." I started biting my cuticle.

The phone rang. Hannah got up and flipped the toggle switch to silence it.

She sat, recrossed her legs, and tightened her lips. "Harvey, I have to ask you some uncomfortable questions."

I put my hands under my thighs to keep them away from my teeth and cleared my throat. "Okay . . ."

"I'm sorry to do this. It's necessary."

I nodded.

Hannah spoke while looking down at the pad. "Do you have any criminal history?"

I laughed. She didn't.

I said, "No. Nothing but a DUI in Virginia."

"The cops mentioned that. What happened?"

"I was in college at the University of Virginia. A bunch of us got drunk after finals. The group decided I was the least drunk, so they elected me to drive home. Accepting that honor wasn't one of my better decisions."

"Bad piece of luck. Virginia is one of the few states that takes DNA for any arrest. Most jurisdictions only take DNA from felons."

"Great. On top of that, they used a needle to take my blood, and I get really freaked out by needles."

Hannah looked up. "I'm not crazy about shots myself."

I felt my pulse quicken from the talk about needles. "Yeah. I was really sick when I was a kid. I had to have a lot of injections."

She went back to looking at her yellow pad. "You have any substance-abuse issues?"

"No."

"Liquor?"

I took my hands out from under my thighs and grabbed the chair arms. "Maybe I've been seriously drunk five times in my life, counting that time in college. I don't even like booze."

"Drugs?"

"Why are you pushing this?"

"I'm not making any judgments. We can't afford to be surprised."

"No drugs. No sex. Just some rock and roll now and then."

She put down her pen. "This isn't a joke. The cops are focused on you. They're building a case."

I realized I was gripping the chair arms so tightly that my knuckles were blanching. I let go. "Sorry. That's just my way of, you know, dealing with stress."

"Where were you the night Sherry was killed?"

"At the Magic Castle. With David Hu. Remember him from high school?"

"Who?"

It was so tempting to get into a "Who's on First?" routine. "Skinny Asian kid who was on the debate team. Remember?"

She stuck the pen sideways in her mouth and spoke through her teeth. "Sort of. He'll vouch you were there all night?"

"Yes."

"Give me his information."

I gave her David's phone number and e-mail. She wrote it down, then flipped back through the yellow pad. Hannah played with a strand of her hair while she studied what she'd written.

I said, "I made a mistake, talking to the cops, huh?"

Hannah looked at me. "In a word, yes."

Ouch. I felt my shoulders slump.

She said, "It's history at this point. Just don't talk to them again. They're allowed to say anything to trip you up. They can even lie, to trick you into saying something, and what you say is still admissible against you. So don't fall for their BS. And don't miss any chances to shut up."

"Okay."

Hannah turned her yellow pad facedown on her lap. "We need to hire a private detective to work on your case."

I jumped up from my chair. "That means you're in?"

She blew out a sigh. "I suppose."

I jumped out of my chair. "Thank you, thank you."

"Sit."

I sat.

Hannah said, "I want letters from your family and friends, attesting to your character. We'll need those to reduce bail if you're arrested."

"Thank you for saying 'if.'"

"I'm going to write the DA, offering to surrender you. That way, they won't just show up and slap you in handcuffs."

"That doesn't sound as good as the 'if.'" I stood up and started pacing.

She said, "Have the police searched your apartment yet?"

I stopped pacing. "They're going to?"

"I want our detective to search it first."

I sat down across from her. "Why do we need a detective?" Which I can't afford.

She uncrossed her legs. "I use an ex-cop. He knows what the police look for. We'll need him to do some other investigating as well."

I have no idea how I'll pay this guy, *but* "Okay."

Hannah said, "By the way, if there's anything in your apartment that shouldn't be, now would be a good time to have a spring cleaning."

I turned up my palms. "Trust me, there's nothing offensive in my apartment except some bird droppings."

Hannah stood up and tossed her yellow pad onto the desk. "One last thing. Are you aware that criminal lawyers get paid up front?"

Uh-oh. "Why's that? So you don't get stiffed if your client ends up in jail?"

"Yes."

I grimaced. "You could have sugarcoated that a little."

"Harvey, do you not have the money?"

"I've got most of it." *If you consider thirty percent to be the definition of "most."* "Maybe we could work out a payment schedule?"

She gave her head a quarter turn, looking at me skeptically. "I've never done that."

"I'm good for it. I've got magic gigs lined up. And I substitute teach. Hey, we magicians really understand devious. Maybe I can do some detective work for your clients."

Hannah rubbed her eyes with her fists. "I have to think about all this."

CHAPTER NINE

Next morning, I called for substitute teaching work.

Zippo.

I asked for Charlie Nelson, the supervisor who usually comes through for me. When he got on the line, I said, "Charlie, I've called for two days and they've said there's no work. Hard to believe every teacher in Los Angeles has broken out with 'healthy.'"

He cleared his throat. "You know the drill. I got seniority issues. I got unions up my ass."

"I need work. I've got some serious bills."

"Well . . . let me look into it." From the tone of his voice, he may as well have said "If I were Pinocchio, you could feel my nose from where you're sitting."

Does he know about the cops? I don't want to educate him if he doesn't. Am I being paranoid? Screw it. "Charlie, is this about the cops?"

I could hear his chair squeal. "I guess maybe someone said something to somebody."

"I haven't been accused of anything. They just asked me some questions. It's not fair."

"Let me look into it."

"You already said that. Charlie, I need this."

"I'll see what I can do."

I clunked down the phone and called Marty Levin, my magic agent. As soon as he answered, I said, "Marty, it's Harvey. I need work."

"And good morning to you, too."

"I mean it. I got bills to pay."

"Oh. That changes everything. None of my other clients have bills."

"Is there anything for me? Anything?"

"Sorry, Harvey. Not in the next few weeks."

"I *really* need this."

He sighed. "All right. Let me shake the trees."

I speak "Marty" well enough to know that meant "Not a prayer."

Later in the morning, I showed up at Hannah's office. I didn't want to call first. If she was going to blow me off, maybe she'd reconsider if I was standing right there.

When I opened the door, she was on the phone, pacing as she spoke. Hannah looked at me, then went back to her conversation.

When she hung up, she said, "Harvey, I can't take your case. I'm already swamped, and you obviously can't afford a lawyer."

I felt my chest tighten. "I'm good for it."

She shook her head. "I'll get you a public defender who won't charge you."

I swallowed. "I don't want a public defender. I want you."

"I'm sorry. It's business."

I nodded slowly, to give myself a few seconds to think. "Okay.

Business. How about this? I'll write you a check for three grand. That's almost all my savings. That means I'm totally committed."

"I told you. Criminal lawyers—"

"Get paid in advance. Look, what will it take?"

She crossed her arms. "Wait a minute. How could you afford Nadler?"

I gritted my teeth. "My mother was going to give me the money."

"And . . ."

I looked at the carpet. "She said she'd only pay for him. Not anyone else."

Hannah rubbed the front of her neck. "Harvey—"

"I don't want Nadler. I want you. I'll work in your office. I'll try to send you business. I'll do your laundry."

I got a crack of a smile.

I produced a red silk handkerchief and held it out to her. "How can you resist someone who makes hankies out of thin air?"

I almost got the rest of the smile.

"Hannah, please. I really need you."

She stared at me.

I raised my eyebrows, trying to looking like a pet store puppy dog who wants to go home with the customer.

Hannah slowly shook her head. "Well, I hate sending anyone to Nadler. . . ."

I smiled, nodding.

She said, "Maybe I could use a little help in the office."

I made a pull-down *Yes!* gesture. "Excellent! I can use my magic skills to find new angles on your cases."

"Nice thought, but what I really need is someone to file, answer the phones, and run errands."

We had something of a negotiation, considering I had no leverage whatsoever. I agreed to work in her office full-time, except for substitute teaching, since that put money in both our pockets. Hannah also agreed to let me off for my magic gigs. That wasn't much of a give on her part, considering I hadn't worked in a month. And most of the gigs were at night.

I lost the last negotiating issue, about bringing my bird to the office.

When I got to her office the next morning, Hannah pointedly looked at her watch and said, "It's nine twelve. My office opens sharply at nine."

Well, aren't we off to a good start? "Sorry."

She waved at the papers lying on her desk, her chairs, her filing cabinet, and the floor. "I'm way behind on filing. Most of these are stacked by client, and they should be in chronological order. Please check to make sure they're correct, then punch them into the proper file. Each file has three sections—one for my notes, one for correspondence, and one for court documents. Got that?"

"Absolutely." Sort of. In truth, my filing skills peaked at stuffing overdue bills in a drawer.

Hannah opened her desk drawer, took out a metal punch that cuts two holes in the top of a page—and handed it to me. She said, "When everything's clipped in, put the files in the cabinet, alphabetically by client. If there are multiple files for the same client, then put them alphabetically by matter, and then chronologically if a single matter has more than one file. I'm expecting a delivery of some documents in the next few hours. When they come, take them to Kinko's and make two copies. They're sensitive materials, so you have to do it personally. Don't just hand them to a clerk."

She picked up the phone and dialed a number.

I looked around at the stacks of papers on every available surface. While Hannah yapped on the phone and paced, I picked the smallest one I could find. The client's name was Arnold. It said: "B and E"—whatever that meant. Oh. Breaking and entering. I sat cross-legged on the floor and started to sort the stuff by dates. Ow. Shit. Paper cut. I sucked on my finger.

It took about ten minutes to get the papers in order and punched. Guess that wasn't so bad. I went to the file cabinet, took out the file, then sat on the floor and started to clip them in. Oh, wait. I forgot I was supposed to separate the correspondence and notes and other crap. I let out a sigh.

Maybe Mom really could afford Nadler. . . .

After I clipped Mr. Arnold into his file, I grabbed another stack and noticed the papers had my name on them. I glanced over at Hannah. She was lost in a phone call. I turned my back to her and took a peek.

At the top was a copy of the police report on Sherry Allen's murder. My pal Sergeant Morton's handwriting could use a Rosetta Stone. Either the victim's address was 4529, No. 9, Kester Avenue in Van Nuys, or he wanted to put 45,299 Jesters in a Vat of Ice. From what I could decipher, she was twenty-four years old and worked with autistic kids. Cause of death was strangulation.

No location for the father of her son. Child turned over to foster care.

I turned the page and saw a photo of the murder scene. My breathing stopped. I quickly looked away.

Then glanced back.

She was nude, lying on her back, tied spread-eagle to the bed. Her eyes and mouth were open wide, like she was shocked that this was happening to her.

How could someone do this to another person?

How could they think my DNA was there?

Hang on. . . .

I studied the picture. Something's off.

What is it?

The way her wrists were tied to the headboard with rope. There's something . . .

What?

I kept staring. There!

The rope. That's it.

I took the photo over to Hannah, who was still yapping on the phone. She gave me a look that said, Why are you not filing?

I held out the photo. She scowled at me, then put her hand over the mouthpiece. "You're supposed to be clipping materials, not nosing into the files. Especially yours, which you can do on your own time."

I said, "She wasn't really tied to the bed."

"Excuse me?"

"Look." I pointed to a small gap in the rope loops around her wrists.

She held up her hand, signaling me to hold on, then finished the conversation. Hannah let out an impatient breath. "What is it?"

I pointed at the photo and said, "Look at the gap in the rope. When Houdini let an audience member tie him up with rope, he flexed his muscles. No matter how tightly they cinched the ropes, when he relaxed, it created enough slack for him to slip out. See that space around her wrists? It's a fake. Maybe some kinky thing. She could have easily gotten loose."

Hannah took the photo, squinched her eyes at it, then looked up. "So she probably knew the killer."

"Exactly. Maybe it was rough sex, but it probably wasn't rape."

"Get me the file."

I grabbed the rest of the papers off the floor and handed them to her.

Hannah thumbed through, stared at a page, then looked at me. "You're right. The coroner said it's not clear whether it was rape or just rough sex."

I grinned, saying, "Let's go look at her apartment."

Hannah backed up. "What?"

"Maybe we'll find something the cops missed."

She laughed. "So, Mr. Sleuth for a Day, you're going to waltz in and solve the case?"

"Yep."

She shook her head. "You can't go to the crime scene."

"I'll wear latex gloves."

"I'm not worried about prints. The cops have already released the scene."

"So what's the problem?"

"There's probably a thousand of them, but let's start with this. Her neighbors see you; then in court, they say you look familiar. In the minds of a jury, that could place you at the crime scene."

"I'll wear a disguise."

Hannah rolled her eyes. "Yeah, that won't be suspicious. Why don't you put on a kimono and tell them you're Japanese?"

"I was thinking I'd go as a dog."

"Unless you use a doggy door, they won't let you in." She shook her head. "You have no right to be there without a court order."

"Then we'll have to rely on my charm."

She twisted her mouth. "Drop the 'we.'"

"Hey. We might find something important. I mean, I might find something important."

"This is stupid. If you're not going to listen to my advice, I can't be effective as your lawyer."

"You wanted a detective to help with the case. Who's better at figuring out mysteries than a magician?"

"If you get caught, you'll be in even deeper shit."

"Then I won't get caught. Look. I already found something in the photo that the cops didn't notice. Who knows what I'll find when I actually go there?"

She stared at me. The phone rang. She didn't answer it. "You committed to working here full-time."

"I get an hour for lunch, don't I? When you go to your mysterious meeting?"

She glared at me.

Why's she so touchy about those meetings? A shrink maybe? Hardly a big deal these days. Isn't having a shrink kinda like making a fashion statement?

Hannah shook her head. "I guess you're free to be an idiot on your lunch hour. I don't want to know about it."

"Then I guess I can't thank you for something you don't know about."

She wagged her finger at me. "If you screw up your case, I'm resigning."

"Okay, okay."

"Be back at two fifteen. Sharp."

Ja wohl, mein Führer.

I grinned as I went back to filing.

She softened her voice. "And be careful."

CHAPTER TEN

As soon as Hannah left for her mysterious appointment, I went to Kinko's, xeroxed the police report on Sherry Allen, and headed home. Standing in front of the bathroom mirror, I twisted open a bottle of spirit gum and took out the little brush that was attached to the cap. I painted my upper lip with the cold liquid, picked up the mustache that I sometimes use onstage, and pressed it onto my lip. The thing smelled like old hair. I looked in the mirror and twisted my lip.

I took the phony can of foam shaving cream from my medicine cabinet and screwed off the bottom, to get to my ultrasecret hiding place that every thief probably learns about in Burglary 101. I fished out my secret "tools" and stuck them in my pocket.

When I got to Sherry Allen's street, Kester Avenue, I parked a block away from her address. No need for anyone to see my car near her building.

I walked toward the apartment house, which was one of

those beige boxes that spawned like paramecium in the 1960s. On the front wall, the name Kester Prince was spelled in wooden letters that were covered with sparkly metal disks. Below the sign was a scraggly palm tree with dried brown fronds, sticking out of a white-rock flower bed.

The building was surrounded by a wrought-iron fence that looked like it was added long after the building went up. Probably when the neighborhood took a nosedive. I stopped at the security gate's phone box and looked at the directory. There were maybe twenty names printed on little cards. Near the bottom was S. Allen.

I picked up the phone and dialed the manager.

A man's voice said, "Yes?"

"Hi. I'm investigating the Sherry Allen incident. Could we talk a few minutes?"

"Are you with the police?"

"No."

"I already talked to the police."

"I know. This will only take a minute."

"Who are you?"

"I'm a private detective. May I come in?"

The door buzzed.

I went into the building. The center hall was dimly lit by coiled fluorescent bulbs dangling from ceiling sockets. The air smelled like damp carpet.

Halfway down, I saw a middle-aged man step out of his door and look at me. He had thinning black hair and loose skin under his jaw that sagged like a canvas pouch. As I got close, I saw a mass of curly hair spilling over the neck of his Hawaiian shirt.

The manager struck out his hand. "Jim Caldwell."

"Horace Kimbel." Close enough. If I get questioned, I'll say I gave him my right name but he misunderstood me.

Jim looked at me, almost squinting.

He said, "Have we met?"

Huh? How could he possibly even think that?

I said, "No." Did my voice go up when I spoke?

He kept staring at me.

The fake mustache felt stiff against my lip.

Caldwell shrugged an *Oh well.* "How can I help you?"

"Could we talk privately for a minute?"

He shrugged. "C'mon in."

I followed Jim into his apartment. The living room had a beige couch with black piping, a wagon-wheel coffee table, and a television on a wheeled cart with wires trailing behind. Decor by Chez Goodwill. One wall had several wooden racks that displayed a collection of spoons with city names on the handles. I'd seen those things in souvenir stores. Always wondered who bought them.

I said, "How many spoons do you have?"

Jim gave a throaty *Ugh.* "Eleven hundred and something. My wife's idea of a hobby." He shook his head. "These are her favorites. The rest are in a couple of old suitcases."

I walked over and looked at the display: Philadelphia Bicentennial, Los Angeles '84 Olympics, New Orleans Jazz Festival.

I turned to him and said, "Nice."

He gave me a look that said, You can't possibly mean that.

I said, "So, Jim. Can you tell me a little about Sherry Allen?"

The door to the hall opened. A short woman with a downturned mouth came in, carrying a bag of groceries. She looked at me like I might be a spoon thief, then hustled into the kitchen.

Jim said, "Why're you asking about Sherry?"

"Like I said, I'm working as a private detective."

"For who?"

I swallowed. "A possible suspect in the case."

"Who?"

"Sorry, I can't say."

Jim stared at me, cocked his head, and squinted.

Finally, he said, "I didn't know much about Sherry. I've only been the manager here about six months. She was living in the building when I got hired."

"You must know something."

"Well . . . She had a little dog. The neighbors sometimes complained about the barking. Otherwise, she wasn't any trouble. Paid her rent on time. Which is more than I can say for a lot of folks around here."

"Did she get many visitors?"

"I wouldn't really know."

"Boyfriends?"

"Sorry."

"Could I see her apartment?"

Jim lowered his eyebrows. "I don't think I can do that."

"Why not?"

"Well, I could be responsible if something turned up missing."

"You can come in with me."

"Sherry's parents are coming to pick up her stuff, day after tomorrow. I'm not authorized to let a stranger in. Maybe you should talk to her parents."

Great idea. I'll just say, "Hello, Mrs. Allen. The cops think I screwed your daughter, then killed her. Would you mind if I poked through her things?"

Shit.

The parents' arrival isn't good news. Once they pick up her stuff, I'll never get to see it.

I raised my eyebrows, pleading. "I'd only need a few minutes. It'd be just between you and me."

Jim shook his head. "Sorry."

"What if I threw in a few spoons?"

He smiled.

I let out a little sigh. "Could I see her rental application?" I figured maybe I could find some info on her friends, employers—that kind of stuff.

"That's also confidential. Look, you seem like a nice fella, but I gotta be careful here. You know, with the cops and all."

"What harm could it do?"

"You know how things are these days. Everybody suing everybody. I could lose my job."

We went on in that vein awhile. I got precisely nowhere.

I said, "Well, thanks for your time."

"Sure." He walked me to the door of his apartment.

I stepped into the hall and turned back. "I'll check back, in case you think of anything."

Jim gave me another "Are you sure I don't know you?" look.

I started toward the front of the building, listening for the manager to close his door.

When I heard the lock catch, I slowed down and glanced back.

Empty hallway.

I stood there a moment to make sure he wasn't coming back out.

When he didn't appear, I walked down the dim hall and stopped in front of Sherry's apartment.

CHAPTER ELEVEN

As I reached for the handle of Sherry's apartment door, I got another idea.

I walked farther down the hall and knocked on the door of her next-door neighbor. No one home. Then I banged on the door directly across the hall from Sherry's. Inside, I heard footsteps. A few seconds later, the door opened and I saw an elderly lady with disheveled hair, wearing a pink terrycloth bathrobe, even though it was almost two in the afternoon.

The woman squinted at me. "Yes?" With an age-spotted hand, she pulled the lapels of the robe tight against her throat.

I said, "I'm sorry to bother you. My name is Horace Kimbel, and I'm doing a private investigation into the unfortunate incident with Sherry Allen."

Her eyes softened. "That poor dear."

"You knew her?"

She squinted at me. "Who are you again?"

"A private detective."

"Can't you get this from the police? I talked to them for over an hour."

I nodded sympathetically. "I'm sorry to ask again. It's important for me to talk directly to the witnesses. How did you say you knew her?"

She nodded. "I babysat Sherry's son, Brandon, sometimes. Sweetest little boy. Do you know how he's doing?"

I shook my head. "I'm sorry, I don't."

She let go of the bathrobe lapels. "Ironic, isn't it? Sherry had to leave her own child so she could help those autistic children? She wanted to go to medical school, you know. She was taking science classes at Northridge."

"Did Sherry get a lot of visitors?"

Ms. Bathrobe sighed. "I'm afraid she was one of those trusting souls who went for a few too many men."

"Did anyone come more often than the others?"

"There was a young man with tattoos who seemed to be here a lot."

I took a step closer. "What kind of tattoos?"

She shook her head. "They all look like scribbles to me."

I tried to keep my voice soft. "Did you remember anything else about him?"

"Spiked hair. I told the police all about this."

I nodded. "Was there anything else you noticed about Sherry?"

"She had a little dog that barked a lot. It used to drive me crazy, but now I find myself listening for him." She looked at me. "Is that crazy?"

I spoke gently. "Of course not."

She wiped her eyes with the sleeve of her bathrobe.

"Did you notice anything unusual on her . . . last night?"

She shook her head, sniffled.

I said, "No one coming or going?"

"No." Her eyes glistened. "I . . . I'm sorry."

She closed the door.

I tried a few more doors, and when no one answered, I went

back to Sherry's apartment, No. 9. *Gotta get in before the parents take her stuff.*

I grabbed the door handle and turned. It rattled in place. I squatted down and studied the lock. Pin and tumbler cylinder. The easiest to pick. Thank you, Mr. Cheapo Builder.

When I was a kid, I read that Houdini worked for a locksmith so he could learn the inner workings of handcuffs, padlocks, and safes. The summer I turned sixteen, I wangled a job at Locks-a-Million, a dumpy little place on Riverside Drive. I saw maybe five customers in eight weeks, but I learned a helluva lot about locks, including how to pick them. I also acquired the lockpick set that now resided in my pocket, even though keeping it without a locksmith license was on the shady side of the law.

I looked both ways down the hall, then pulled the tools out of my pocket. I took the tension wrench, which looked like a miniature hockey stick, stuck it in the bottom of the keyhole, and turned it slightly to keep tension on the pins. Then I took the pick, a metal instrument with a hook on the end that looked like a dentist's pick, and inserted it all the way into the keyhole. I maneuvered the pick until I could feel it engage the first pin; then I pushed until it lined up with the shear line. Keeping the tension on the cylinder, I carefully moved the pick forward to the next pin and fiddled with it until I felt the pin line up.

A bead of sweat ran down my forehead, then veered into my eye. *Ahh!* That stings. If I wipe it, I'll lose the two pins I already picked. *Ow!* I blinked rapidly.

I looked down the hall. Still clear.

I got another pin lined up.

Then the next. Almost there . . .

My cell phone rang. *Shit.* I can't have someone come out to look for whatever is ringing.

I let go of the pins, pulled out the picks, and answered the damn thing. "What?"

Hannah said, "Did I not tell you to be back at two fifteen sharp?"

I looked at my watch. Two twenty. *Ooops.* "I'm really sorry."

Hannah said, "Get back here. Now. Otherwise, you have no job and no lawyer."

She hung up.

I looked at Sherry's door, looked at the cell phone.

I stuck the lockpick tools in my pocket and went out the building's back door, so I wouldn't pass the manager's apartment.

CHAPTER TWELVE

When I got back to the office, Hannah set down her pen. "Why were you late getting back from lunch? That is unacceptable."

I smiled sheepishly. "It took a little longer than I thought to, you know, do that thing you don't want to know about."

She closed her eyes and slowly shook her head. "I don't suppose I should ask if you learned anything?"

I told her about the manager and the neighbor, then said, "I'll be having lunch again tomorrow out of the office. Stay tuned for further developments."

"What you do on your own time is your business. Just remember. You have a lunch *hour*."

"Okay, okay."

Hannah opened her desk drawer, took something out, walked over to me. She handed me a business card that read *Daniel Labs*.

Hannah said, "I've asked the cops for a split of the DNA from the crime scene so we can have it analyzed by our own expert. You can leave early to pick it up from the downtown police department at this address." She handed me a piece of paper. "You'll need the case number written at the bottom. Then take the DNA sample to the address on the business card. I phoned ahead and made all the arrangements at both places."

"Anything else?"

She looked at me. "Pray they find a discrepancy."

Late in the afternoon, I got to the downtown police headquarters and found a small room whose door said EVIDENCE RELEASE CENTER. Behind a window made of thick bulletproof glass, a tired-looking woman in a blue uniform pushed a red button. The speaker inside a metal wall box shrieked, then her tinny voice said, "Can I help you?"

My mouth felt a little dry. "I'm, uh, here to pick up some evidence."

"Case number?"

I read the number off Hannah's sheet.

She said, "Put your driver's license in the drawer." A metal drawer underneath the window slid out at me, like one of those bank teller operations.

I fished the license out of my wallet and set it down.

She pulled the drawer toward her, picked up my license, and studied it. Then she got up and went into a back room.

A man in a beige messenger uniform with greased black hair and stained armpits walked up beside me. He smelled like a pitchfork full of manure.

The man smiled at me. "Pickin' up some evidence?"

No, I'm in the Evidence Release Center to grab some cheeseburgers. "Yeah."

"Me, too. Two rapes and an assault. Whadda you got?"

I started breathing through my mouth to avoid the smell. "Parking ticket."

He screwed his forehead in puzzlement.

Through the tin speaker, I heard, "Mr. Kendall?"

I turned away from Mr. Dung Heap, still breathing through my mouth.

The woman behind the window said, "Please sign the receipt."

The bank drawer opened. Inside was a receipt, my driver's license, and a clear plastic Baggie with a strip of yellow tape on it.

I scribbled my name on the receipt, grabbed the license and Baggie, and left her to Mr. Manure, who stepped up to the window. Good thing for her that it's made of thick glass.

As I walked down the hall, I examined the clear plastic Baggie. Inside was a tiny piece of cotton, smaller than a pencil eraser. A strip of yellow tape printed with the words *Los Angeles Police* ran up one side of the Baggie, over the stapled top, and down the other side. Someone had written on the bag itself, across the tape, with a felt pen. Case number, date, and an undecipherable signature.

I held the Baggie carefully in my fingertips and walked to my car. After placing it gently on the passenger seat, I drove through heavy afternoon traffic to the Pacoima address on the lab's business card.

It turned out to be a squat brick building on Glenoaks Boulevard, surrounded by a cracked parking lot with weeds growing through the asphalt. I squinted at the building. Is this the right place? I can't see an address number.

I looked closer. The sign on the door said DANIELS LAB.

I drove into the lot, parked my car, and went into the building.

Whoa. The temperature in here is subarctic.

My bare arms bristled. This some kinda lab thing? To preserve dead bodies or something?

Behind a counter, a man stood up. He had a nose that looked like it had been given a quarter turn clockwise. As I stepped closer, I saw that the pin on his white coat said *David*.

David said, "Help you?"

"I'm delivering some evidence for analysis." I rubbed my hands for warmth. Is my breath visible?

"Name?"

"Hannah Fisher."

He looked through several loose pages, then back at me. "Maybe it's under a case name?"

I shifted my weight from one foot to the other. "Um, Kendall?"

He looked at the papers again. "Yep. Got it."

I quickly handed him the Baggie, got a receipt, and hurried outside. It felt great to be back in the heat of a seventy-degree day.

As I walked toward my car, I saw a woman standing next to the open door of a black Dodge Neon, taking off her white lab coat. She looked about my age, with short black hair, bright blue eyes, and a slight overbite. Now that the lab coat was off, I saw that she wore a loose-fitting checkered blouse over denim jeans. Is she wearing a bra?

The woman noticed me watching and held my gaze. Her mouth formed a little smile.

I smiled back.

She slowly rubbed her bare arm.

We kept looking at each other as I walked over to her.

I said, "You must work here." Could I have possibly found a worse cliché?

She smiled with that overbite. "Guess the white coat gave it away?"

I laughed a little too much. "What do you do?"

"Lab work. Titrating liquids, capillary electrophoresis, and similar exciting things. What brings you to beautiful downtown Pacoima?"

I looked down at the cracked pavement, then forced myself to look at her. "I'm working for a criminal lawyer. Dropping off some evidence for analysis."

She raised her head in an *Ah.*

I said, "You worked here long?"

"Just a few months. I left my prior job over a moral issue."

I took a step closer. "What happened?"

She held out her hand. "I'm Carly Banks."

"Harvey Kendall." I shook her hand. She didn't let go of mine.

She said, "Your hand's cold."

"Yeah. It's about three degrees in there. That to preserve chemicals or something?"

"No. The lab director likes it that way. Took me a month to get used to it."

She was still holding my hand.

I cleared my throat. "So, what happened to your other job?"

She slid her hand out of mine, crooked her index finger in a "Follow me" gesture, and walked around behind her car. When I got there, Carly pointed to a bumper sticker: ABORTION IS MURDER.

Uh-oh. Religious freak?

She said, "I worked for two years at a university, doing stem-cell research. Then I came to believe that dealing with the aftermath of abortions was wrong, so I felt like I had to quit. When I left, I wasn't exactly quiet about my feelings, and that didn't go over so well with the academic community. Since they all know each other, I couldn't get a research job, even outside the stem-cell area. So this was the best I could do. I'm sure things'll quiet down in time. Meanwhile, I'm the only Ph.D. here at the lab."

"All because you talked about your views on abortion?"

"Uh-huh."

"Whatever happened to free speech?"

She twisted her mouth and raised her eyebrows as if to say, Don't be naïve.

I said, "You, um, said you 'came to believe' abortions were wrong. Was that . . . I mean, was it because of . . ."

She smiled. "A religious awakening? No. I'm an agnostic."

I wrinkled my forehead. "So why did you take such a strong stand?"

She walked back to the open door of her car. I hurried behind.

Carly said, "I gotta run. I'm meeting someone." She reached into the pocket of her blouse and pulled out a business card, then leaned inside the car and grabbed a pen. Carly wrote on the back of the card and handed it to me. "Here's my cell phone. Buy me a cup of coffee sometime, and I'll tell you all about it."

I looked at the card. *Carly Banks, Ph.D.,* along with the Daniels Lab information. I flipped it over to make sure her personal number was really there. Nice handwriting.

Carly gave me a smile with that overbite, her top teeth sensually touching her bottom lip.

CHAPTER THIRTEEN

Next morning, when I walked into Hannah's office, she said, "It's five minutes after nine."

"My watch says it's nine exactly." Give or take five minutes.

"Harvey, you've been late both days you've worked here. I expect you here on time."

Prepare for disappointment. "Sorry."

She gave me a curt nod. "Don't do it again."

Hannah spent the morning on the phone while I worked through the filing, which seemed to grow faster than I was putting it away, like the insect monsters in some space movie.

She left for an appointment late morning, so I took the opportunity to extend my lunch hour a bit and drove toward Sherry's apartment. On the way, I called Dr. Carly from the laboratory on her cell.

When she answered, I said, "Dr. Banks, this is the barista

from Starbucks, and there's an incredibly charming young man here who's insisting on buying you a coffee tonight."

She laughed. "You don't waste any time, do you?"

"One of my better qualities. How about it?"

"Well, since you had the barista call me, I don't see how I can refuse. But not tonight."

We arranged to meet at the Starbucks in Westwood the next night.

She said, "There's one embarrassing thing."

"I like embarrassing things."

"Well . . . I've forgotten your name."

I parked a block away from Sherry's apartment, in the opposite direction from where I'd parked the day before, and walked toward her building. How do I get in? Not a good idea to alert Jim, the Hawaiian-shirted apartment manager. Can't pick the security gate's lock out in the open. Maybe buzz Ms. Bathrobe? I didn't get her name. Do a random buzz? That never works. Even if it does, they're suspicious.

Maybe the old "Wait for someone to go in and grab the gate." How do I stand around and not look like a stalker?

I walked slowly past the building. The lock on the security gate was better made than the ones inside. It'd take a long time to pick. I looked around. Don't see anyone heading for the gate.

I turned the corner, walked a half block, and turned down the alley behind Sherry's building. The rear of the apartment house was built with an overhang held up by round black metal pillars, with several cars parked under the eve. The back door was wrought-iron mesh. Same kind of high-security lock as the front gate. Neighboring apartments looked down on it. Can't pick it without risking an audience.

I started to circle the block, then stopped.

Hmm.

The cars.

I walked back. Wonder if any of the cars have alarms? Probably not the battered Ford from the seventies. There. That Kia looks pretty new. It's parked all the way into a space, so the neighbors can't see me if I stand in front of it.

I went around the side of the car next to the wall, turned myself sideways, and inched forward. The car was too close to the stucco wall. Couldn't quite get to the front. I squeezed as far forward as I could manage and got my foot on the bumper. I stepped hard, then let it go. The car bounced a little.

No alarm.

I stood up on the bumper and bounced up and down.

Kept going.

Harder.

The alarm shrieked out an escalating *whooop.*

Ow. That is seriously loud.

I scoogied out of the tight space, hurried over beside the Ford, and squatted down. The Kia alarm switched to a pulsing buzz.

Is this stupid? What if the apartment manager comes out?

The alarm went back to a whoop.

Where's the car owner? Are these people deaf?

The back door of the building rattled, then swung open. A woman carrying a small child stepped out, both of them grimacing from the noise. She looked around, frightened, then held her keys toward the car.

Go. Now. While her attention is on the car. I straightened up, sidestepped along the wall, caught the door as it closed, and hurried into the building. I heard the car alarm stop. My ears were still ringing.

I took a few steps down the dim hallway, then stepped into

the stairwell. Don't want that woman to see me when she comes back.

I heard the metallic groan of the back door, then the woman's voice talking as she went past. "Shhh, honey, it's okay."

Steps going farther down the hall.

Jangling of keys.

Door open.

Door close.

The hall went quiet.

I waited a few moments, then peered around.

Empty.

I stepped softly as I walked to Sherry's apartment, continually swiveling my head.

When I got to her door, I took the lock picks out of my pants pocket and squatted down. After looking up and down the hall one last time, I stuck the wrench in the bottom of the keyhole, inserted the pick, and started working the pins.

Got the first one.

I checked the hall again. Still clear.

Worked the next pin.

My thighs burned from the awkward stance. I let out a breath I didn't realize I was holding, then wriggled the pick until the last pin lined up.

The cylinder gave way in a slight turn.

Yes!

I used the tension wrench to turn it all the way. The latch opened.

I pushed the door just past the catch, then pulled my tools out of the lock.

As I straightened up, my knees cracked. I froze. Did anyone hear that?

I gave one last glance up and down the hall, then stepped inside and shut the door.

CHAPTER FOURTEEN

Inside Sherry's apartment, I leaned my back against the door and tried to steady my breathing. Blood whooshed loudly in my ears.

In the dark apartment, I groped along the wall, feeling for a light switch, then stopped. If someone looks through the window, will they notice her lights are on? Can you see lights in the daytime?

I waited for my eyes to adjust, looking around. Her place smelled like dusty rags.

Against a living room wall, I saw a bookshelf made of raw planks and cinder blocks. The wood sagged under a mass of paperbacks and an old television. Next to that was a yellow crib. I took a few steps toward the crib. Mounted over the bare plastic mattress was a mobile of multicolored fish, hanging dead-still. I remembered that Sherry had an eighteen-month-old son. I took another step. There was dust on the crib's rails. Dust on the mattress. Even on the fish. I found myself wondering if this little boy will even remember his mother. I turned away from the crib.

Against the opposite wall was a couch. An end table was

crammed with photos in clear plastic frames. I walked over to it. Two of the pictures were larger than the others. One showed Sherry in ski clothes, standing in the snow with an older couple. Gotta be her parents. They look just like her. Sherry had her fingers in a V behind her father's head, making rabbit ears. The other large picture was a photo of Sherry with a toddler on her lap, both of them grinning. A tiny white Maltese looked up at them.

A lot of the smaller photos were pictures of Sherry with different kids. Maybe the autistic ones she'd worked with? They didn't look any different from normal kids. Most were smiling. Some were playing with blocks. Another sat staring at a train set.

The rest of the pictures were of Sherry with different men. In every photo, she was touching the man: her head on his shoulder, or hugging him around the waist, or holding his hand. In each one, she was looking at the camera with that sexy look I'd seen in the photo that the cops showed me.

I went into the kitchen. The air smelled of rotting food. I took a deep breath and held it.

The sink was full of dishes caked with food. On top of the pile was a tiny bowl, painted with a clown holding a red balloon that said *Brandon*. Beside the sink was a box of organic wheat cereal with its flaps standing up. A stream of ants pulsed down the side of the box, across the counter, and onto the floor. On the linoleum was a small red dog dish, heaped with tiny kibble pellets. It said *Misty* on the side. Why was it full? Did the dog stop eating when she . . .

I left the kitchen and let out my breath. To my right, I saw the open bathroom door. In front of me was the closed bedroom door.

I took a step toward the bedroom, then stopped.

What am I doing here?

I feel like a ghoul.

I half-turned around.

No. I have to be here. The cops are trying to hang this on me.

How could they think I did something like this? I'm starting to feel like some guy in a 1950s horror film who's telling everyone that the aliens are coming and they're all smiling at him and saying, "Sure, sure" while they call the men in the white coats with nets and . . .

Shit. I could really swing for this. I'm the only one who knows I didn't do it. Except the real killer, who's not likely to stand up in court like Jean Valjean in *Les Miserables.* My shirt felt wet against my chest.

If I don't figure this out, there's a good chance nobody will.

I turned back and stared at the off-white door, which was warped enough to leave gaps where it should be flush with the frame.

I took a step.

Stopped.

Can I really go into the bedroom where she was murdered?

There could be something important in there. According to the manager, her parents are coming tomorrow.

I took another step.

Wouldn't the cops have found everything important?

Am I going to see something gross? I don't do well with blood.

I reached for the door handle, then stopped my hand in midair.

C'mon, Harvey.

I forced myself to put my fingers on the knob. The metal felt cold.

Should I really be doing this? Hannah said it was stupid. Why am I paying her if I'm not going to listen?

The handle squeaked as I turned it.

I took a deep breath and opened the door.

CHAPTER FIFTEEN

As I stepped inside Sherry's bedroom, I half-expected to see the outline of a body painted on a bloody mattress.

I let out my breath.

Just messy sheets. The crumpled fabric was printed with little smiling unicorns.

No ropes on the headboard.

I looked around the room. In one corner was a chair, heaped with teddy bears, a Barbie doll, and a stuffed sock decorated as a monkey. Near to the chair was a desk, with wires stretched halfway across, their plug ends laying limply inside the dust outline of a laptop. Did the cops take the computer? If not, was there a burglary? The door to the hall didn't look forced. No broken windows. Maybe the killer took the computer because he wanted it to look like a robbery? Maybe because he didn't want anyone to know what was on it?

I walked over and carefully opened the desk drawer. A mess of pens, chewed pencils, Scotch tape, Post-its, and paper clips.

When I finished looking through the desk, I walked over to her dresser, which had an open red-lacquered jewelry box sitting on top. A thick gold necklace was draped over the side of the box. In the black velvet divider were a few rings and jeweled pins.

This couldn't have been a robbery. They'd have taken the jewelry, even if there's nothing valuable.

I opened the top drawer of the dresser. Inside were three cut-glass bottles that smelled of flowery perfume.

The next drawer held her underwear and bras. I started to go through them, then stopped myself.

Hannah was right. There's nothing here. I took all this risk . . .

I let out a breath and closed the drawer.

As I straightened up, I noticed something.

Hang on. . . .

I squinted at the jewelry box. There was something odd about it.

What?

Onstage, the wooden boxes that make people disappear sometimes have hidden compartments, designed to fool the eye. It's done by painting them with a forced perspective, and it's very deceptive. But I've seen so many trick boxes that it's obvious to me.

That's what's wrong here. The jewelry box has more space than you can access from the top. Not much. But definitely something.

Is there a hidden compartment? I tried lifting up the velvet dividers.

Wouldn't budge.

Everything looked solid. I took out the jewelry, picked up the box, and studied the construction. I tilted it to the side and heard something slide.

Aha.

I quickly tilted the box the other way. Whatever was inside thunked against the wood.

If it got in there, there's a way to get to it.

I looked at the sides of the box. I turned it over and felt around the bottom. Checked the sides again.

Wait. . . . A gap where one of the corners met was a little bigger than the others. I fidgeted with the back panel. C'mon.

Nope.

I put both thumbs on the side panel and tried to slide it sideways.

Nope.

I pushed in the other direction.

When I applied upward pressure, I heard a click. The panel slid up an inch. Yes!

I could see a small space under the velvet divider tray. I opened my palm and tilted the end of the box against it.

A computer thumb drive, about the size of a toenail clipper, fell into my hand. I put down the jewelry box and took the thumb drive to the light by the window. The writing said *2.0GB.* A drive that size can hold a lot of data.

I went back to the box and pushed down the wooden panel. Then pushed harder. What, is it stuck?

I heard the metallic turn of a lock in the next room, then the creak of hinges.

Sherry's front door.

The manager's voice said, "Mr. Kimbel, I'm here with the police."

CHAPTER SIXTEEN

I heard footsteps coming toward Sherry's bedroom.

As I stuffed the thumb drive into my pants pocket, one of the lock picks slivered under my fingernail and stabbed into the quick. *OW!*

I pulled my hand out and shook it.

The lock picks. Shit. Not a good thing for the cops to find on me.

I am good and truly fucked.

The footsteps grew louder.

I grabbed the jewelry box, forced the secret panel back into place, scooped up the jewelry, and dumped it on top.

Just as I set down the box, an olive-skinned policeman walked in, followed by the manager. The manager turned on the lights. I squinted in the sudden brightness.

The name tag on the officer's shirt said *Morales.* The radio on his shiny black utility belt squawked.

The manager pointed at me. "That's him, Officer. One of the tenants saw him sneak in the back door. When they called me, I recognized his description. He'd been asking about Sherry Allen, so I listened at her door and, sure enough, I heard him inside." The manager squinted at me. "I see you shaved your mustache since yesterday."

Ooops.

Morales looked at me, then around the room. He noticed the jewelry on the dresser.

The officer took a step toward me. "May I see some identification?"

"Yes, of course." I fumbled my wallet from my back pocket and held it out.

He didn't take it. "Remove your license, please."

I opened my wallet, reached behind the clear plastic window, and grabbed the end of the laminated license with my fingertips. When I tried to pull it out, my grip slipped off. I wiped my fingers on my pants, managed to get a better hold, and pulled.

Is the damn thing glued in?

I scissored it until it was loose, then handed it over.

Morales looked at the license. The manager looked over his shoulder, then up at me. He narrowed his eyes.

Guess he noticed my name isn't Kimbel.

The officer handed back my license. "What are you doing here, Mr. Kendall?"

I tried to hold his gaze. "I'm a suspect in Sherry Allen's murder. I wanted to look at the crime scene."

The manager's eyebrows went up.

The cop said, "You understand breaking and entering is a crime?"

I said, "The door was unlocked."

The manager said, "No, it wasn't."

I said, "Yes, it was. Otherwise, how could I get in without breaking the door?"

The manager pointed a finger at me. "I double-checked it last night. After you came snooping around, bothering the other tenants. This apartment was locked up tight as a drum."

"I'm telling you, it was open."

The officer held up his hand to stop our volley. "Mr. Kendall, have you taken anything?"

"Absolutely not. I just looked around. I was only here five minutes before you arrived."

The manager said to the policeman, "Mrs. Horst, the lady across the hall, saw him fooling with the lock."

Morales squinted at me. "That true, Mr. Kendall?"

"I had to give it a few turns, that's all. Look, I'm sorry about this. The manager said Ms. Allen's parents are taking her things tomorrow. I wanted to see the apartment before it was emptied."

"You know there are procedures for this kind of thing?"

I grimaced, forcing a smile. "I guess not."

The officer's radio cackled.

He said, "You haven't taken anything?"

"Nothing."

"Would you mind emptying your pockets?"

The thumb drive and the lock picks suddenly felt like they were burning my leg. "Um, of course not."

The manager moved closer to the cop.

I reached inside my shirt pocket and pulled it inside out. Then I tucked it back in. I stuck my right hand into my pants pocket and grabbed my keys and coins. I stuck my left hand into the left front pocket, which had the lock picks and Sherry's thumb drive. I palmed the picks and drive, just like I do with coins in my magic act.

I took out both hands at the same time, pulling my pants pockets inside out. As I did, I let the coins "accidentally" fall. The officer's eyes went to the floor. While he was distracted, I dropped the picks and thumb drive into the shirt pocket I'd already shown him was empty.

I said, "Sorry. I'm a little nervous." With the insides of my pants pockets dangling over the seams, I held out my open palms, then turned my hands over and back.

He said, "Back pockets, please."

I turned around and pulled out my back pockets. With my back to him, I took the contraband out of my shirt pocket and put it back in a front pocket as I stuffed the inside back into my pants. I didn't want him noticing any bulges in the shirt.

When I turned around, the officer stared at me.

His radio screeched with static.

Morales said, "Get out of here, Mr. Kendall."

"Yes, sir." I squatted down to get the coins and keys.

The manager said, "You're not going to arrest him?"

"I have no evidence he took anything. There's no sign of a break-in."

"What about trespassing?"

The cop said, "With all due respect, sir, I've got a few more serious crimes to worry about." He motioned his head toward the door. "Mr. Kendall, I'll escort you out of the building."

I got back to Hannah's office a little after two.

She wasn't back from her mysterious meeting, so I unlocked the door, turned on the lights, and went inside.

Did the filing papers have babies while I was out?

I let out a sigh.

Hmm. I've got a few minutes before she gets back from her meeting. . . .

I sat down at her desk, glanced at the closed office door, and turned on her computer. Before it finished booting, Hannah came through the door. I sprang up.

She said, "What are you doing?"

"I . . . uh . . ."

"Don't you ever touch my computer without asking. There's sensitive data on there."

I threw up my hands in surrender and stepped away from the desk. "Sorry."

She scowled as she moved between me and the computer.

I reached into my pocket, grabbed the thumb drive, and held it out on my flat palm. "I went somewhere you don't want to know about and found this. The cops missed it."

"You . . . what?" She stepped closer and took the device.

I said, "It's a thumb drive."

She turned it in her fingers. "I can see that. What's on it?"

I suppose I could have plugged it into my ass to read the data, but I thought it'd be easier to use your computer. "I dunno. I was about to look."

Hannah studied the thumb drive, then looked at me. "Where did you find it?"

I told her about the jewelry box.

She cocked her head, as if asking, Are you really that clever? "How did you get into her apartment?"

"I don't think you want to hear about that."

She let out a breath.

I said, "Aren't you proud of me?"

Hannah set the thumb drive carefully on her desk. "Actually, this is quite problematic."

"What do you mean?"

"I mean, the cops didn't find it. So the only way we can prove it was in Sherry's apartment is for you to testify."

"You don't think they'll believe me?"

"That's not the issue. I never put murder defendants on the stand. It opens you up to cross-examination by the district attorney."

"I don't care. I didn't kill her."

She shook her head. "It's not about what you did. It's about how you look to a jury when you're under the knife of a prosecutor. On top of that, if there's anything on this device that incriminates you—"

"There won't be. I didn't know her."

"If there's anything on here that incriminates you, then I'm ethically obliged to give it to the police."

"Before we spin out thirty-two theories, why don't we stick the damn thing in the computer?" I gestured for her to take the seat in front of the screen.

Hannah sat down and plugged the thumb drive in a USB port. I came around behind and leaned over her shoulder to watch.

The device showed up as *G:* drive. Hannah ran the mouse pointer over it and double-clicked. Only one folder: *Sherry Personal.* Hannah clicked on it. A box popped up, asking for a password. We both said, "Shit."

I said, "You know anything about computer hacking?"

"I've got a techno weenie who can do it, but he's not cheap. It's worth trying a few guesses. Passwords are usually something people can easily remember. Personal data, like their birthday, Social Security number, or address. Most of that should be in the police report."

I walked toward the file cabinet. "I'll get it."

She shook her head. "I can't do this now. I'm on a deadline."

"Maybe I could—"

"Do your filing." Hannah took the thumb drive out of the computer and put it on her desk. "You can play with the thumb drive on your own time."

She started typing.

I said, "Someone took Sherry's computer. Can you find out if the cops have it?"

She answered without looking up. "I'll check. Start punching." Hannah grabbed her briefcase off the floor, put it on the desk, and clicked the two latches with her thumbs. "I've got to finish my brief in the Oliver Desmond case and file it within the next hour and a half."

"Oliver Desmond? That rich kid who killed the basketball player's son?"

"*Allegedly* killed him."

"You're his lawyer?"

"Yes."

I nodded repeatedly. "Wow, that's a really high-profile case."

She smiled despite herself. "I have to hurry. There's a press conference in two hours."

"And you're talking to the press? This really is the big time."

She picked up her purse. "I wouldn't normally talk to the press at all, but there's so much negative coverage of this case that I have to get our side out there."

"Cool. Where are we going?"

"*I'm* going to the downtown courthouse. You're staying here and filing."

As soon as Hannah left for the courthouse, I grabbed Sherry's police report and looked up her personal data. I stuck the thumb drive in Hannah's computer and thought about passwords Sherry might have used.

Let's start with her address.

When the box came up, I typed in the numbers of her address. A line of asterisks crawled across the screen. I hit ENTER. *Invalid Password.*

Maybe the address backward. *Invalid Password.*

Phone number.

Backward.

Address with apartment number.

Slices of her Social Security number.

Shit.

I leaned back and rubbed my eyes, telling myself I'd better get some filing done before the dragon returns to her lair.

I took out the thumb drive, shut down the computer, and picked up a stack of loose papers.

Hannah got back around five o'clock, swinging her briefcase.

I said, "How'd it go?"

"Not bad. I'll be on the news at six."

"Wow. That's really cool."

She waved the air like it was no big deal, but her mouth had a little grin. I said, "Let's go watch the news."

She narrowed her eyes, looking annoyed that I was trying to slough off work, but I could tell she was thinking about it.

Hannah said, "I've got a lot to do."

"C'mon. How often are you on television? We'll go to one of the local bars. Maybe someone will recognize you and we'll get a free drink."

She set her briefcase on her desk. "Let me see what I can get done in the next half hour."

As I grabbed a stack of papers, she said, "Harvey?"

I looked over at her.

I said, "Yeah?"

"I have to talk to you about your filing."

Uh-oh. "What about it?"

"You've got to be more careful. Misfiled is worse than unfiled."

And a penny saved is a penny earned?

Hannah said, "I found three documents out of date order. One document was in the wrong file. Fortunately, I came across it while I was looking for something else. Do you realize I could have wasted hours looking for those papers? All that a lawyer can sell is her time."

"Sorry."

"It shakes my confidence in your ability to do things properly."

Truth is, I thought, I'm not exactly Mr. Anal-Retentive, so putting me in charge of filing was a little like hiring a plumber to do your heart transplant. On the other hand, I can't afford to pay Hannah's bills, so here I am.

I put up my hands. "I filed things in the same order as the piles." *I think.*

She furrowed her brow. "I'm pretty sure things were stacked perfectly. In any event, you've got to double-check. I can't afford to have paperwork out of place."

"I'll do my best."

Hannah looked directly at me. "Harvey, this isn't charity. In exchange for reducing my legal fees, I expect you to take this work seriously."

I nodded, then went back to filing.

A little before six, Hannah and I walked into Captain Jack's Paradise, a bar located in the great seaport of North Hollywood, about twenty miles from the nearest waterfront. The Captain's front door had a round porthole riveted into place, to get you into that nautical mood right away. Inside, the ceiling was hung with rusty lanterns, rope fishnets with gray cork floaters, and a plastic pelican. Behind the bar was a pirate chest dripping with strings of pearls. At least the bartender wasn't wearing an eye patch.

When we sat at the bar, I asked for fizzy water and Hannah

ordered a Diet Coke. *Big surprise.* Ms. Control Freak doesn't drink liquor. I grabbed a handful of nuts from the bowl, then pushed it in front of Hannah, saying, "Want some?"

She recoiled, as if I'd thrown a snake at her. Hannah shook her head vigorously and shoved the bowl back at me.

I said, "You okay?"

"I don't eat nuts anymore. If I get started, I can't stop."

Guess the old Fat Hannah still lives inside.

I ate my handful of nuts, aware of Hannah watching me chew. I dusted the salt off my hands, then pushed the bowl in the opposite direction from Hannah. Her eyes followed it.

I said, "Was it hard to lose all that weight?"

"Yes. It took me almost two years."

"Good discipline."

"Not really. It's . . . well, never mind."

"Never mind what?"

She tightened her lips and shook her head.

I said, "How long have you had the weight off?"

"Three and a half years."

I started to reach for the nuts, then pulled my hand back. "Has losing weight changed your life?"

Hannah crossed her legs. "Only in every single respect."

I turned toward her on the stool. "Like . . ."

She ticked off each point with a finger. "I can look at a turnstile and not worry about getting through. I can fit in an airline seat, and I no longer need a seat belt extender. Men look at me differently. I get cold more easily. Hard seats hurt my ass, because I lost my padding. I can buy clothes in a normal store. In the beginning, I felt vulnerable because I didn't have a layer of protection around me. I—"

The bartender said, "Here you go, folks." He clunked the drinks in front of us. Hannah grabbed her Diet Coke, put her lips on the straw, and took a measured sip.

I said to the bartender, "Can you put on one of the local news stations?"

He didn't move. "There's a ball game at six."

"We only need to watch for a few minutes."

"Why?"

I almost said "Some people actually care what happens outside this bar." I settled for "There's a story I have to watch for work."

The bartender twisted his mouth to the side, then said, "Only a few minutes." He lumbered over to the TV and turned the round dial by hand.

As he walked back, I said, "Could you turn the sound up a little?" If it was any lower, it'd trigger the closed captioning.

He gave me a "Why are you being such a pain in the ass?" look, then went back and nudged up the volume.

The news logo came on. Hannah sucked down most of her soft drink. She glanced around to see if anyone else was watching the TV. No one was.

Lead story was the President's visit to France. Then a shooting in Monterey Park.

The bartender came over. "You done yet? Some of the regulars want the game."

"Just a few more minutes." I fished out five dollars that I couldn't afford to spend and gave it to him. It quickly disappeared into Captain Jack's treasure chest.

The bartender walked away and started wiping a glass with a white towel.

Hannah said, "Let me pay for that."

I shook my head. "It's okay." Keep insisting—on the third time, it's okay for me to cave.

"No, really. I know you're a little short."

"It's okay. I got it." Once more and it's yours. . . .

She nodded. "Well . . . thanks."

Well . . . shit.

On the TV, an Asian announcer stood in front of some huge concrete steps, holding a microphone labeled *KABC*. Hannah sat up.

The announcer said, "The attorney for Oliver Desmond, the teenager accused of shooting and killing the son of Lakers forward Alex Hedges, was in court today, attempting to suppress key evidence. The attorney, Hannah Fisher, daughter of famed criminal lawyer Bruce Fisher, had this to say. . . ."

Hannah came on the screen, surrounded by bunch of hands pointing microphones at her like the rifles of a firing squad. I glanced over at her. She was staring intently at the screen. The bartender didn't seem to notice she was on TV.

On the screen, Hannah blinked heavily and sounded very stilted. "Mr. Desmond is wrongly accused of this crime, as we will prove in court. He is a victim of scapegoating in a case where the police were under public pressure to quickly produce a suspect. So much pressure that the prosecution is trying to introduce illegally obtained evidence. We feel deeply for the victim and his family, but Mr. Desmond is innocent."

I glanced at Hannah wondering why you try to suppress evidence against someone who's innocent.

Up came a still picture of Desmond. He was an African-American teenager with Mike Tyson–like tattoos over most of his face and mug-shot numbers across his chest. His eyebrows were lowered, his lower lip was plumped, and he stared at the camera like he was on the verge of spitting at it.

I said, "That's the son of a rich guy?"

"Shhh."

The district attorney came on the screen, standing next to Hedges, the basketball player whose son was killed. Compared to Hedges, the DA looked about four feet tall. The DA started rambling about there being no doubt of Desmond's guilt.

When he finally shut up, the picture went back to an in-studio Hispanic announcer who said, "In other news, the city of Santa Monica has a new park, and an Inglewood man recovers his son's pet turtle from a storm drain. Those stories and more, right after this."

The station went to commercial. I turned to Hannah. "You were great."

"I thought my voice sounded weird."

"It's always weird to hear a recording of your own voice. Everyone sounds different inside their own head. Probably the way it resonates or something."

"I mean, didn't I sound kind of stiff?"

Pretty much. "You were great. But I gotta say that kid doesn't look like he comes from a rich family."

"He's adopted. His father is a real estate entrepreneur and a very kind man. He's given millions to charity. Oliver's been troubled since he was a little boy. When he was six, he climbed on the roof of the garage and wouldn't come down until the fire department dragged him off. When he was nine, he ran away from home on his bicycle for three days. At twelve, he beat up a boy at school so badly that—"

"Okay, okay, I get it." I took a huge gulp of my fizzy water.

Hannah said, "Everyone's entitled to a defense, no matter who you are. And I give Oliver's parents a lot of credit. They've stood by him through everything."

I wondered if he'd do a little better if he took the consequences of what he did, but I guess no one's interested in my parental advice. I polished off the drink and fought the urge to burp up the bubblies I'd just gulped down. "Won't the jury kinda hate him?"

She nodded. "Yes. That's the challenge here. If I get him off, I've really done something."

Like let a killer out on the street? "Why did the newsman mention your father?"

Hannah smiled. "My dad's also a criminal lawyer. He's the reason I decided to practice law. You remember the Mulholland stalker?"

"The guy that chopped up smooching kids while they were parked up on Mulholland?"

"Yes."

"I remember all right. My parents told me every detail, trying to scare me away from parking up there. Worked pretty well. I took my dates for a romantic outing in the Costco parking lot."

"Dad got him off. Despite all the publicity. Despite all the cries for his blood."

I wondered if I should ask whether he was guilty. Not much upside in that question. "Your dad must be amazing."

She beamed. "He's the best. When I was about ten, Mom took me to court to watch him. He has this deep, resonant voice. He looks directly at whoever he's addressing. Puts his whole focus on them."

I nodded. Why's that sound so familiar? Ah. Michael Nadler.

Hannah swiveled toward me on her stool.

Have we ever sat this close to each other?

She said, "I still remember sitting in that courtroom. I saw how his clients looked at him. They knew he was the only thing between them and jail. I saw the respect he got from the judge. I saw how the jury watched him. I knew right then I was going to be a criminal lawyer. I never once wavered from that decision."

I took my black plastic straw out of my drink and rolled it between my fingers. "I was ten when I decided to be a magician." Well, actually, I was torn between being a magician, an astronaut, and a rock star.

"Why magic?"

I scooched a little closer to her. She smelled like vanilla. Was that perfume? Shampoo?

I said, "My mother took me to something called the Renaissance Pleasure Fair. It's this medieval festival that goes on for a few weeks every year. Mostly it's a bunch of booths selling quill pens and harlequin hats and other crap from the Middle Ages. But they've also got entertainers walking around, like minstrels playing lutes, white-faced mimes, and beanbag jugglers. So while we're wandering around, I see this guy wearing one of those poofy red Rembrandt hats."

Hannah picked up her glass and tried to get another sip of Diet Coke. The straw sucked air. She set it down and ran her tongue over her lips.

"This guy had a little table in front of him. It was covered in black velvet with long gold fringe. He put green and red balls on the table, covered them with clay cups, and made them change places. He took out a blue metal bucket that was painted with red stars, then pulled coins from the air and clinked them into the bucket. He finished by putting an egg into a multicolored patchwork bag, then taking out a live chicken that was flapping its wings."

Hannah leaned her elbow on the bar, put her chin on her palm.

I said, "I wouldn't let Mom take me away from the magician. I watched his show over and over. I couldn't figure out how he did it. After an hour, Mom gave up and left me there. When she came back, I insisted on seeing it just one more time. The magician, who'd noticed this little twerp watching him, asked if I wanted to learn a trick. I practically jumped in his arms."

She smiled. "Do you remember which trick it was?"

I gave her an "Are you kidding?" look.

Hannah said, "Show me."

I reached into my pocket and took out one of the vintage

fifty-cent pieces. "He used a quarter, because my hands were so small. It went like this." I did a simple palm, pretended to drop the coin in my other hand, then opened my fingers to show it was empty.

She shook her head, smiling. "It's in your other hand."

"Well, it amazed a ten-year-old." I made a move that disguised my dropping the coin into my shirt pocket. Then I showed her both hands were empty.

She widened her eyes.

I said, "I've improved since then."

She smiled. "That was cool. How'd you learn more tricks?"

"I bugged my parents for months, until they got me a magic set for my birthday. I showed my appreciation by making them watch the same magic show six hundred times."

"What kind of tricks were in the kit?"

"The usual joke-shop cheapos. A little slide drawer that makes coins disappear. A red plastic thing that looks like a chess bishop but opens at the top. You put in a black ball, and when you open it a second time, it's gone. I also got these little twisted metal puzzles that came apart if you knew the secret. They weren't really magic, but they came with the set. I could never get them apart."

Hannah wriggled forward in her seat. "Show me another trick."

I got another coin and held it up in my fingers. Then I pulled out a silk handkerchief, draped it over the coin, and let her feel it was really inside. I twisted the handkerchief around it, then pulled the coin through the fabric. She squinted skeptically. I opened the handkerchief to show there was no hole in the middle.

She started clapping. "You're good."

The bartender appeared. "You done with the news show?"

I said, "Not quite." I figured we'd only gotten about four dollars' worth.

When he walked away, I said, "This is just the small stuff. I've invented some big tricks that'll blow away the professionals. I've got one being built right now. All I need is a break, and I'm on my way."

She nodded. "You'll do it."

I felt my face flush. "Thanks."

Hannah upended her glass, shook out an ice cube, and started crunching it in her mouth. She said, "I hope Oliver Desmond's case will be my big break."

"How good is his case?"

Hannah swallowed the ice. "It's got problems. The cops claim they stopped him for driving without headlights, then found incriminating evidence."

"How incriminating?"

"Incriminating enough."

"Like the murder weapon?"

She shifted in her chair. "I can't say what it was."

Bull's-eye! I said, "How can you knock out the evidence?"

"I think they really stopped him for DWB."

"What's DWB?"

"Driving While Black. He was in an expensive car in an upscale neighborhood late at night. If I can show they had no probable cause to stop the car, then nothing they found can be used as evidence at the trial."

"How do you prove they didn't have the right to stop him?"

"He says his lights were on, so at the moment, it's his word against the cops'."

I nodded. "He doesn't exactly look like the best witness."

"I would never put a murder defendant on the stand, even if he was a church bishop. I'm trying to figure another angle."

I grabbed some peanuts, felt her eyes on me, and put them back. "How's it going?"

Hannah said, "I called my father and kicked around some strategies. He says it's not important whether or not I win. The main thing is that the publicity will build my reputation."

There's a fine view of the American legal system.

Hannah said, "Dad coached me on how to talk to the press. He even made a few calls to make sure I got reporters down there."

Aha. Maybe the announcer's mention of Dad wasn't a coincidence. . . .

Hannah leaned forward. "He may be right about the publicity being more important than the case, but"—she narrowed her eyes—"I'm going to kick the DA's ass."

CHAPTER SEVENTEEN

After the bar, I left Hannah to her ass-kicking and drove toward Herb Gold's warehouse in Valencia. Herb is the top builder of magical illusions in the world. Fortunately, he keeps rock-star hours, opening at noon and running until eight or nine, or whenever he feels like knocking off. His warehouse is about forty-five minutes from my apartment on a good day.

This was not a good day. The 405 freeway was moving about six miles an hour, which turned out to be NASCAR speed compared to the traffic when I hit Interstate 5. Not that I was in a hurry to deliver the news I had for Herb.

Well over an hour later, I parked in front of Herb's two-story concrete warehouse and looked at my watch. A little after eight. The sonofabitch better still be here.

I climbed the concrete steps to a gray metal door and shoved the intercom button. An overhead security camera glowered at me.

Herb's voice came through the intercom. "Yeah?"

"Herb, it's Harvey."

"Password?"

"Stuff it up your ass."

"Close enough." The lock made a loud buzz.

As I grabbed the handle, I noticed Herb had installed a shiny new lock—an expensive tubular one. Couldn't pick that with my simple tools.

I pulled open the heavy door and stepped into a high-ceilinged warehouse that was as long as a football field and smelled like wet paint. In the distance, I heard the *thoop-thoop* of a nail gun.

I looked for Herb among the magic props in various stages of construction: a ten-foot-tall guillotine, a red-and-gold mummy case, a chrome-barred tiger cage, and a silver-specked pyramid.

There. I spotted Herb at the far end of the building, wearing a dust mask and working a pneumatic drill whose orange hose coiled to the ceiling. He was a big man, weighing maybe two fifty or so, with drooping gray eyes and jowls like Jabba the Hutt. He laid the drill on a table, pulled his mask down around his neck, and lumbered my way. I tried to smile. As he walked, the hammers dangling from either side of his leather tool belt flopped like the ears of a bull elephant.

When Herb got to me, he stuck out a huge calloused mitt. I grabbed hold and watched my hand disappear into his. It felt like I was shaking hands with a rawhide chew toy.

Herb said, "Wait'll you see this." He turned and yelled something in Spanish. Three men scrambled to an area near us and grabbed hold of chains that ran up through pulleys attached to the ceiling I beams.

I said, "Herb, I need to tell you—"

He yelled at the men, waving his hands like an ape conducting an orchestra. The men heaved the creaking chains. A glass trunk leaped into the air, then swayed on the chains, like the pendulum of a stopping clock.

I felt my eyes widen.

My Crystal Fantasy trick! The aluminum wasn't polished. One of the glass panels was cracked. But this was *my* trick. The trick *I* invented. For the first time ever, I'd be able to make an assistant vanish from a glass trunk hanging right over the heads of the audience.

A shot of laughter burst out from my throat. *My* trick. Something that came from a spark in my head. No one in the thousands of years of magic had ever thought of this. My idea. Months of perfecting the design, working with Herb on the plans.

Now it was *real*. Hanging right there in front of me. I could touch it. Perform it! I shook my head.

Herb pointed at the trunk with a thick finger. "Look at that damn thing. I defy anyone to see the gimmick. Even some schlub who's ten feet under it. Whaddaya think, Harvey? Huh? Huh?"

"It's . . . it's . . . Wow!"

Herb grinned. He gave the workers a sign to lower it. The chains rasped against the pulleys as the trunk seesawed to the floor. Do they have a good grip on those chains? It clunked against the concrete harder than I would have liked.

Is it okay? Did anything break?

I turned toward Herb, who was still staring at the trick, grinning. In the background, I heard the whine of a band saw. The air suddenly smelled like sawdust.

I said, "Herb, we gotta talk."

He looked at me. "Huh?"

"We gotta talk."

"So talk."

"Not here."

He clopped a hand on my shoulder and steered me across the floor, into a small woodshed in a corner of the warehouse.

Inside was a metal desk, scattered with ballpoint pens that carried advertising slogans, a broken yardstick, and a splay of loose nails. On the wall behind the desk was an electric wall clock that said *Pechowski's Plastics*.

Herb closed the door. "Talk to me."

I swallowed. "Herb, I've run into some financial problems."

His eyebrows lowered. "Meaning . . ."

The wall clock hummed loudly.

I said, "I can't give you any more money for the trick right now."

Herb crossed his arms over his chest. He half-sat his butt against his desk. "You know, Harvey, I started building your trick ahead of other guys who pay full boat."

"I promise I'll pay you. I came out here to tell you this personally, right? I'm not some flake."

"Nice manners don't keep my lights on."

Herb's eyes burned into me. I heard the scrape of his desk moving backward under his weight.

I said, "I wanted you to know right away. You know, so you could stop work for now."

"I already spent more for parts than you gave me."

"I'm good for it." *Assuming I'm not in San Quentin.* "You know how great my trick is."

Herb shook his head. "Kid, you got your priorities wrong. This trick is your ticket to the top. Hell, my workmen have been jabbering about the damn thing ever since they saw the plans. Those guys ain't even impressed by forty-four-inch tits."

"Yes, but—"

"David Copperfield was in last week to pick up his new trick. Even he was blown away. I dunno what else you're doing with your dough, but you're a horse's ass if you don't put it here. It'll pay you back fifty times."

"Copperfield liked it?"

"*Loved* it. David Blaine's coming in two weeks. Betcha dollars to donuts he'll feel the same."

I sighed. "I know you're right. I just don't have the money right now."

Herb pushed up from the desk and took a few steps forward.

I felt myself take a half step back. He said, "You know this won't be good for our future relationship."

My eyes went to the claw hammers on his belt.

He took another step toward me.

I forced myself to stay put.

His breathing grew louder.

Should I run?

No. I'm a dead man, no matter what I do.

But I don't have to be a wimp about it.

May as well get in his face.

I straightened up, looked directly into his eyes, and took a step forward. I said, "Herb, I can't be the first magician to have money problems. I'm going to make it big, and if you work with me now, you'll be my builder for life. If you don't, I'll remember that. And I agree with you. It won't be good for our relationship."

Herb's nostrils flared. His eyes narrowed.

Either I've impressed him with my balls, or he just remembered he can snap my neck like a chicken's.

Herb clenched his fists.

Don't move, I told myself.

Are my hands shaking?

He lunged forward and grabbed my neck in a headlock. I flailed my arms, trying to hit any part of him. My fists glanced off his overalls. Using both my hands, I grabbed his arm that was holding my head and pulled so hard that my muscles quivered. His grip didn't budge. I twisted my head. My neck chafed against his shirtsleeve. "Herb! Let go of me!"

He started laughing.

Herb dug noogies into my scalp with his knuckle. "What am I gonna do with you, you little pisher?"

He let go so suddenly that I fell on the floor.

CHAPTER EIGHTEEN

Next morning, I wandered down the aisle of a Walgreens on Riverside Drive. Hannah had called and woken me up early to say that the best use of my skills would be to buy her some lightly scented panty liners on my way to the office.

I walked along the feminine-hygiene section.

I don't think I've ever been on this aisle before.

The shelves were stuffed with bulging plastic packages of panty liners—pink, yellow, pastel blue. Lots of unscented but not one that was lightly scented.

I let out a sigh. Do I have to get a salesperson? That'll be fun. Asking for help with panty liners. It could be the second-most embarrassing drugstore incident of my life. First place goes to a night when I was sixteen and wanted to discreetly buy a package of condoms. I waited a half hour until I could get alone in a checkout line with a male clerk. He scanned the box four times and couldn't get a beep. So he grabbed a flexible chrome microphone, pulled it to his mouth, and told the store, "Price check on Trojan Ribbed, SuperSensitive."

I came to the end of the feminine hygiene aisle. *There.* On the bottom shelf. Lightly scented panty liners. I grabbed the package and held it down at my side as I walked to the front.

The checkout clerk didn't smirk when the package moved toward him on the rubber conveyor belt. Neither did the old lady behind me.

The bar code beeped on the first try. *Whew.*

As I drove to Hannah's office, my cell phone rang. "Yo."

"Harvey, it's Marty."

My magic agent, if you consider someone who hasn't gotten you work for three months to be your "agent."

I said, "Hey."

"I got a gig for you next week. It doesn't pay much, but—"

"I'll take it."

"Crappy little convention. They only got a hundred bucks."

I spoke loudly into the phone. "I'll take it."

Marty laughed. "Man, if you were a chick, you'd always be pregnant."

"I can use the money right now."

"Fine, fine. You didn't even let me tell you the best part. There's a Vegas promoter who's going to be in town. He books five different casinos. I think I can get him to the show."

"Excellent!" I made a pull-down gesture. "I still want the hundred bucks."

"Yeah, yeah. And for God's sake, be on time."

Whistling, I walked into Hannah's office. She was sitting at her desk, forehead scrunched, studying the computer screen. I set the panty liners on her desk. She didn't look up.

I said, "Here's your diamond bracelet."

She kept her eyes on the monitor as she rapidly tapped the keyboard. "Mmm."

I said, "I had a hard time finding 'lightly scented.'"

"Mmm-hmm." The keys clicked under her fingers.

"You didn't tell me which scent to get, so I made an executive decision."

She stopped typing and looked at me, squinting in confusion. "There's more than one scent?"

"Uh-huh."

"What did you get?"

"Tuna fish."

Hannah whacked me on the arm so fast that I didn't see it coming.

Ow! Shit.

I rubbed the throbbing spot. That girl can wallop.

Between Hannah's smack and the remnants of Herb's noogie, it's gonna be a great day.

Hannah said, "If you weren't being such an asshole, I'd have told you I've been working on the password for Sherry Allen's thumb drive."

I stepped behind her to look at the screen. *Invalid Password.*

She swiveled her chair to face me and rubbed her eyes. "I can't get it. We have to hire a hacker."

I leaned closer to the screen. "What have you tried?"

"Her address, birth date, Social Security number. Forward and backward. I tried her name, her son's name, her parents' names."

Guess I don't need to mention that I already tried most of those. Though I only did the numbers. Why didn't I think of using names?

I said, "You try brothers? Sisters? Grandparents?"

"I don't have those. We need the hacker."

"We can't afford a hacker."

She shook her head. "Maybe I'll just give this to the cops."

"Don't you want to know what's on it first?"

"We don't seem to have that option."

"Can I try?"

She smirked. "If you want."

What was important to Sherry? What could I tell from her apartment? That chair full of stuffed animals. I said, "Try Teddy. Try Barbie."

Hannah turned back to her keyboard and punched them in. "Nope."

"Monkey."

Seemed like she was hitting the keys harder. *Invalid Password.*

What else? Sherry had pictures of boyfriends. Pictures of a . . .

I said, "Hang on. I saw a dog dish with a name painted on it. It was . . . Melissa. No. Misty."

She typed in *Misty.* The file opened.

Hannah looked at me like I was a three-year-old who'd just solved a calculus equation. "Very good."

We both leaned into the computer screen.

It showed two file folders: *Personal* and *E-mails.*

Hannah said, "The cops said they have her computer. The only things on it were songs, photos, and some papers she wrote for college. They checked her online e-mail account. The in-box and out-box were empty, and the trash was dumped. Maybe she backed up her e-mails before she erased them."

I twisted my mouth to the side. "Who backs up e-mails?"

"Someone who has a reason to save them."

She opened the *Confidential* folder. There were four files, titled *Ellison, Sutton, Michaels,* and *Bragg.*

She clicked on *Ellison.* It read, "June 14. Babysat for Randy Ellison, 8:00 to 10:30 P.M. Although he hugged me last time, this time he didn't acknowledge my being there. The entire evening, he stacked blocks, tore them down, restacked them, tore them down."

Hannah clicked on Bragg.

"June 16. Babysat Helen Bragg. She echoed my speech. I said, 'Hello, Helen.' She said, 'Hello, Helen.' She drew circles over and over on the same page for an hour. When her parents got back, I heard them arguing outside the front door. Her father said he can't afford Helen's therapists. He's working an extra job and he's exhausted. Her mother said Helen will grow out of this. It's just a phase."

Hannah scrolled down the screen, passing similar entries. "This is obviously her journal of the autistic kids. And none of our business." She closed the file and clicked on the *E-mails* folder, then opened a file.

The first was an e-mail from someone named Linda, telling Sherry about a ski trip to Mammoth.

I said, "That's pretty mundane. Why would she go to the trouble to back it up, then hide it?"

"Maybe they're not all so mundane. Maybe someone was snooping around her computer and she didn't want them to see the e-mails."

I glanced at Hannah, who was staring at the screen.

She opened another e-mail. A note from a social worker, asking if Sherry would take on a mildly autistic child named Arthur.

I said, "Will the cops fingerprint her computer keyboard?"

"Not likely. With all that banging around, it's hard to get a good print off computer keys. Besides, it would only mean someone used the computer." Hannah opened another e-mail. She pointed at the screen. "Aha."

I leaned in.

The e-mail was from Sherry. Addressed to KL186. She wrote, "You're making me nuts. Stop hassling me. Do I have to call the cops?"

It was dated February 20.

Two days before she was killed.

CHAPTER NINETEEN

We scrolled down to the beginning of the e-mail chain with KL186. The first was dated three months before Sherry died.

Just as Hannah clicked on it, the office door opened. We both looked up, like a couple of kids that'd been caught playing doctor behind the house.

A distinguished-looking man with gray hair, combed back perfectly, strode in. He wore a tailored gray stripe suit, gold watch, and rep tie. As he walked, he swung a shiny black alligator briefcase.

Hannah jumped up. "Daddy!"

Her father carefully set down his briefcase, then held his arms out to his sides. She ran to him, grinning like a toddler. He hugged her and picked her up. Hannah bent her knees, sticking out her feet as he swung her back and forth.

When he put her down, he said, "I sure couldn't do that when you were a little girl."

Hannah's shoulders slumped.

Wow. Has this asshole been ragging on Hannah's weight for her whole life?

Hannah turned to me, forcing a smile. "This is my father."

I walked toward him, saying, "I kinda figured that when she called you 'Daddy.'" I stuck out my hand. "I'm Harvey Kendall."

He gave me a firm shake. "Bruce Fisher." I got the same power stare that I'd gotten from Nadler. Do they, like, teach that in law school?

Actually, there was one slight difference between him and Nadler. Old man Fisher also had an "Are you banging my daughter?" look in his eyes.

Bruce said to Hannah, "I was in the neighborhood. Can I take my media starlet to an early lunch?"

She perked up. "Sure." Hannah went back to the desk and grabbed her purse.

He said, "While I'm here, let me see your motion to suppress in the Desmond case."

Hannah dropped her purse, opened a file on her desk, took out the papers, and handed them to her father. He took a pair of rimless half-glasses out of his coat pocket and started to read. Hannah watched him intently, shifting her weight back and forth.

Her father turned the page. "Mmm."

She bit her lip, looking at Bruce like a figure skater waiting for the Olympic judges to hold up their signs.

He nodded slightly.

Hannah rubbed the front of her neck.

He turned another page.

Bruce finished the document and handed it to her.

He said, "Not bad. You've got a typo on page three, line sixteen. Courts hate that. And I would punch up the reference to *People versus Anandale*. Put your emphasis there."

Hannah dropped the hand holding the papers limply to her side.

Her father smiled. "C'mon. We can discuss strategy over lunch."

She threw the papers on the desk, picked up her purse, and whispered to me, "Stay off my computer."

As she walked off with her father, I heard him say, "You were a little stiff on the news show. Memorize what you're going to say beforehand. When you read something, the audience can tell."

Jeez. Welcome to the Self-Esteem-Squashing Theater.

After the door closed, I waited a few minutes to make sure they weren't coming back, then sat down at the computer keyboard and hit the space bar to knock off the screen saver.

Shit! She passworded the damn thing.

What, she doesn't trust me?

I took a guess at her password and hit ENTER.

Guess *BITCH* isn't it.

I let out a sigh.

Thanks, Hannah. Daddy waltzes in, makes Dumbo fat jokes, eviscerates your work, and you take off with him like a teenage girl running to the football captain's convertible. Leaving me and my murder case hanging.

Maybe those e-mails have something time-sensitive in them.

It's my neck that might get stretched here. Seriously stretched.

Hannah got back at her usual two fifteen, looking glum. I said, "Does your father always treat you like that?"

She took a half step back. "What do you mean?"

Ooops. "I, well, you know . . . criticizing your work."

"He's a brilliant lawyer. I couldn't achieve half of what I've done if he didn't push me to do my best."

From the look on her face, she meant maybe half of that.

Hannah said, "Did anyone call?"

"Yeah. A slug of press people." I handed her the yellow pad on which I'd written the names. "Also, some guy named Terence Lund. He said he's a corporate lawyer and he's got an emergency for one of his clients. I tried your cell, but you didn't answer."

Hannah grabbed the phone and dialed. "Terence? Hannah Fisher." She started pacing.

After a few back-and-forths, she stopped at her desk, leaned over, and wrote on a yellow pad. Hannah scowled; then her mouth formed a little smile.

She said, "Okay, I'll take care of it. Listen, why don't you just do a memo to all your male clients. Tell them if they go down to Whoreville on Sunset, there is no such thing as a gorgeous young blond woman who's down on her luck and trying to make a few bucks. Those are all undercover cops."

She hung up, shaking her head, then dialed a reporter and repeated what she'd said about Desmond on television.

I started filing.

The phone rang and Hannah picked it up. After listening a moment, she said, "Yes, this is the Hannah Fisher on television."

Guess her dad was right about getting business from the publicity. I punched the stapler on a stack of papers, then clipped them into a file.

Hannah hung up and called another reporter.

I kept punching papers, looking over at her. When do we get back to those e-mails?

After the last call, she picked up some papers and started reading.

I cleared my throat.

She didn't look over.

"Hannah?"

She answered without looking up. "Yes?"

"When do you think we can get to Sherry's e-mails?"

Hannah looked surprised. Her face said, Oh, I forgot, but I can't admit that, and if I drop what I'm reading, that's admitting it, so how do I gracefully handle this?

She looked at me, then looked at the papers in her hand. Hannah slowly moved her hand up and down, like she was judging the weight of the papers, then dropped them on the desk. "C'mon over."

I hurried over and stood behind her as she started to type in her screen-saver password. Can I steal it by watching her fingers?

Nope.

She opened the file on the thumb drive and went back to the e-mails from KL186, the guy who Sherry told to buzz off or else she'd call the cops.

In the very first e-mail, KL186 wrote her, "Amazing running in to you today. Thank God for our three cheese and pepperoni pizza. Let's hook up. Kev."

Sherry wrote back. "How's Tuesday?" She gave him her phone number.

I said, "Too bad he didn't give her his info."

"Maybe he does later on. Looks like he works in a pizza place."

"Or met her in one."

In the next few exchanges, they talked about the movies, nightclubs, music, and the like. In one e-mail, he said, "Come this way tonite. We'll do the boardwalk."

I said, "Boardwalk probably means Venice Beach. They have a lot of pizza places there."

Hannah nodded, pulled up the next e-mail.

More idle chitchat.

We came to an e-mail written a few weeks before Sherry died. She wrote, "We can't do Wednesday. My father may come by."

Kev answered, "I totally get it. Don't need to live that scene again."

I said, "Kevin obviously knows her father. Maybe we can find him through the dad."

Hannah looked up at me. "Doesn't sound like they're real close."

The next note was dated a few days later. Sherry wrote, "Kev, we gotta cool it a little."

After a few "Why?" e-mails and "Just because" responses, she said, "I think we should see other people for a while."

Kev kept begging for an explanation. Did he do something? Did her father find out about them?

She finally admitted she was seeing someone else. She owed it to herself to see if this other man was "the one," even though there were "some issues."

Kev wrote back, "If this is the old guy you were talking about, I can't compete with money. But he can't love you any more than me. Please. See me one last time. Then I'll never bother you again."

Kevin resent that last e-mail six times, pleading for her to see him.

Sherry didn't answer for two weeks. Finally, she wrote the one we'd seen before, dated two days before her death. "You're making me nuts. Stop hassling me. Do I have to call the cops?"

Hannah looked up at me. "So Kevin maybe works in a pizza place. It's possible he just ran into her there, but he said 'our' when he mentioned the pizza, which sounds like he works in a restaurant. Maybe this place is on the boardwalk, maybe not."

I nodded. "Well, it's more than we had an hour ago."

Hannah rolled her chair back from her desk and rubbed her eyes. "We've got to give this to the cops."

"I want to see Kevin first."

She stopped rubbing her eyes and blinked at me. "What? You're Rambo now? Gonna bring in the bad guys yourself?"

"Shouldn't we know what he has to say before the cops do?"

"The cops probably have his name already. I'll bet her dad gave it to them."

"Looks like dad didn't know they'd gotten back together."

"You don't know that."

"No, but I'm the one volunteering to walk up and down the Venice boardwalk, asking if they've got any three-cheese pepperonis with a side of Kevin."

Hannah stood. "Did it occur to you that this could be dangerous? If this kid's a killer, he might not appreciate your snooping around."

"Then I'll have to rely on my charm."

She gave an exaggerated headshake. "May I remind you that you have a commitment here? It would take your entire lunch hour just to drive there and back."

"Which is why I'll be going on the weekend."

The phone rang.

Hannah snatched the handset, jerked it up to her ear, and said, "Hannah Fisher." She listened for a moment, then glared at me.

I cocked my head in a "What is it?"

She turned her back to me and finished the call. All I could make out was a few uh-huhs.

Hannah swung around and slammed down the phone. Her eyes burned into me. "Is there something you forgot to tell me about your visit to Sherry's apartment?"

"What do you mean?" Did my voice crack?

"Something like 'being questioned by a cop for breaking and entering.' What the hell do you think I mean?"

"Hey. No big deal. I handled it."

She crossed her arms over her chest. "You *handled* it?"

"Yeah. He asked a coupla questions and went away. Let me tell you how I hid the thumb drive when I emptied my pockets. See—"

Hannah's face flushed. "Did you think the cop wouldn't mention your little visit to the detective working your case?"

"Well . . ."

She stabbed her finger at me. "That was Sergeant Morton on the phone. He wanted to thank you for stopping by. The apartment manager said you looked familiar. Morton said he'd never have known that if you hadn't shown up. Why the hell would the manager think you look familiar?"

I shook my head, turned my palms up. "I have no idea. I've never seen the guy before in my life."

"Yeah. And you never knew that dead girl with your sperm in her vagina."

I stepped toward Hannah. "Look. I didn't do this. I don't care how it looks. If you don't believe me, you can bail." I'm not even close to meaning that.

She stood there, seething.

I held her gaze. Don't break eye contact. I felt the corner of my mouth twitch.

Hannah spoke evenly, though her tone was laced with storm warnings. "The evidence says you're a killer."

I shrugged and raised my eyebrows in a "Guess I can't argue with that one."

She said, "Whether you're guilty or not—"

"I'm not."

"—you're entitled to a defense." She tightened her jaw. "What was the first thing I told you when we started?"

"That criminal lawyers get paid in advance?"

"No, smart-ass. I told you that I can't afford to be surprised. If you expect me to continue, I need you to tell me everything. I mean *everything*."

I nodded. "Sorry. It's an occupational hazard of magicians to hide things."

"Stop with the cutesy bullshit. You could lose twenty years

of your life, if not more, and you're acting like this is some high-school prank."

"Look. I'm sorry. I told you I deal with stress—"

"Yeah, by turning into an adolescent. I don't have time for your crap. If you're not serious about this, then I can't be."

"Listen!" My voice rose, surprising me and, from her face, her as well. "Of course I take it seriously. If I don't act like it, I'm sorry. I'm scared shitless, okay? That what you want to hear?" I felt my hands shaking.

She said, "I don't want to hear anything except that you are being one hundred percent straight with me. Now is there anything else? If there is, spill it. This is your last warning."

I bit my cuticle. "No. Nothing."

Hannah narrowed her eyes. "If you aren't straight with me from here on, we're done."

I raised my hand like in court. "I swear."

She turned away.

I went back to filing, but my stomach kept churning. Hannah tapped away at her computer keyboard. Every clack spiked a drumbeat headache into the back of my eyeballs.

Around four in the afternoon, I said, "Say, Hannah . . ."

She kept typing and spoke without looking up. "Yeah?"

"I need to leave a little early."

She stopped typing and looked over. "You're not going to look for this Kevin, are you?"

"No. I'll do that tomorrow. On my *weekend* time. There's a better chance he'll be there on a Saturday anyway."

She tightened her mouth. "Why do you want to leave early?"

Let's see . . . the truth or a more appealing story? "I'm meeting someone from the lab who's working on my DNA testing.

She offered to educate me about the process, so I thought it'd be a good idea."

"Great idea for your own time. Not mine."

I tightened my mouth in an expression that said, Well, maybe there's one other little thing. . . . "And, uh, okay, well she's kind of attractive."

Did Hannah stiffen a little?

I said, "I'll make the time up Monday. Or on the weekend."

Hannah sighed. "All right. It's a slow day, so go ahead, but don't make this a habit. And I expect you to make it up."

I stood up. "Thanks."

She went back to her computer. "Good luck with Little Miss Double Helix."

CHAPTER TWENTY

After work, I parked near the Starbucks in Westwood just before six thirty. I was actually early! It was only because I miscalculated the traffic on Coldwater Canyon, but I'd take it any way I could get it.

As I walked into the store, I thought about coffee shops being the perfect spot to meet someone new. Cheap enough that you won't blow more than a few bucks before you know where you stand. Enough people around that no one can throw a scene. Easy to beat a retreat if your date shows up with a drool cup.

I took a seat at one of the tables and watched the glass door.

Where the hell is Carly? She's late.

I looked around at the people typing on laptops. Glanced at my watch.

This is rude. How could she be late?

Ah. There she is.

As she came through the glass door, I stood up and waved. She squinted, ticked her head, and started toward me.

I went over to meet her, then we got our coffees and sat down.

Carly took a sip through the hole in the white plastic cup

lid, set down the cup, and smiled with her overbite. I love that overbite.

I said, "So. I've lived up to my end of the bargain and bought you coffee. Tell me how you came to feel so strongly about abortion that it cost you your career."

She settled back in her chair. "Don't you have a cause you're so passionate about that you'd sacrifice your job?"

"Of course." *Not really.*

"What is it for you?"

"You first." While I try to think of something, hoping you'll forget about that question.

Her eyes twinkled. "In other words, you'll show me yours if I show you mine?"

I pulled my chair closer. "I like the way you think."

Carly leaned in. "I grew up as a liberal. Still am, in most areas. I always felt women had the right to decide about abortion for themselves. Though I have to admit I never gave it much thought. I also believed the goal of stem-cell research outweighed any ethical questions about using the aftermath of abortions."

I nodded.

She clasped her hands on the table, interlacing her fingers. "Then my sister got pregnant."

Carly told me about her older sister Lynn, a trim woman with high cheekbones, who had been a track star in high school. Lynn was working in an upscale dress shop when she met Ted, a chef in the French restaurant next door who rode his bicycle ten miles to work each day. Lynn was thirty-six when they got married. She was also two months pregnant, which she laughingly blamed on her biological clock.

A few months later, Carly threw a baby shower at their parents' house. The ladies sat in the living room, which was filled with sweet-smelling flowers. Lynn started to untie the pink ribbon on her first present, then suddenly dropped the gift and ran out of the room.

Carly ran after her. She found her in the bathroom, throwing up. Quietly, Carly ran water on a linen towel and handed it to her sister. Lynn, still bent over, patted her face with the wet towel and said she was so embarrassed. It was the heavy smell of flowers that made her sick. Carly said it was just part of being pregnant.

Lynn sat on the closed toilet, taking deep breaths. They could hear the women chattering in the next room. After a few minutes, Lynn stood, checked herself in the mirror, and gave Carly a quick nod that said everything was okay. As she turned to leave, she wrenched around and threw up on the floor. Her chest heaved in spasms. Carly saw blood in her mouth.

Carly took her to the doctor, who said it was an inflammation of the stomach lining. Probably stress-related. He said the baby was showing signs of distress. The doctor told Lynn to go to bed for at least two weeks. Possibly for the rest of her pregnancy.

Lynn took a leave from her job and stayed in bed. Ted took good care of her for the first few days, but within a week, he was getting agitated. He said he was exhausted. Working all day, taking care of her all night. How would they get by without her income? They had a mortgage on the condo. Credit card loans. No cushion for the baby expenses.

A few weeks later, around six in the morning, Carly got a phone call from her mother. "Get to the hospital. Lynn went into premature labor."

Carly sat in the waiting room with her parents, their eyes jittery.

The baby was so early. How far along was she? Not even thirty weeks?

Ted came out in a yellow paper gown, a surgical face mask pulled down around his neck. He wasn't smiling.

He said it was a girl. She was very small. Under two pounds.

He left them and went back inside.

Carly and her parents went to the nursery window. Through the plate glass, they saw tiny Brenda lying in a Plexiglas box. She was not much bigger than the nurse's hand. The baby had wires taped to her body, an IV in her umbilical cord, and an oxygen mask covering her pink face. Brenda's eyes were squinted shut. Her mouth opened and closed like a tiny fish.

As they watched, Brenda's body began to shake so violently that one of the wires came loose. A monitor buzzed loudly. Carly's mother shrieked. An attendant ran to Brenda, shouted something they couldn't hear through the glass, then wheeled the baby into the next room.

Carly ran to a nurses' station. She demanded to see a doctor. The man behind the desk made a phone call, then politely said he couldn't tell her anything.

They went to Lynn's room. Lynn was lying there alone. Ted had gone back to work. Not wanting to upset Lynn, they chit-chatted, trying to act like nothing had happened. From Lynn's eyes, she knew better. She didn't ask.

Carly kept going to the nurses' station. They said Lynn's doctor would be in shortly.

Over an hour later, a somber woman in a white coat opened Lynn's door. The doctor asked the family to leave. Lynn looked panicked. She said she wanted them to stay.

The doctor nodded, then spoke matter-of-factly. "Brenda had a convulsion. It sometimes happens."

Lynn's eyes widened. "Is it . . . serious?"

The doctor didn't look at her. "We've done an MRI and a CAT scan. I'm sorry to have to tell you this. It shows severe cerebral hemorrhaging."

Lynn's eyes teared. "What?"

"Hopefully, we can control the seizures with IV medication. Your baby will need constant monitoring. She'll have to be on oxygen for quite some time."

Lynn started to cry. "Did I . . . did I do something to cause this?"

The doctor shook her head. "Absolutely not. No one knows what causes it. Unfortunately, it's more common with premature babies."

Lynn's face was streaked with tears. She said, "If we give her medication, can she have a . . . a normal life?" Lynn grimaced, bracing herself for the answer.

The doctor sighed. Her face softened. "It's too early to know exactly what will happen, but there is very severe brain damage."

Carly's mother grabbed her husband's arm for balance.

Lynn said, "How will that . . . affect her?"

"She will be severely disabled. There's a high probability she'll be paraplegic. Possibly quadriplegic. With damage this extensive, her life expectancy may not be more than a few years."

Lynn sobbed, shaking her head. "No, no, no."

Carly's mother buried her head against her husband's chest. He tightened his face and stood straight, rocking in place.

Little Brenda was in the hospital for two weeks before her condition stabilized. They sent her home with an array of IV tubes and monitor wires. On that first morning, Lynn placed the baby in her crib, being careful not to dislodge the wires. She gently covered Brenda's head with a clear Plexiglas cube attached to a hissing oxygen machine. Lynn stood there, watching her baby for most of the morning. Brenda hardly moved.

Over the next few days, Lynn and Ted argued about money. He said the bills were bad enough when she quit her job. Now there were hospital bills for God knows how much. Some of it wasn't covered by insurance. Lynn said they'd have to scrape by. She obviously couldn't go back to work. She had to watch Brenda.

Carly thought money wasn't the real issue. She thought Ted blamed Lynn for the baby's problems, despite what the doctor said. He also resented how much time Lynn was spending with Brenda.

Ted started coming home late. He started drinking more. Sometimes, Lynn drank with him. Their arguments escalated to yelling at each other.

Then they stopped talking.

One night, Lynn woke around three A.M. It wasn't a noise that woke her. It was the lack of one. She didn't hear the hum of Brenda's oxygen machine through the intercom.

Lynn reached for Ted. He wasn't in bed. She felt a spike of adrenaline and jumped up.

She ran to Brenda's room. Why was the door closed? Lynn threw it open and saw Ted with his hand on the oxygen machine. He jumped back, eyes wide. Then he straightened up. The machine started to hum.

Ted said, "I . . . didn't hear the machine, so I came to check it. I think I got it working." He looked at the floor.

Lynn rushed to Brenda. The baby wasn't breathing.

As Carly finished the story, she was crying. I glanced around the coffee shop. The other people were all involved in their own conversations. No one seemed to notice.

I jumped up, grabbed a handful of paper napkins, came back, and handed them to her. She wiped her eyes with one, crumpled the napkin, and sniffled. "Excuse me. I'm sorry."

I put my hand on hers and spoke softly. "I understand."

Carly nodded. She picked up another napkin and said, "Lynn

pulled me aside after Brenda's funeral and told me what Ted had done. I knew she was in shock. She used the same tone of voice that she'd use to describe a lunch with her girlfriends." Carly dabbed her eyes. "I started to say something, but Lynn cut me off. She said that she'd called one of the women in the dress shop and asked about a job. Did I think she should go back to her old job? I said she should do something about Ted. Call the police. She said, 'No. Better that it's buried with Brenda.'"

"A few weeks later, Ted left her. You know what he said to her?" Carly looked directly at me, eyes red. "He said, 'Brenda was premature. What happened was no different from aborting a baby who wouldn't have made it.'"

Carly said, "After that, Lynn sat for hours in Brenda's room, next to the empty crib. She never turned on the lights. If I stayed with her for a few hours, I could eventually get her up. She'd vacuum the house, or dust the living room, then go back into Brenda's room and sit again. Sometimes she'd say how easy it would be to take some pills and just go to sleep. When I told her not to talk like that, she got this sad smile and said, 'Don't worry. I don't have the energy to do anything about it.'"

Carly closed her eyes. Her mouth tightened, like she was in pain. She opened her eyes and looked at me. "My mother and I gathered up all the pills in Lynn's house. Even the aspirin. Lynn sat longer and longer in the baby's room. Eventually, we couldn't get her up at all. She hardly ate. She soiled herself sitting there. Finally, my parents had her hospitalized. She's still in there."

Across the room, a loud woman said something about Fred's nose. The girls at her table laughed.

Carly sat up straight. She smoothed her skirt with her hands. "So that's what got me thinking about abortion. In a bizarre way, Ted was right. What *is* the difference between killing a newborn child and killing a fetus? Why should it be legal to kill a child before it's born and illegal afterward?"

I blinked repeatedly.

She took a sip of coffee.

When I spoke, my voice felt like it was resonating inside my head. "I can't imagine how horrible that must have been."

She smiled. Her tears were dry now, her voice stronger. "It's been a source of strength. It's what keeps me moving on the path of outlawing abortion." Carly looked straight at me. "How do you feel about abortion?"

I shifted in my seat. "Well, I certainly see both sides of it."

Her eyes crinkled as she grinned. "C'mon. Pick a side."

"Well, I haven't—"

"Don't be a wuss."

I sighed. "I guess it comes down to whether you think abortion is murder. It certainly seems like murder if you abort the day before a healthy baby is born. Not so much if you abort a few minutes after conception. In between, it gets fuzzy."

Carly drummed her fingers on the table, smiling impatiently. "And your answer is . . ."

"Bottom line, it's a balancing of the fetus's rights and the mother's right to decide the course of her life. Those are such emotional issues that I don't know how to solve it just on logic. Everyone has to make a personal decision about how they feel."

"You're still wimping out."

"There's no clear answer here. May never be."

"Of course there isn't. That's why both sides are so passionate. C'mon. Where are you on this?"

I let out a sigh. *Guess I gotta be honest.*

This may be a very short date. . . .

I said, "Since there's no clear answer, I think each woman should have the right to decide for herself."

I clenched my teeth, waiting for her wrath.

She still had that little smile.

I said, "Are you upset I feel that way?"

She shrugged. "A lot of the world thinks like that." Carly put her hand on mine. "Guess I'll just have to work on you a bit."

I pulled my chair closer to the table, making sure I didn't dislodge her hand. "I've always prided myself on having an open mind."

She took her hand away and looked at her watch. "Ooops. Guess I'll have to work on you some other time. I'm late for an appointment." She pulled her chair back and stood.

An appointment on a Friday night? Is this one of those fifteen-minute dork drops that coffeehouses are so perfect for? I stood up and said, "I'll call you again?"

She smiled and left.

CHAPTER TWENTY-ONE

Next morning, the phone woke me up. Without looking, I fumbled it off the hook.

Hannah said, "How was your date?"

I rubbed those crackly things in my eyes. "You're calling me on a Saturday morning to ask that?"

Sounded like her phone clunked. "I've been thinking about your incident at the apartment. That could really hurt your case."

I ran my hand through my tangled hair. "You said that yesterday."

"Are you serious about looking for this Kevin?"

I sat up and yawned. "Yes. I'm going today."

"I think I should go with you."

"I don't need a handler."

"Actually, you do."

I already have a mother, thank you. "Look, this is very nice of you, but—"

"If we find this guy, I want to make sure you don't do more damage to your case."

"Hannah—"

"Pick me up at the office in an hour."

I walked into Hannah's office, wearing a red shirt, black magician's jacket with sequins, and my bird, Lisa, on my shoulder.

Hannah, deep in computerland, didn't look up until I was standing next to her. When she saw me, she jumped in her seat. Looking me up and down, she said, "Have you lost your mind?"

"Been to the Venice Boardwalk lately? It's full of chain-saw jugglers, fire-eaters, and Rollerblading Mohawks. It'll be easier to talk to people if I look like this."

"Like Long John Silver in drag?"

"Hannah, meet Lisa. Lisa, Hannah."

Hannah looked at the bird. Lisa ruffled her head feathers, stepped closer to my neck. Hannah said, "Is she . . . friendly?"

"Want to hold her?"

She stuck out her hand. I put Lisa on her finger. Lisa looked back at me, as if she were asking, Who the hell is this bitch?

Hannah stroked the bird's chest with the index finger of her other hand. Lisa's eyes went to Hannah's finger, like it was a fat worm.

I grabbed the bird and said, "Let's go."

As we got to the parking lot outside Hannah's office, I saw a very overweight woman laboring herself out of a blue Chevy. She had short brown hair, layered chins, and perspiration stains under the arms of her flowered blouse. The woman grabbed the top of the car door and used it to help herself stand, then reached into the front seat and pulled out a bulky brown paper grocery bag. She hugged the bag to her chest with both hands, turned, and saw us. Her mouth spread into a warm smile.

Hannah said, "Hi, Mom."

I almost missed a step.

Mom? Bruce Fisher, of the haute couture, is married to this woman?

Hannah's mother, still hugging the grocery bag, pushed the car door shut with her rear end. She started toward us and said, "Hello, dear." Despite her size, she walked with a youthful bounce.

When Mrs. Fisher got to us, she spoke in a melodious voice. "And who is this handsome young man?"

I smiled. "Harvey Kendall. I'm helping in Hannah's office."

Mrs. Fisher's eyebrows went up, maybe with the hope that her daughter was finally interested in someone. Or maybe it was the bird on my shoulder.

Her smile broadened. "Nice to meet you, Harvey. I'm Louise Fisher."

I stuck out my hand to shake hers, then realized she couldn't do it with the grocery bag, so I reached for the bag, but she wouldn't release it, so I kind of grabbled her fingers where she was holding the bag, gave a little shake, then took back my hand.

Hannah said, "Mom, you're supposed to call before coming by."

"I know, dear, but you're always here on Saturdays, so I brought you some lunch. I made chili last night, with those Southwestern spices you love so much. It's always better the second day, after all the flavor seeps in. I threw in some fresh-baked oatmeal cookies."

My stomach lurched toward the bag.

Hannah said, "You know I don't eat sweets anymore."

"With all the weight you've lost, you can indulge yourself now and then."

Hannah looked at her watch. "Harvey and I are late. Thanks for bringing the food." Hannah took the bag.

Mrs. Fisher looked at Hannah. She blinked rapidly.

Hannah said, "Bye, Mom." She leaned down and kissed her mother on the cheek.

Mrs. Fisher smiled. She nodded at me, turned, and walked slowly back to her Chevy.

As we started toward my car, Hannah gave me the bag. Through the paper, I felt the warm chili container. I could smell the oatmeal cookies. My stomach screamed *Rip it open and bury your face in it.*

She said, "You want the food?"

Yes! A day without a frozen dinner. "I couldn't do that. She made it for you."

"I'll throw it away if you don't take it." Hannah went around my car, toward the passenger side.

Balancing the bag, I opened the driver's door and looked at Hannah over the car roof. "Why would you throw it away?"

She opened the door. "I'm sticking to healthy foods these days."

"So why does your mother bring you this kind of stuff?"

"She can't accept the fact that I've changed my eating habits. Mom keeps trying to get me back as a binge buddy." She ducked her head and climbed into the car.

"Well, okay. Thanks." I pushed the driver's seat forward and started to put the food in the backseat.

Hannah said, "Could you put it in the trunk?"

"Huh?"

"I don't want to smell it the whole time."

"You don't like the smell?"

"I love the smell. Put it in the trunk."

I put the bag in the trunk, then got in the car and pulled the shoulder belt across my chest. "You think your mother is trying to sabotage your diet?"

"Yes."

"Why would she do that? Isn't she proud of your weight loss?" I started the car and put it in gear.

"Mom equates food with love. If I reject her food, she thinks I don't love her. So I take the bag every week, then toss it."

"Have you tried telling her to stop?"

"Only a few hundred times."

As we drove, I listened to the whoosh of the air conditioner.

I said, "Your mom and dad are really . . . different."

Her head snapped toward me. "Are you saying that because my mother is a big woman?"

Well . . . yeah . . . "No."

Hannah looked out the side window. "She didn't look like that when they got married."

Why do I feel like I'm walking on dynamite? I said, "I'm not talking about her looks. She just seems more . . . down-to-earth. You have to admit, they're pretty different."

Hannah blew out a breath. "Well, the truth is, my father also thinks they're pretty different. He left her fifteen years ago."

We didn't talk until we were a few miles from Venice Beach.

I said, "Is it a good sign that I haven't heard from the cops?"

"Not really. Most likely, it just means they're still building a case."

"You always know how to make a guy feel better." I turned into a public parking lot.

She half-turned toward me in the seat. "You want the truth, or you want sunshine pumped up your ass?"

"Maybe throw a little light into my small intestine?"

After I parked the car, Hannah, Lisa, and I walked a few blocks down Venice Boulevard and turned onto the Boardwalk. It was jammed with people, as it usually is on sunny spring weekends, with loud conversations, music from radios, and the scrape of Rollerblades. The air smelled like cotton candy.

We passed Muscle Beach, where an African-American man bench-pressed a bar that was loaded with enough iron disks to flex the bar like a hunter's bow. A man in a turban roller-skated past us, playing an electric guitar that was wired to a small amp on his back.

We headed north on the Boardwalk, weaving through the crowd. In the front window of a tattoo parlor, a handwritten sign offered a 10 percent discount before noon. Probably a safe bet. Its customers weren't likely awake by then.

I said to Hannah, "Have you noticed that no one's looked at me twice?"

She kept walking, eyes straight ahead.

We found the first pizza joint, which was more like a serving counter. I walked up to the window. Hannah edged in front of me and said, "Is there a Kevin who works here?"

The frizzy-haired man behind the counter said, "You a cop?"

"No. Is Kevin here?"

He adjusted the white paper hat on his head. "You look like a cop."

"I'm not a cop."

A big guy behind us said, "Speed it up."

Hannah spoke louder. "Is Kevin here?"

"Never heard of him, Officer."

Hannah huffed away.

I hustled to catch up with her, then said, "I'll take the next one."

A few doors down was a white wooden structure with screened windows. Its faded sign said NERO'S RETREAT. I walked up to the woman behind the outdoor serving counter. "Hey, is Kevin around?"

She screwed her mouth to the side. "Who?"

"You guys have a three-cheese pizza?"

"Only if you want the same cheese three times."

"No one named Kevin works here?"

"Sorry. What's he look like?"

Hannah smirked at me.

I said, "About six foot three. Bald. Tattoo of a goat on his forehead."

The woman shook her head. "No one here like that, dude."

As we headed down the walkway, I saw a crescent-shaped crowd forming. A skinny man with a giant Adam's apple, wearing a dented black top hat, stuck his arms into the long sleeves of a straitjacket. He stood next to a twelve-foot-tall metal contraption that looked like an Erector set on steroids. Dangling from a pulley at the top of the device was a rope with an iron hook on the end. A blond woman in sequined leotards cranked a handle on the machine, lowering the hook.

I said to Hannah, "Hang on a sec."

She looked at the guy in the straitjacket, then at me. "I don't have time for this."

"Only a sec."

She looked at her watch. "Thirty seconds."

The skinny man invited a large man in a red-checked lumberjack shirt to tie the straps on the straitjacket. Lumberjack put his foot in the small of the thin man's back and pulled the canvas tight. I noticed how the thin guy braced his arms to pick up some slack, just like Houdini did. He knows what he's doing. That'll give him room to wriggle free.

Lumberjack's face reddened as he fastened the leather straps into the belt hooks. Skinny said, "Now, could you please tie my feet?"

The assistant handed Lumberjack a length of rope. He took it, squatted down, and tied the escapist's feet together.

From behind me, Hannah said, "Ten seconds."

Without looking back, I waved for her to hold on.

The assistant grabbed the rope dangling from the tall machine and pulled it over to where the magician was standing. She attached the iron hook at the end of the rope to the ties on his feet, then went back to the contraption and turned the crank. The roped tightened. The magician squatted, sat, then laid down on the ground. The assistant kept cranking. His feet went up in the air, then the rest of his body. The top hat fell off.

Hannah said, "Glad to see your case is less important to you than a sideshow."

I said, "Just a second."

The magician went up higher, swaying on the rope. His assistant stopped cranking when his head was about five feet from the concrete.

I saw him give her a nod, though the audience probably didn't notice. She took out a cigarette lighter, flicked it on, and lit a torch.

The assistant said, "It took Houdini two minutes and forty-four seconds to get out of a straitjacket." She walked over to the escapist, raised the torch, and held it up against the rope just above the magician's feet. The rope caught fire. The crowd gasped.

The magician started writhing like a butterfly in a cocoon.

The assistant said, "It takes two and a half minutes to burn through the rope. If Les doesn't get out in time, he can't use his arms to break the fall. He'll go headfirst into the pavement. Last year, a magician didn't make it. He cracked his skull and is still in a coma. Anyone mind if I take up a collection in advance?"

She dunked the torch in a bucket of water. The flame hissed out.

The crowd stared at the struggling magician. The assistant scooped up the magician's top hot and walked through the crowd. Still watching the escapist, people absently tossed money into the hat. The rope blackened. Strands popped out.

I reached into my pocket and gave her a dollar that I couldn't afford. She looked at Lisa and my jacket, then gave me a wink. Did she know I was one of them?

I saw the magician make a lurching move. I could tell he was free of the jacket, though he kept it around him for effect. He watched until she'd made the last collection, then he tossed it off.

The crowd cheered. Lisa flapped her wings. She likes applause.

The magician pulled his upper body toward the hook on his feet, like he was doing a sit-up in the air. Wow. He's got incredible abs. Just like Houdini.

The rope burned to a thin strand.

The audience was focused on the magician. I shot my eyes between him and the assistant. Just as he got hold of the foot hook, the assistant threw a hidden lever on the lifting machine. The burning rope snapped. As the magician fell, he straightened up and landed on his feet. The crowd cheered.

This guy is good. I started forward to congratulate him, then glanced back at Hannah.

Gone.

I'm in deep shit.

Maybe I can take a second to congratulate him. Magicians like to know they're appreciated by other magicians.

A bunch of people had gotten in ahead of me. I tried to push in. Got elbowed in the ribs.

C'mon, move it.

I looked at my watch. I shouldn't piss off Hannah any more than necessary.

I waved at the magician. Didn't catch his eye.

I looked at my watch again.

Maybe I'll catch his next show.

I gave him one last wave. He didn't see it.

I started up the Boardwalk, glancing back.

I found Hannah two pizza parlors down the way. As I walked in, she was talking to a bald man behind the counter, who was shaking his head. Hannah turned and walked past me. I hurried outside and tried to get alongside her. She can really move.

When I caught up, Hannah stopped. She turned to face me. "I don't know why I'm giving up a Saturday if you're more interested in a street entertainer than you are in your own case."

I took a half step back, panting from the run to catch up with her. "That magician had a technique I'd never seen before." Well, not for a while anyway.

"Great. I'm sure you can get extra privileges by doing tricks for the prison guards."

"Hey. I'm a professional magician. I have to keep up with the latest techniques. Don't you read the newest law cases?"

"Not when I'm doing client business." She took off, walking fast.

I hurried alongside. We both looked straight ahead.

Lisa nibbled at my earlobe. I pushed her away. She came in for another bite.

Hanna and I tried three more pizza places, which proved equally Kevin-free.

We next walked into Vesuvio, a tiny redbrick building that smelled like pizza dough. There was a white Formica counter, with a menu board hanging above it, and two wooden picnic tables covered with plastic red-checkered tablecloths. A spiky-haired man walked up to the counter when he saw us. He wore a white apron over a wifebeater undershirt, and his arms were so inked with skulls, barbed wire, and jungle cats that it looked like he was wearing a colored shirt.

The man looked at Lisa and said, "Cool bird." When he spoke, I saw a stud glint on his tongue.

"Thanks."

He took a pencil from behind his multipierced ear, opened an order pad, and flipped over the top page. "What'll you have?" Despite the warrior tattoos, his voice was gentle.

I looked up at the menu board.

There it is! Right under the Romana Special.

Three-Cheese Pizza.

I smiled at the guy. "Is Kevin around?"

He looked at Hannah, then back at me. He squinched his eyes. "Who are you?"

"Harvey Kendall. This is Hannah Fisher. We're private investigators."

"What do you want with Kevin?"

"Just some information. You're Kevin, right?"

Keeping his eyes on me, he put the pencil behind his ear, let go of it, and gave a single nod.

CHAPTER TWENTY-TWO

Kevin looked at Hannah, then at me. "Is she a cop?"

Hannah said, "No. We're working for one of the defendants. Someone who didn't do it."

Kevin looked back and forth between us. "How come you're here before the cops?"

She shrugged. "Frankly, we're ahead of them on the case."

I said, "Help us find the sonofabitch who did it." I watched him closely, looking for a defensive reaction. Didn't see one.

Kevin yelled toward the back. "Ernie, can I take a few minutes?"

A man with a stubbled gray beard stuck his head over the kitchen counter. "Make it quick."

We went outside and sat at a concrete table whose red-checked plastic tablecloth flapped in the ocean breeze. A thick crowd of people milled past us.

Kevin picked up a glass shaker of red pepper flakes and tilted it to the side, forming a red-flecked slope.

Hannah said, "How'd you meet Sherry?"

He turned the shaker, reengineering his slope. "I used to

babysit for her when she was ten. I'm five years older than her." He spoke so softly, it was hard to hear him over the crowd noise. I leaned in closer.

Kevin said, "Her father was a single dad. Real protective, you know? He never liked me much, but I lived in the neighborhood and I was cheap."

Hannah said, "When I was little, a neighborhood boy used to babysit me. I had the biggest crush on him."

Kevin smiled. He leaned forward and set down the pepper shaker. "Yeah. Guess it's an older-man thing."

Good, Hannah. You're relaxing him.

She said, "How'd you get back together?"

Kevin told the story we'd pieced together from the e-mails. Sherry came into his restaurant with a girlfriend, he waited on them, they exchanged info, he followed up, and they started dating.

I said, "How'd her old man feel about that?"

He drew back from the table. *Ooops.* Did he just figure out that we knew more than we were telling?

Hannah kicked me under the table. *Ow.* I moved my leg away from her.

She spoke soothingly to Kevin. "Where'd you go on the first date?" He kept looking at me, then turned back to her.

"Raz. This club in Hollywood."

As he talked about his dates with Sherry, I could see him loosening up.

Okay, Hannah. I won't miss any chances to shut up.

While he told Hannah about his date with Sherry, I reached into my jacket pocket, took out a piece of smooth white rope, and laid it on the table. Hannah glanced at it, looking puzzled, then went back to talking to Kevin.

I saw Kevin's eyes go to the rope, then back to Hannah.

While they spoke, I started tying the rope into a loop knot.

Exactly like the one around Sherry's wrists. As the knot took shape, I watched Kevin for a reaction. He glanced down at the rope, looked up at me like I was some kind of whack job, then went back to Hannah.

Hannah gently worked him up to the subject of Sherry's father.

Kevin said, "The old man didn't like me when I was a kid. Probably thought I molested her or something." He looked back and forth at us. "I'd never do anything like that."

Hannah and I were both shaking our heads. "Of course not."

Kevin said, "Both me and her figured it was better if her old man didn't know about our hooking up again. I mean, you know, unless it got real serious or something." He picked up the pepper shaker and tapped the side, quivering the flakes.

Hannah said, "What's he like? Her father?"

"Tough guy. High-school boxer, I think. Scared the shit out of me when I was little." His mouth formed a shy grin. "Guess he still does, a little."

"You said he was really protective?"

Kevin blew an upward puff of air from the side of his mouth, meaning "No shit, Sherlock."

She said, "Did he find out about you?"

He shook his head. "Not unless she told him. Which I seriously doubt."

"What happened over the last few weeks?"

Kevin clunked down the pepper shaker. "She wanted to break up." His eyes got wet.

Hannah nodded sympathetically.

Kevin told a story consistent with the e-mails. She stopped answering his calls, then sent an e-mail saying they should see other people. She said something about dating an older man. Kevin didn't know who he was.

He said, "I loved her. I told her this was bogus. You know,

breaking up by e-mail and all that. I said she should tell me to my face. So I kept bugging her until she agreed to see me."

"Did she?"

"Yeah."

I sat up straight. So did Hannah.

That wasn't in the e-mails.

Hannah said, "When?" Her voice had a little quiver.

"The night before she . . ." He bit his lower lip and looked away.

The plastic tablecloth snapped in the ocean breeze.

Hannah said, "What happened?"

A customer walked past us, into the store. Kevin jumped up, ran inside, and stood behind the counter. We followed him in. Hannah was watching him closely. Does she think he's going to run?

Kevin wrote up the order, then came back to us. We walked outside and sat at the table again.

He looked around. "Sherry said I could come by her place. No fooling around, she said. Just one last conversation." His eyes filled with tears.

I said, "I'm sure she cared about you."

Hannah kicked me again. *Okay, okay.* I slid away from her.

Kevin said, "We talked for a long time. I couldn't get her to tell me what was going down. She just said she was dating somebody. Wouldn't tell me who. Anyway, I'm crying, and telling her I love her, and then I sit next to her. Then I try to kiss her, and she says, 'No,' but I can tell she doesn't mean it, so pretty soon, she really doesn't mean it, and we ended up, you know . . ."

The sounds of the crowd seemed to get louder.

Hannah said, "You think she was going to get back together with you?"

"I dunno. I hoped so. Until that guy came in."

Hannah and I both said, "What guy?"

A bell inside the restaurant dinged. Kevin jumped up and ran inside. We went to the door and watched him grab a pizza off the kitchen counter, slide it off the round metal tray into a white cardboard box, and hand it to the customer.

From the kitchen, a gruff voice yelled, "Break's over."

Kevin said, "I just need a second."

"I don't pay you to sit around."

Hannah walked toward the back. She said, "We'll be happy to order something. Please give us a minute with Kevin."

A gray-bearded man's head came over the counter. "Who're you?"

Kevin looked terrified.

Hannah put on a purring sexy look.

Hadn't seen that one before. Kinda nice.

She said, "I'm his cousin from Ohio. Just in town this afternoon. Please, sir, I'd love a few more minutes to visit."

The old man looked at her. He stared for a few seconds, then waved the air in a "Get on with it."

Hannah ordered a three-cheese pizza. Kevin put in the order, and we went back to the table.

Hannah said, "So who walked in on you?"

"I know. I shoulda called the cops. I was just, well . . ."

Hannah patted his hand. "I understand. You were overwhelmed."

His voice quavered. "Am I gonna get in trouble for not calling them?"

"We'll help you with that. Tell us about the guy. It was a man, wasn't it?"

He nodded. "I don't know much."

"Just tell us what you do."

"Well, we were, you know, going at it in her bed. Then I hear her dog bark. I didn't think much of it until I hear this guy's voice in the room. He yells, 'Slut!' I roll over to get a look but he's gone. I hear her apartment door slam."

Kevin pulled at one of his earrings.

Hannah said, "Was the dog barking the whole time?"

"No. Just a couple of barks before he came in. Then it stopped."

"What happened next?"

"I asked her who that was. She wouldn't tell me. Sherry started yelling at me. She said I'd fu—screwed everything up, and told me to get the hell out. She actually hit me. First time she ever hit me." He started crying.

The bell inside dinged. Kevin grabbed the front of his T-shirt and pulled it up to wipe his eyes. He then jumped up, went inside, and came back with Hannah's three-cheese pizza.

As he set it down on the table, Kevin whispered, "Ernie says I'm gonna get fired if I don't get back in there."

"Where were you the next night?"

He stiffened. "The night she was . . ."

"Yes."

He shook his head. "Working. Right here. You can ask Ernie. There were some regular customers who can vouch for that, too."

"I believe you." Hannah stood. "Kevin, you need to tell the police what you know. Ask for Sergeant Morton. He's working this case. Tell him I said to call." She gave him her card.

He looked down at her card, then up at her. "This says you're a lawyer. You told me you were an investigator."

She took the pizza. "I do both."

As soon as Kevin went back inside, Hannah dumped the pizza in an oil-drum trash can.

Didn't you think I might have an opinion before you chucked it? I could smell the hot cheeses.

As we walked back toward my car, I said, "What do you think about Kevin's story?"

"The intruder was almost certainly the new boyfriend. Assuming Kevin is telling the truth and there really was an intruder. Kevin could've killed her because she broke up with him."

"You think he was lying?"

"On instinct, no. But you never know. We'll see if his alibi is solid."

I explained why I'd made a knot like Sherry's while we were sitting there.

She said, "Ah. I thought it was the equivalent of weaving baskets in a loony bin."

I said, "He didn't react to the knot."

"Might have been too subtle."

We passed the straitjacket magician, who was packing up. I really should congratulate him. I looked at Hannah. Her face was lined with thought. Maybe I'll congratulate him next time. . . .

I said, "Sherry's neighbors complained about the barking dog. If it was a quick bark and then it stopped, the dog probably knew the intruder. She lived in a security building. The intruder had to be someone with a key to the building and her apartment."

"Consistent with the 'other lover' premise."

"Or her father. Or like you said, Kevin did it and there was no intruder."

We walked up Venice Boulevard. I said, "Kevin's story doesn't really help me, does it?"

"He didn't see who came in. It's impossible to pin someone's voice on a single word." Hannah kept looking straight ahead. "So you could have been the intruder."

CHAPTER TWENTY-THREE

Hannah and I drove down Washington Boulevard, away from Venice Beach, and got onto the 405 freeway. As we picked up speed, I said, "Why'd you keep kicking me under the table at the pizza place?"

"Why do you think?"

"Because I was screwing up whatever line you were on?"

"Right. You have to make people comfortable before you interrogate them. Start with nonthreatening questions. Get them in a talking mode. You kept cutting to the chase. Like when you asked about her father early on. We knew that was a touchy subject from the e-mails. Did you see how he reacted?"

"Yeah."

She said, "It's like, when you first meet a girl. Five minutes later you don't say 'Let's hop in bed.'"

"You don't?"

Hannah punched me. *Ow.*

We got off the 405 and onto the 101.

Hannah looked at the road. "Do you think I look like a cop?"

"Huh?"

"Do I look like a cop?"

I grinned. "Yeah. You could be on *Law and Order.*"

"I'm serious. Three people asked me that today."

I shook my head. "Nah. You were just all business suited-up on the Boardwalk. May as well wear a sandwich board that says UPTIGHT."

Her head snapped toward me. "You think I'm uptight?"

"Course not."

Compared to, say, the Pope.

As we neared the Laurel Canyon exit, Hannah said, "Do you mind stopping at my apartment for a minute?"

"No problem." I'd love to see you in your natural habitat. "Why?"

"We're running late. I've got to change clothes."

I shifted in the seat. "Like for a date?"

"Something like that."

I looked over at her. She was staring straight ahead.

I said, "Who's the lucky guy?"

"Get off on the 134, then turn left on Cahuenga."

Hannah lived in a three-story apartment building on Cahuenga, just north of Riverside Drive. It was an old Spanish building that was pretty well kept-up, if you ignored the six-foot-long cracks in the stucco. Her living room had overstuffed red furniture with toothpick legs, sitting around a kidney-shaped glass coffee table. Real fifties vibe. In a corner of the living room was a blond-wood desk stacked with piles of papers. I looked away from that area. Don't want her getting any ideas about my organizing that shit.

Hannah went into the bedroom and shut the door. I wandered over to her bookshelf. Top row was a bunch of law books, some with yellow *used* stickers on them. Contracts. Civil Procedure. Torts, whatever those are. I opened the torts book to a random page. Lisa shifted on my shoulder, as though she were reading along with me. Some legal case about fireworks in a subway station.

Below the law books were a bunch of thin paperbacks, all titled *Double Crostics*. I put back the torts book and pulled out one of the paperbacks. Tricky kind of crossword puzzles. Next to that were books with logic problems. I opened one called *Figure This Out.*

"If a caterpillar crawls to a leafy bush at a speed of nine inches per hour, eats until it is full, then returns over the same distance at only three inches per hour, what's its average speed for the full trip (not counting the eating time)?"

Hmm. Gotta be . . . nine plus three, divided by two, equals six. I flipped to the back. Huh? The answer is four and a half. How?

I heard the bedroom door open, jammed the book back on the shelf, and spun around so quickly that Lisa flapped her wings to keep her balance. From the dark bedroom, Hannah's voice said, "What are you doing?"

I looked over, but I couldn't see her. "Just looking at your bookshelf."

"If you were a dog with that expression, I'd be checking the rugs."

"The rugs are fine. But I did take a dump on your sofa."

Maybe I heard a chuckle. At least she's too far away to hit me.

Hannah came through the door, wearing a tight-fitting black dress, a pearl necklace, and dangling pearl earrings. Her face was smoothed with makeup.

"You look . . . wow."

She checked her watch. "Let's go."

When she got in the car, I could smell her vanilla perfume.

As we drove back to her office, I said, "So where are you going tonight?"

"Dinner."

"Where?"

"Don't know."

She turned on the radio.

When we got near to her office, I said, "You want me to walk you in?"

"So you can see my mysterious date?"

"No, so I can make sure you're okay."

"I can take care of myself."

"Then how will I see your mysterious date?"

I drove into her parking lot and saw a silver Mercedes parked diagonally across two spaces, puffing out neat white clouds of exhaust. I stopped a few car-lengths away.

Hannah opened the door. "Thanks for the lift."

"Certainly, madame. Will that be all for the evening?"

"That will be it, asshole." She climbed out and shut the door.

I sat there, watching her walk away. Lisa seemed to be staring, too. The driver's door of the Mercedes opened. Out stepped a man who looked maybe ten years older than Hannah. He wore a dark suit and had perfectly combed hair. What kind of guy takes the time to put every hair in place? He probably smells like a cologne factory. The man pecked Hannah on the cheek, then walked around and opened the passenger door. Hannah got inside without looking back at me.

I turned the key in the ignition and heard a screeching grind. Shit. The motor was already running. I threw the car in gear, jammed the wheel all the way to the left, and U-turned out of the parking lot.

When I got home, I took Mrs. Fisher's food bag out of the trunk, went into my apartment, and set the food on the kitchen counter. My stomach rumbled.

With Lisa still on my shoulder, I took out the cookies, which were wrapped in Saran. They were soft enough to indent where I touched them. *Excellent.* I gently placed them on the counter.

I reached into the grocery bag and lifted out a huge Tupperware container of chili. *Whoa.* This could feed a family of six for a month. I peeled off the top, spooned some into a cereal bowl, put it in the microwave, and hit the timer. After giving the cookies one last glance, I went to the living room and turned on the TV.

Another Saturday night with my bird and the television. Wonder how Hannah's enjoying her escargot with her Mr. Perfect Hair? I'm sure he's very attentive when he's not studying his own reflection in a crystal wineglass.

I plopped on the couch with an exhale, grabbed the remote, and channel-surfed.

Some guy fishing.

Click.

Soap opera in Spanish.

Click.

Big-band singer.

Click.

How can there be nothing on two hundred channels?

Lisa shifted on my shoulder.

Maybe I should call Carly. I'm pretty sure she wanted to see me again. What's the worst that happens if I call? She turns me down. What's a little humiliation if you might be going to jail for the rest of your life?

I leaned over for my phone on the end table, stretching my arm so far that I felt my shoulder socket strain. My fingers were just a few inches away. . . . No way I was getting up. I wriggled my fingers, leaned farther. *Yes!* I hooked the cord and pulled it toward me. The phone crashed onto the floor. Lisa flapped her wings as if to say, What the hell?

I pulled the cord, reeling in the phone. It started screeching at me. In the other room, the microwave beeped.

I hung up the phone, went to the kitchen, and took out the steaming bowl of chili. Man, those spices smell good. I took a spoon from the drawer and scooped a bite. My mouth watered as I slid it in.

As I chewed, my eyes involuntarily closed. *Oh . . . My . . . God.* This is the best-tasting food I've had in a year. Maybe ever . . .

I opened my eyes and slurped in another mouthful. Then another, and another. Is it okay to just drink it? My spoon scraped the bowl. I'm already finished? Are the sides of the bowl too steep to lick?

I grabbed the Tupperware, refilled the bowl, and stuck it back in the microwave. C'mon. Hurry up. I eyed the cookies. You're next, boys.

While waiting for the chili, I went back to the living room, fell on the couch, and called Carly's cell.

She answered right away.

I said, "Hi. It's Harvey."

"I hoped you'd call."

"You did?"

"I enjoyed our coffee."

I sat up on the couch. "I enjoyed it, too." Boy, I can really dish out the clever lines.

I stood up, pushing the phone hard against my ear. "Well . . . actually, my plans tonight just fell through. I'm sure you're busy, but I thought . . ."

"My plans got cancelled, too."

The microwave beeped in the kitchen.

I started pacing with the phone. "I heard about this new movie, *Heather's Last Love.* It's supposed to be a three-hankie chick flick."

She laughed. "Actually, I prefer action movies."

A girl who likes action films? I said, "Terrific. How about the new Will Smith film in Century City?"

"Perfect."

"I already had dinner, but I'm happy to get you something at the food court." Fast food is about all I can squeeze out of my current budget.

"I already ate."

I'm in love. . . .

I hung up, smiling.

I took the chili out of the microwave and poured it back into the Tupperware container. The cookies seemed to be calling my name, so I unwrapped them and took a bite. Just the right consistency of squishy and crunchy. *Wow.* I wonder if Mrs. Fisher would like to adopt a magician.

I started to put the cookies away.

Maybe just one more bite . . .

After finishing the cookies, I jumped in the shower, closed my eyes, and let the powerful spray shoot needles at my face. I turned up the hot water and took a deep breath of the steam.

Wow. Going from alone to a date in sixty seconds.

I opened my eyes.

Almost too easy . . .

How come?

Wait a minute. . . .

Is Carly only seeing me because she wants to convert me to her antiabortion cause?

I turned around and let the shower hit my neck.

Is she the front for some cult? Do they want to Svengali me into firebombing abortion clinics?

I turned back to face the water spray.

What the hell. Everybody's got some kind of agenda.

Including me.

I've been celibate so long that my sweat smells like semen.

CHAPTER TWENTY-FOUR

During the action flick, we gasped, laughed, and cheered at the same scenes. I managed to touch elbows a few times, but not much more. Maybe we should've seen the chick flick.

As we walked out of the theater, Carly said, "I live nearby. You want to come over?"

Lemme think that over for two or three seconds. "I'd love to."

I followed her black Dodge Neon to a large apartment building on Malcolm Avenue in Westwood. After I parked on the street, she met me at the front door, and we went to her apartment on the second floor.

When she opened the door, I half-expected to see pictures of dead fetuses hanging on the walls. *Whew.* Over the couch was a framed print of a nighttime street with a daytime sky. Next to that was a pen-and-ink drawing of lizards climbing in and out of a piece of paper. Magritte and Escher. Two of my favorites.

Carly dropped her purse on the coffee table. "You want something to drink?"

"Water?"

"Have a seat."

I sat on the couch and watched her go into the kitchen. She took a plastic bottle of water from the refrigerator and unscrewed the top with a snap.

Carly came back to the living room and handed me the water. Am I leaving fingerprints on the water bottle?

She kept standing. Her mouth formed a little smile as she said, "You want to smoke some grass?"

Well, well.

I hadn't smoked since high school. Can't say I loved it. Made the top of my scalp feel like it was under anesthetic. On the other hand, it seemed awfully rude to turn her down. Especially if it got her all . . . relaxed.

Is it smart to get stoned while I'm under investigation by the cops?

Carly raised her eyebrows in a question. She bit her lip with that sexy overbite. Her eyes twinkled.

I didn't see any cops following me here. . . .

I cleared my throat. "Sure."

She smiled and went back into the kitchen. I got up and followed along. She opened the freezer and took out a package of frozen spinach. Carly opened one end, pulled out a pouch of icy spinach, then stuck her hand all the way into the box. She came out with a rolled-up Baggie of marijuana and held it out to me. "You want to roll the joint?"

Not unless you want it to look like a pregnant worm. "Go ahead."

She opened a kitchen drawer and took out a packet of cigarette papers. Carly pulled one out, folded it in a V shape, dropped in the grass by sifting it with her thumb and forefingers, then rolled it into a joint. She looked at me as she slowly ran her tongue along the glue.

"C'mon." She motioned with her head for me to follow her back to the living room.

As we walked, she said, "My folks were really into sixties music. You mind if we listen to some?"

"I love the sixties. My mom's from that era, too."

"Yeah? I'm named after Carly Simon."

"You did better than me. I'm named after a great-uncle who was a school janitor until he won five hundred grand in the lottery. I suspect my folks were hoping for a few bucks out of the deal. All we got was a name that made me the butt of every grammar-school kid's joke."

She giggled. "What sixties music do you like?"

"Pretty much all of it."

"Could you be a little more specific?"

Is this a test? To see if I really know the sixties? "Buffalo Springfield. Jimi Hendrix. The Doors. Joni Mitchell. Jefferson Airplane."

"Good ones. Let's go with Joni. *Ladies of the Canyon?*"

"Cool. I mean, groovy."

Carly got up and put on the music. She lit a large amber candle on the coffee table, turned off the lights, and sat next to me on the couch. Our legs were almost touching.

She put the tip of the joint against her lips, like she was going to light it, but instead slid the whole thing into her mouth, then pulled it out slowly through her lips. It hung from her mouth, all shiny-wet.

I settled back into the couch. Carly took a wooden match from a holder on the coffee table and struck it against the table leg. As the match flared, it lit her face in a yellow glow. She touched the flame to the tip of the joint and sucked in smoke. I watched her chest expand. Were her nipples standing up when we came in?

Carly kept the smoke in her lungs and handed me the joint. I reached for it. How do you hold this thing? Thumb and . . . forefinger, right? I forced a smile. Took the joint.

Put it in my mouth.

Sucked in a little toke.

Ow! That burns. *Don't cough.* Don't—

I hacked out a raspy cough, spraying smoke.

Carly laughed. "Been a while, huh?"

I tried to stop coughing. "That obvious, huh?"

She took the joint, held it against my lips, and said, "Gently. Just take in a little."

I took a small breath through my mouth.

Did I get any? If I ask, I'll lose the smoke.

Whatever.

Most important thing is to get her relaxed. Right?

After a few more tries, I could definitely feel something. The top of my head was tingling. Is that, like, normal? No way I'm gonna ask.

The music sounds awfully good. Do the notes always feel like they're vibrating your cells?

Carly said, "How long have you worked for a criminal lawyer?"

I shifted around on the couch so I could face her. "Just a few weeks. My real gig is magic."

Carly turned toward me and curled her legs up under her. How do women do that?

She said, "Magic?"

"Yeah. I'm a magician."

"Like, a professional?" She sucked on the joint and handed it to me.

I waved away the joint. Since I'm already floating a couple of feet above the couch, I'm probably good.

She put it in the ashtray. *Whew.*

Carly said, "Where do you do magic?"

"Oh, shows here and there. I'm a member of the Magic Castle. You heard of that?"

She shook her head. "Uh-uh."

"It's a private club for magicians. I perform there sometimes. My goal is to work in Vegas. That's the big time for magicians, you know."

"Show me a trick."

"Thanks to your weed, I'm not sure I could even touch my nose."

She plumped her lips into a pout. "C'mon. I really want to see one."

"Carly . . ."

She raised her eyebrows, turned down the corners of her mouth. "Please . . ."

I let out a sigh. What the hell. If she's as high as I am, it shouldn't be too hard to amaze her. "You got a deck of cards?"

She jumped off the couch, quick-stepped to her desk, opened a couple of drawers, rummaged through, and came back with a pack of cards.

I took it from her. *Aaargh.* It was poker size, not bridge. I opened the flap and took out the ratty deck. The cards were bent, the edges worn. Forget double lifts. The design on the back is a bunch of flowers that won't look the same upside down.

Carly climbed back on the couch, curled her legs under her, and leaned toward me. I couldn't help looking down her blouse. Couldn't see much in the low light. The lower part of my body was doing just fine with the available information.

I pretended to shuffle the deck, while in fact I was arranging the cards. Then I gave it a few false shuffles that kept them in order. The cards felt like they were sticking to my fingers.

I fanned through the deck and said, "Pick a card." She took the one I forced on her. "Don't show it to me." I looked away, through the open door to her bedroom. She had a bed without a headboard, covered with a paisley bedspread. On the wall behind it was a black-light poster, a vibrantly colored drawing of a motorcycle rider flying toward you. *Awesome picture.* If I was any more stoned, I'd be ducking. I haven't seen a black-light poster since Mom put her collection in the garage about ten years ago. Guess Carly is a legitimate sixties throwback.

She said, "Harvey?"

"Oh. Sorry." I turned around and told her to put her card back in the deck. As I closed it up, I dropped most of the cards. *Shit.* Some of them went between the couch cushions.

Carly helped me dig around until we collected them. I put them on top of the deck and awkwardly squared up the cards.

Since I couldn't give her the same card again, I had to restack the deck. I went through my phony shuffling, then forced her to take another card. This time, I got it back in the deck without mishap.

I handed her the cards and said, "Don't tell me your card. Spell out your card's number by putting one card facedown on the table for each letter. So if you had a five, you'd put down four cards for F-I-V-E."

She dealt off three cards.

I said, "Now spell the suit the same way. Like if it's clubs, you put down five cards."

She dealt off six cards.

I said, "Okay. What was your card?"

"You want me to tell you?"

"Yeah."

"Two of hearts."

I said, "Turn over the next card."

She flipped over the two of hearts. Carly's eyebrows went up. She looked at me, looked back at the card. "Wow. You're really good."

I said, "Take a look at this. You spelled H-E-A-R-T-S using

these cards." I flipped over the five cards she'd used to spell the suit. They were all hearts.

"Harvey. That's—"

"And"—I flipped over the three cards she'd used to spell the number—"you spelled T-W-O using the other three twos."

Her mouth fell open. She started clapping. "That's . . . awesome! How'd you do that?"

"I used a trick deck."

"Oh . . . Hey, it's my deck." She giggled. "C'mon. How'd you do it?"

I gave her the old magician's line. "I did it very well."

Carly scooched closer. "Guess I'll just have to charm the secret out of you." She put her hand on the back of my neck and massaged.

Ohhh.

Still massaging, she leaned her head onto my shoulder. Her hair smelled like strawberry shampoo.

Joni Mitchell sang "Morning Morgantown."

Carly stopped massaging my neck, took hold of my arm, and ran her hand up and down my biceps.

Now what? I started to put my arm around her, then stopped. All that shoulder movement would jar her head. Will she pull away? She's hardly acting like she's going to pull away. I started to move again. Stopped.

What's the worst that can happen? Back to Saturday nights with my bird?

I left my shoulder where it was and carefully reached over with my other hand. I stroked her face. She *mmm*'d under my touch. Her skin was so smooth. I felt a warm bulge stretching my pants. It's been so long that this could be over before I get undressed. What do you do to make it last? Don't guys, like, think about baseball or something? I don't know anything about baseball.

I lifted my shoulder and put my arm around her. She moved in rhythm, waiting for my arm to fall in place, then settled her head against my chest. Does grass always speed up your heart? Can she feel it through my chest? She rubbed my stomach.

I leaned down to kiss her. Her mouth came up to mine. *It's been so long. . . .*

Oh man. She tastes delicious. I closed my eyes.

Wait. I don't want to miss this. I opened my eyes. Hers were still closed.

We kept kissing for at least three Joni Mitchell songs. I moved my hand down to her blouse. Grabbed the top button and tried to wriggle it through the fabric. I twisted it the other way. Squeezed the damn thing with my fingers.

Are these buttons, like, sewn closed? Maybe grass isn't so good for fine-motor coordination. I tried another one-hand twist. Am I wrinkling the fabric?

I brought my other hand around. Carly laid back on the couch, looking amused. Using both of my hands, I got her top button open, then the next, and the next. Her blouse fell to the sides, leaving a strip of bare skin down the middle. I saw that her belly button was an outie.

Carly whispered, "Do you have protection?"

Not unless you count the condoms that have been in my dresser since the Pleistocene era. I said, "Um . . ."

"Don't worry. I've got some."

She got off the couch and took my hand. Her open blouse fluttered as she led me into her bedroom. When we got through the door, she reached against the wall and turned off the light.

We laid down under the black-light poster and pulled off each other's clothes. Carly turned on her side, away from me. I heard the slide of a drawer in her bedside table. She rolled back with a foil packet and tore it open. I laid on my back.

She unrolled the condom onto me. That feels so incredibly . . . *too good.*

Hold on. Not yet. This has to last.

Wonder how the Dodgers are doing this year?

Carly laid on her back and pulled me on top of her. I easily slid inside. Oh man. I remember this. Just like riding a bicycle.

We started to move. She *mmm*'d softly.

Hold on, Big Guy. Make it last. Make it last.

Take me out to the ball game. . . .

I moved harder. Her face beaded with tiny droplets. She closed her eyes and started to moan.

Hold on. Hold on. Think about something else. Think about . . .

How safe are these condoms? What brand are they?

I craned to see the name on the crumpled packet. Couldn't make it out in the low light. Not that I'd know one from the other.

The poisons have been building up in my system for six months. Am I going to deliver such a gusher that it'll crash through the condom membrane?

Carly moaned louder, saying, "Yes! Yes!"

I pictured millions of sperm screaming toward her ovum. I saw one of them plant a stake. I pictured the cells fertilizing and dividing inside a woman who probably believes that life starts before I even come.

I'm not ready to be a father. I can barely support my bird.

If I stop now, it's not murder in anybody's book.

If . . .

I went limp.

It took Carly a few pumps before she realized she was pretty much on her own.

She stopped moving, opened her eyes.

Carly blinked at me and said, "You okay?"

"I . . . well . . . it's been a while."

Carly reached down and touched me. She gave me a couple of squeezes, as if she couldn't believe anything could be that soft.

I rolled over on my back. "I think the grass made me a little sick."

She propped herself on one elbow. "I'm sorry. It's usually great for sex." She trailed her fingers lightly over my chest. Down my stomach. Lower.

She took hold of me, gave me a few strokes.

I closed my eyes. *Relax.*

She stroked a little harder.

I really want it to get up. I really want . . .

I could feel myself flapping loosely.

I said, "I'm really sorry. This hasn't happened to me in years."

She let go of me and rolled over on her side, facing away from me.

I sat up. "I feel terrible."

"It's okay." Her tone didn't sound like she meant it.

Carly reached down to the floor, grabbed her blouse, and draped it over herself.

I said, "I hope you'll give me another chance."

Still facing away, she said, "No big deal. I gotta get up early tomorrow anyway."

CHAPTER TWENTY-FIVE

Sunday morning, I dragged my ass out of bed around eleven. I took a step, stopped, wobbled in place. My head throbbed. My tongue had grown four sizes.

I didn't think you could get a hangover from grass.

Wrong about that one.

I stumbled toward the bathroom, gently touching my forehead with my fingertips. *Ow.*

I stepped into the shower and turned it on.

I felt a little better when I got out, but it still seemed like I was walking through Jell-O.

After some black coffee, I drove to the Magic Castle's Sunday brunch. Gotta get my mind off my body.

I watched some of the close-up magicians. My head still pounded. I decided I'd better eat something. I went upstairs to the buffet and sneaked a few bites off the serving table without paying.

Just as I was grabbing a sweet pickle, Herb Gold, the magic-trick builder, came over. He clapped a catcher's-mitt hand on my shoulder and said, "Listen, bubbie. I've been thinking about your situation."

I backed up a little. "I promise I'll pay you."

"Yeah, yeah. What I mean is, I think Copperfield might buy your trick."

Ron Wilson, one of the senior magicians, walked by in his Scottish-plaid coat. He waved at us. I smiled at him and waved back.

Herb said, "You hear me?"

I looked at him. "I heard you. The trick's not for sale."

"I know. It's just that, you know, since you're having some financial problems, this could be a way out."

"You said it yourself. That trick is my ticket." I tossed the pickle in my mouth and crunched on it.

"He'd probably pay twenty-five grand."

I stopped chewing. *Holy Shit.* "Twenty-five grand?"

I've never had that kind of money in my life. That'd take care of Hannah, and then some.

No more punching and filing.

I could sit back and wait for the right magic jobs.

Twenty-five grand?

I'm not getting any substitute teaching jobs. Magic work doesn't pay much even when I can get it.

The pickle juice tasted sour in my mouth.

On the other hand, I've got a gig coming up, and Marty said he can get a Vegas promoter to come see me. If he likes me, I'll get better work. Then I'm on my way. Besides, my trick is brilliant. Even Herb thinks so. Copperfield obviously does, too. I may never have an inspiration like that again.

I swallowed the pickle chunks. "Can't do it."

"Maybe I could get him to thirty g's."

Thirty g's? "Herb . . ."

"Kid, just think about it."

He winked at me and walked off.

When I got to Hannah's office on Monday morning, she was on the phone. I took a stack of papers from her out-box and started sorting them into piles on her desk.

I looked around at the stacks of papers in the office. I'm actually making a dent in the filing. If she'd just stop churning out more crap.

Hannah ended her phone call and immediately punched a blinking line, like a chain-smoker. I picked up a sorted pile and banged it on the desk to square it up. She didn't seem to notice. I banged it harder. She kept talking.

When she got off the phone, I said, "How was your weekend?"

"You mean, how was my mystery date?"

Yes. "No. I mean, how was your weekend?"

"Fine. And yours?"

"Fine. So who was Prince Charming in the Mercedes?"

"His first name is None. Last name . . . Of Your Business."

"Ah. I think I know his sister."

In the afternoon, when Hannah got back from her daily meeting, she dialed into her voice mail. After listening a moment, she gasped, then slammed down the phone.

I said, "What?"

Her eyes were wide with panic. "That was a message from my sister. My father's in the emergency room."

"What?"

Hannah quickly dialed. She stood and shifted her weight from foot to foot. "Susan? What happened? Where is he?"

Hannah closed her eyes in a "Thank goodness" expression, then opened them. "So they're sure it wasn't a heart attack? Okay. I'll be right over." She shook her head. "No. I want to come." She twisted the phone cord tightly around her hand. "Yes. Now."

She hung up, snatched her purse, and spoke as she hurried out, "Cover the office. Not sure when I'll be back."

A couple of hours later, Hannah called me at the office. "Could you please grab the Desmond file and bring it to my father's house?"

"How's your dad?"

"The chest pains turned out to be massive indigestion. Knocked him out, though."

"Is he feeling better?"

"He's bitching constantly, so he must be. On the way over, would you mind stopping at Barnes & Noble? I want to get him some books. Grab a pen and I'll give you the titles."

Bruce Fisher lived on Bristol Avenue in Brentwood, just north of Sunset Boulevard, in a neighborhood of huge homes on estate-size lots. Carrying Oliver Desmond's file and the books Hannah wanted, I walked up a brick pathway to a sprawling two-story Spanish house. It had beige stucco walls, a red-tiled roof, and decorative wrought iron surrounding the tall windows. *Man.* He must have over an acre of land. All this from keeping people out of jail?

I climbed the front steps and pushed the bell. Through the thick oak door, I heard the Westminster chimes, then the padding of footsteps. A young woman, around Hannah's age, opened the door. Her straight black hair caught the light as she studied me with emerald green eyes. She wore black jeans and a red-checkered blouse that was tied in a knot just above her bare stomach.

I said, "Hi. You must be Hannah's sister."

"Actually, I'm her stepmother."

"And I'm . . . Humiliated." I felt my face flush.

She laughed. "You're hardly the first to make that assumption."

Or the last.

She stuck out her hand. "Gillian Fisher."

"Harvey Kendall. I work with Hannah."

She smiled at me. I smiled at her.

Gillian cocked her head. She said, "Would you like to come in?"

"Oh. Right. Thanks."

I stepped into a two-story entry hall with a sweeping staircase of red-tiled steps flanked by a black wrought-iron railing. The walls were hung with oil paintings of cowboys spurring horses, sprinkled with a few Navajo rugs.

Gillian said, "Hannah and Bruce are upstairs. First door on the right."

I walked up the bare tiled stairs, conscious of my steps echoing in the massive hall. At the top, the first door was open. Before I got there, I heard Bruce's booming voice.

"Well, based on all that, Harvey may go down."

I stopped still in the hallway.

Hannah said, "I know. It doesn't look good."

I fell back against the wall and spread out my palms to steady myself.

Well, fuck me. She's just been humoring me? She needs the fees that bad?

If my own lawyer thinks I'm gonna swing, I am in the deep end of an Olympic-size swimming pool of shit. My heart started thumping like it wanted out of my chest.

Fuck.

Bruce said, "You think he did it?"

Her nanosecond hesitation in answering seemed like a couple of hours. "Not really. Hopefully, I can attack the DNA evidence. I'm waiting for the lab results. Without DNA, their case is very weak."

I let out a breath. When you're about to drown, even a toothpick floating by looks pretty good.

Hannah's father said, "You might want to plead him out. Now let's talk about this Desmond case."

She said, "The DA offered Desmond voluntary manslaughter and five years."

I pushed off the wall and walked through the open door, into a large bedroom. Bruce lay propped up in a four-poster bed, wearing a black silk bathrobe over striped pajamas. Wonder if those pj's are monogrammed. Neither he nor Hannah noticed me. I stopped just inside the door.

Bruce said to her, "Take the plea bargain."

"I'm not so sure."

"Cut your losses. Move on to the next one."

So much for the old man's warrior spirit. . . .

Hannah said, "Yes, but—"

"The public's got blood in their nostrils. You've got a client with a history of violence who looks like a Maori warrior that'd eat your eyeballs for a snack. Chuck it and move on."

Hannah shook her head. "Something's not right here. They wouldn't be offering this kind of deal if they weren't worried. I've got a gut instinct they're hiding something."

"After all these years, I've got a pretty good gut for these things, too." He smiled as if he were pacifying a crying four-year-old so he could get out of the house for a fancy dinner. "Mine says cut your losses."

Hannah looked pained, as if the words had slapped her face.

I said, "Hi." Their heads turned my way.

Bruce said, "Hello, Harvey. Nice to see you."

He's good. Remembering my name from one meeting?

Hannah looked worried, as if she sensed that I'd heard them discussing my case.

I said to Hannah, "I brought you the stuff you wanted."

She came over, took the Desmond file and books from me, and went back to her father. Hannah gave him the file.

He glanced at the file's label, then set it on the bedside table. "I'll take a look when I'm feeling better."

She looked at the file on the table, then back at her father. Hannah said, "I got you a couple of books. Here's a collection of essays on world economy that I heard about on NPR. And this is an exposé on the CIA's Cold War tactics." Hannah held out the books with an expression that said she feared these meager gifts weren't worthy of His Holiness.

He took them, set them on top of the file on his bedside table, and said, "Thanks."

Hannah took a step back.

Bruce said, "Are you still working on that assault case?"

Her face brightened. "Yes. The illegal search issue is so complex that it could be on a law school exam."

He nodded. "I've given it some thought. Maybe you can argue—"

Behind me, I heard a woman's voice. "How you feelin', Daddy?" Bruce's face lit up in a broad grin.

I turned to see a tall blond woman bouncing into the room, swinging a plastic bag. *Wow.* She must be almost six feet tall.

The woman was wearing a sleeveless lime green dress, and she was so thin that I could see her shoulder bones pushing against the skin. In contrast, her breasts were quite uplifting. Perhaps a little help from the Tit Fairy?

She looked me up and down, as if I were a statue she was thinking of buying. "And you are. . . ."

"Harvey Kendall. I work with Hannah."

Hannah said, "Harvey, meet my sister, Susan." Hannah's tone suggested that I wasn't going to enjoy the experience.

I looked at the blonde. *This is Hannah's sister?* She doesn't even look like a fourth cousin. How'd the dumpy Mrs. Fisher produce a six-foot anorexic?

I said, "Nice to meet you, Susan."

Susan gave me a polite nod, then walked away like she'd decided I was damaged goods. She went to her father's bedside, leaned over, and kissed him on the cheek. Susan opened the plastic bag she was carrying and took out a handful of magazines. "Daddy, I got you the latest copy of *Cigar Aficionado.* Also a *People,* a *USA Today,* and an *Enquirer.*"

Bruce grinned. "Excellent. Some trashy reading." He took the magazines and patted her hand.

Hannah's shoulders slumped.

Susan sat on the bed and began massaging Bruce's feet through the covers. Hannah's gaze burned into her sister.

Hannah said, "Dad, you want to hear about the search and seizure?"

Susan leaned into the massage. Bruce said, "Let's talk about it later." He lolled his head back, closed his eyes, and *mmm*'d.

Hannah turned and walked out. Did Susan's smile just broaden?

I spun around and hurried after Hannah.

She was already down the steps, on her way to the door. I hustled to catch up. She ran outside. I hurried after.

Hannah was unlocking her car when I finally caught up. Slightly out of breath, I said, "Are you okay?"

She flung the car door open, hard enough to make it bounce back. "I'm fine."

"You don't look fine."

Hannah stared at me, blinking rapidly, like she was debating whether to open the floodgates. Then she looked away.

I said, "What's up with the scrawny blonde?"

She chuckled, looked back at me, and shook her head. "Do you always say whatever floats through your brain?"

"Pretty much. Your sister's a kiss-ass, and your father laps it up like kitty milk. Bet he always has."

Hannah gave a pained laugh. She leaned against her car and let out a breath.

From the yard next door, I heard the whine of a lawn mower. The air suddenly smelled of cut grass.

Hannah said, "In high school, if I came home with four A's and a B-plus, my father would say, 'What happened with the B-plus?'"

I stuck my hands in my back pockets. "If I'd gotten a single A, my mother would've taken an ad in the *L.A. Times*."

She looked past me at her father's house. "My sister never got above a C, but that was okay, because he said she had 'other strengths.' That was his code for 'She's thin and popular.'"

"Hannah . . ."

"My father went to every football game when Susan was cheerleading. He even rearranged business trips so he could watch her prance around in her short skirt."

Having met the current Mrs. Fisher, I figured he was probably more interested in the other cheerleaders.

I said, "He's got to be proud of you. Harvard Law? How many people do that?"

"He did. And he was on the *Law Review*. I didn't make that."

The lawn mower next door whined in a lower key as it

chugged away. I said, "I'm sure he loves you. Maybe he's one of those guys who has a hard time showing it."

Hannah grabbed me in a hug. I was so surprised that it took me a moment to put my arms around her. I felt her body shudder against mine. I held her. The sound of the lawn mower next door whined closer. I looked over and saw the brown-uniformed gardener give me a thumbs-up.

Hannah let go and stepped back, looking down at the street. She sniffled. "Thank you."

"Sure."

She started to get into her car.

I said, "You okay to drive?"

"I'll see you at the office."

She closed the door.

I got to the office before Hannah, unlocked the door, and went inside.

Where is she? Should I have followed her? She didn't look like she should be driving. . . .

A few minutes later, Hannah walked in, looking past me.

I said, "Feeling better?"

She stiffened. "I'm fine. Sorry I melted down back there."

I put my hand on her shoulder. "I'm glad you let it out."

She dipped her shoulder out of my grip. "Harvey, we need to keep our relationship professional." She sat at her desk, picked up the phone, and started to dial.

Oh . . .

"Of course."

For the moment anyway.

I cleared my throat. "So. Speaking as a professional. How does my case look?"

Hannah stopped dialing, still holding the phone. "Well . . . you know it's got some problems."

I blinked rapidly.

"Do you think I'm going to. . . ."

She said, "Let's see how the DNA comparisons come back. Then we can discuss it."

"How long will it take to get the lab results?"

"A few more days. Maybe a week."

I nodded. "We'll beat this, right?"

Hannah hung up the phone and looked at me. "You know that nobody can give you that kind of assurance."

"But you think we will, right?"

"I certainly hope so. I'll do my best." She bit her lower lip.

I started pacing. "What can I do? I feel useless just sitting around."

"Nothing at the moment."

"Hannah, I'm getting the distinct feeling that there's a python tightening around my chest. Did you know that pythons don't crush their prey? They just tighten up on the chest every time their victim exhales, so the person can't take another breath, and then he suffocates."

"That's pleasant. Harvey, I wish there was some magic answer—no pun intended—but sometimes there's nothing you can do but wait." She picked up the phone and dialed.

I said, "I'd like to take off a few hours tomorrow."

She looked at me. "To do what?"

"Not sure you want to hear about this one, either."

She hung up the phone. "I want to hear about everything."

"Okay." I raised my eyebrows, as if asking, Are you sure? She kept staring at me.

I said, "I want to talk to Sherry Allen's father."

Hannah threw back her head in an "Are you nuts?" gesture.

"What? Walk right up, tell him you're a suspect, then ask if he'd share some intimate facts about his daughter?"

"Maybe I won't mention the suspect part."

She rolled her eyes. "Great idea. It'll make you look very credible when he testifies how you tricked him while he was mourning the death of his child."

"Okay, okay. I'll work on the technique. Can I have a couple of hours off?"

"No." Hannah blew out a sigh. "But you can come along while I interview her father if you promise to shut up."

CHAPTER TWENTY-SIX

After work, as I drove to the Magic Castle, I started to call Carly on my cell phone. It'd be rude not to call her. I don't want her to think my nonperformance was her fault. I really would like to see her again. Maybe without the grass.

Will she hang up on me?

I dialed her number. Voice mail. I hung up without leaving a message.

That was dumb. She'll see my number on her Missed Calls list.

Maybe she saw my number and that's why she didn't answer.

I really should call back and leave a message. Should I say something clever?

Like what?

"I'm really *UP* for seeing you again?" Dumb.

"I'm so sorry about Saturday night." Wimpy.

"Would you mind getting your tubes tied before our next date?"

Better stick to plain vanilla. I dialed her number again. While her recorded voice told me to leave a number, I cleared my throat. After the beep, I said, "Hi, Carly. It's Harvey. I'd really love to see you again. Give me a call. Or I'll call back."

How dumb did that sound?

I sat at the Magic Castle bar with my pal David, the investment banker, and said, "I took your advice and called Hannah Fisher."

"How is she?"

"Thin."

He looked at me. "Fat Hannah? No shit."

I explained how I was working in her office to pay my legal bills.

David said, "I thought indentured servitude was illegal." He took a swallow of whiskey. "How's your case going?"

"You haven't heard from the cops, have you?"

"Nope."

I leaned in toward him, then glanced around to see if anyone was listening. He leaned in closer.

I spoke just above a whisper. "David, you ever have any problems, like . . . performing?"

His wispy mustache thinned as he smiled. "I assume you don't mean performing magic?"

"The other kind of magic."

He nodded. "It's happened once or twice."

I moved nearer to him. "What did you do?"

He looked around, then whispered, "First, you slap your dong against the bedpost three times. Then—"

"C'mon. I'm serious."

He straightened up, dug a chunk of ice out of his glass with his fingers, and threw it in his mouth. David crunched on the ice and leaned in toward me. "I just slowed things down. Took it easy so there wasn't any pressure. That worked really well."

I nodded.

Ever do it with a right-to-lifer?

Next morning, when I walked into Hannah's office, I saw Sergeant Morton sitting in her guest chair. I stopped in the door. *Oh shit.* Am I getting arrested? My chest thumped. Should I turn and run?

Hannah said, "Sergeant Morton was just telling me about the father of Sherry's son."

Morton stood and looked at me. "Since you were nice enough to have her boyfriend call, I thought I'd give you a little something." His tone didn't sound like the gift was coming from his heart.

I kept my eyes on Morton as I took a few steps into the office.

He said, "Abner Raymond. That's the father of her kid. Former heroin addict turned rehab counselor. He managed to sleep with every vulnerable girl that he helped get sober. Guess he switched addictions from junk to sex."

Hannah said, "Is that how he met Sherry?"

Morton sat down. "Nope. She was clean. At least as far as we know. Abner stuck around until she was about six months pregnant, then disappeared. Probably thought she was too fat."

I saw Hannah wince.

Morton said, "According to the neighbors, they yelled at each other a lot. We didn't get any abuse calls."

Hannah said, "A lot of battered women don't contact the authorities."

Morton looked annoyed that she was schooling him in something so obvious. He said, "At any rate, we're trying to run him down. Oh. We checked out the boyfriend Kevin's alibi. Three people saw him working the night Sherry was killed." Morton stood. "I'll take that thumb drive, please."

She told him about the thumb drive? I took a half step back.

Hannah opened her desk drawer and handed it over. Morton held up the device, squinted at it, then pulled out a plastic Baggie and dropped it in. I watched the Baggie disappear into his pocket.

Morton gave me a little grin as he walked past. "See you later, Mr. Kendall."

As soon as the door closed, I said, "Did you hear that 'See you later'? He was threatening me."

"Don't be so jumpy. His coming by was a good thing."

"Well, it scared the shit out of me. Why didn't you warn me?"

She started typing on her computer. "He just showed up. Cops do that. Sort of like cats."

I started pacing. "What did you mean, it's a 'good thing'?"

Hannah didn't look up from her typing. "It gave us a chance to cooperate by giving him the thumb drive. The more cooperative we are, the less guilty you look."

"Why'd you tell him about the thumb drive?"

She punched a few keys with her index finger. "He wanted to know how we found Kevin."

Still pacing, I said, "What if we need that info again?"

Hannah looked up at me. "You don't think I made a copy of the data?"

I stopped pacing and put up my hands in surrender. "You're the boss. When do we see Sherry's father?"

She stood and picked up her purse. "Now."

CHAPTER TWENTY-SEVEN

As we drove toward Sherry Allen's father's house in Panorama City, I said, "You think Sherry's father could be the one who walked in and said 'Slut' while she was in bed with Kevin?"

Hannah glanced over at me. "Possibly. But the Slut Man ran out. If it was her father, wouldn't he have had it out, right there?"

We turned onto Van Nuys Boulevard. I said, "Maybe he's smarter than that. Maybe dad sulked off and worked himself into a rage. Then he came back the next day, argued, and killed her."

"She was lying nude, spread-eagle, with someone's semen in her. How does dad fit in that scenario?"

"Maybe it was Kevin's semen."

"He said they didn't get that far."

"Maybe he's not telling the truth. So say it was Kevin's semen—"

"Which happens to match your DNA?"

"—which the cops screwed up in testing the DNA. She kicks Kevin out. Dad comes back and strangles her."

"Well, if that's true, this won't be a very friendly visit with dad."

We turned onto Wyandotte and found Roy Allen's house a few blocks up. The one-story tract home had a gray composition roof, black bars over the windows, and a green garden hose snaking across the front yard. Inside the open garage door was a red Corvette with its hood up and a thick black pad on the fender.

As we walked toward Allen's house, my cell phone rang. Hannah glared at me. I took it out of my pocket and saw the name Carly. *She called back!* Am I forgiven? Or is she going to tell me to never call her again?

This isn't exactly the best time for a *tête-à-tête*.

I put the phone in my pants pocket. I could feel the rings vibrate against my leg until it died.

Walking up Allen's driveway, I heard the clank of metal in the garage. Next to the car was a red metal tool chest on wheels, with several drawers half-open. A hand reached around the hood, grabbed a wrench from one of the drawers, then disappeared. We stopped in front of the garage and waited for the man to notice us.

More clanking.

Hannah said, "Mr. Allen?"

A head popped up and looked around. Allen's face was deeply lined, like someone who'd spent a lot of time in the sun. His straight gray hair hung across his eyes, dripping sweat. Allen squinted at us, raised his forearm and used it to wipe his brow, then came toward us. He had almost as many tattoos as Kevin. A dagger, an eagle, the name Jenny.

Allen came closer toward us, carrying the wrench in his hand. "Can I help you?" His voice had a Southern twang.

Hannah said, "I'm Hannah Fisher, a private investigator working on your daughter's case. This is Harvey Kendall."

Allen looked at Hannah, then at me. He squinted, studying my face. "Ain't we met?"

I said, "No, sir." I felt Hannah looking at me.

He wagged the wrench at me. "I know I seen you before."

I shook my head. "We've never met."

His eyes went hard. "Hang on. The cops showed me some pictures. You was one of 'em."

Hannah spoke evenly. "That's right, Mr. Allen. Harvey is a suspect in this case. He's innocent."

Allen backed up, holding up his palms toward us, like he was trying to keep us away. "I ain't supposed to talk to you. Not without the po-lice."

"It's perfectly fine to talk to us. You can call Sergeant Morton, if you like."

He kept backing away. "I got nothin' to say I ain't already said."

Hannah stepped toward him. "We all want the same thing. Which is to find your daughter's killer."

Allen's lower lip trembled. He closed his eyes tightly. When he opened them, he said, "I cain't talk about it no more. Up 'til yesterday, I ain't hardly been outta the house." He squeezed his eyes shut, opened them, blinked rapidly.

Hannah said, "We understand."

He pointed the wrench at her. "Don't you try mollycoddlin' me like that. You ain't—"

I stepped forward. "Mr. Allen."

Hannah shot me a look.

I said, "I lost my father. I know it's nothing like losing a child, but I couldn't get out of bed for three days. I couldn't leave my house for two weeks. My mother took it even worse. I swear to you, I never knew your daughter."

He tightened his grip on the wrench. "Why'd the cops have your picture?"

"Like she said, I'm a suspect. Would I come here and face you if I was her killer?"

Allen blinked at me. He looked at Hannah. Looked back at me.

Hannah said, "Can we please just chat for a few minutes?"

He shook his head. "I done told the cops everythin' I know."

Hannah said, "The cops have dozens of homicide cases. I only have one."

He pointed the wrench at her. "You ain't interested in findin' her killer." He threw his head my way. "You're just interested in gettin' this guy off."

Hannah spoke soothingly. "You're right. My primary job is to get him off. Still, I might find her killer in the process."

He lowered his hand, dangling the wrench at his side. "Well, leastways you're honest." Allen slumped his shoulders, looked at the ground. "Truth is, I ain't seen Sherry much over the past year. I was in Seattle when she was kilt. I don't know nothin' that can help y'all."

He turned around and slowly lumbered into the garage.

As we drove off, I said, "What do you think?"

"I'll ask Morton if they verified whether he was in Seattle. If so, he's obviously not the Slut Man."

I let out a sigh. "I certainly don't get the vibe he's a killer. Though I guess the really good killers don't give off that vibe." I scratched my scalp with my fingernails. "So where are we?"

Hannah glanced over. "You want a straight answer?"

"Not necessarily . . ."

"The apartment manager recognized you. Her father recognized you, though that was probably from the photo. The father of Sherry's son, with his sleazy past and abusive temper, can maybe create reasonable doubt. Too soon to tell."

I felt a sharp pain in my stomach. I pressed on the spot with my index finger. "I didn't do anything. That's got to come through."

"As between you and God, you're golden." Hannah drove onto the 101 freeway. "I need to talk to your alibi David Hu. We have to prove you were at the Magic Castle that night. Anything to put doubt in the jurors' minds."

She swerved into a faster lane.

I rolled down the window a couple of inches, got a rush of air on my face, and said, "What else can I do?"

"Pray the DNA tests are faulty."

CHAPTER TWENTY-EIGHT

That night, as I walked down the hall toward my apartment, I saw something taped to my door. It was a white envelope with my name handwritten on the front. I peeled it off the door, ripped it open, and unfolded the paper inside.

3-DAY NOTICE TO PAY RENT OR QUIT.

It went on to say that my rent was overdue. *Like I didn't know that?*

If I don't pay up in three days, I'll be evicted.

I crumpled up the notice, went inside, and threw it on the floor. Lisa fluttered in her cage. I took her out and put her on my shoulder. She bit at my earlobe. I pushed her aside.

I sat on the couch and dialed Carly's cell. While it rang, I practiced what I was going to say.

"Hi, Carly."

I cleared my throat.

"Hello, Carly."

Pitched my voice lower. "Carly? It's Harvey."

She answered, saying, "Hi, Harvey."

Thank you, caller ID.

I said, "I . . . uh . . ."

"Me . . . um, too . . . I . . ."

"Well, I wondered . . ."

"Yes. I'd . . ."

Lisa backed a few steps down my shoulder.

I stood up. "I'm doing a magic show tomorrow night. Just a crappy little convention. You said you wanted to see some tricks, so I thought maybe you'd like to come along. I mean, I know it's short notice and all that, but—"

"I'd love to."

Carly and I arrived at the Culver City Convention Hall just before my show. We went into the auditorium, which was a small gym, and saw clusters of middle-aged men holding red plastic cups while yapping at each other. The air smelled like beer. Uneven rows of empty folding chairs were arranged in front of the closed stage curtains.

Hmm. Carly's the only woman here.

I said, "You want to watch from backstage?"

"No, I want the full effect of the show."

"The only ones out here are these conventioning Moose-Heads, or whatever they're called."

Carly chuckled. "I can handle myself." She gave my arm a little squeeze.

I said, "I may have to raunch up the show to get their attention."

"I'm a big girl."

"Well . . . okay." I glanced at the stage. "I've got to go back and get ready."

"Break a wand."

She turned and walked off. I watched her hips swing.

I went outside to the U-Haul trailer hitched to my car, unloaded the two rolling metal trunks, and used one to push the other as I wheeled them inside. I first took out my magic table, with its black velvet top and gold fringe, then unpacked the tricks and set them up.

When I finished, I walked to the front of the stage, leaned against a proscenium pillar, and pulled aside the thick velvet curtain to peek out.

None of the men were looking toward the stage. No doubt they'd rather tell fish-gutting stories than watch some doofus like me.

Where's Carly? Some guy already got her into his cab-over camper?

Where's my agent, Marty? And the Vegas promoter?

I studied the Moose-Heads. A bearded guy laughed so hard that he sloshed beer over the side of his cup. Most of these guys are shiny-eyed from the booze. Gotta do something to get their attention right away. Still no women besides Carly. Definitely raunch it up.

I let go of the curtain.

Someone behind me yelled, "Harvey!"

I turned around and saw my agent, Marty, walking my way, wearing his BriteSmile grin. He had gel-induced spiky hair and wore brown loafers without socks. In his right ear, a wireless cell phone earpiece blinked with a blue light. Beside Marty was a balding man with a ponytail who was working an Android phone with his thumbs.

Marty said, "This is Bernie Schulman."

Bernie gave the Android a few more thumb taps, then slid it into his pocket. He stuck out his hand. "Marty says you've got some talent."

I smiled at him. "I do."

Bernie chuckled. "I like guys with confidence. Show me what you got, kid." He clapped me on the arm and walked off.

Marty yelled after him. "Catch up with you, Bernie." He grabbed my arm and pulled me aside. Marty leaned in close and whispered, "Why are the cops asking about you?"

My breath caught. "What?"

"The cops. They called me right before I left tonight."

"Why would they do that?"

"You tell me."

I shifted my weight to the other foot. "Well, they've been talking to me about this misunderstanding. No big deal. What did they ask you?"

"They wanted to know where you were. Right that second."

"What did you say?"

"I said I didn't know."

"Good." I looked around. "Did you, um, tell them about my show tonight?"

"Well . . . yeah. They're the cops." Marty leveled his gaze at me. "That a problem?"

What the fuck do you think? "No . . ."

He straightened up, then held out his fist so I could give him a fist bump. "Knock 'em dead!"

Couldn't you pick another word, douche bag?

I fist bumped him, then straightened my posture, smoothed down my sequined jacket, and adjusted the knot of my shooting-star tie. I reached inside my coat and stroked Lisa, who was snug in her secret pocket. Finally I walked over to my magic table and checked the tricks one last time. Because I'd decided to raunch up the act, I'd substituted a couple of the props.

Are the cops out there waiting for me? How am I going to do a show with that on my head?

A squat hall manager came up to me and said, "You're on."

I threw my head toward the audience. "Nobody's sitting down."

"They'll sit when we open the curtains."

"Isn't somebody gonna say the show's starting?"

He stared at me. "Sure. 'The show's starting.' Now get going, Houdini." The man shuffled off to the side.

I stepped forward and cleared my throat. In my peripheral vision, I saw the hall manager grab a curtain rope and heave it hand over hand. The pulleys squeaked as the curtains slid open.

The gym lights were up at full blast. The folding chairs were empty. I saw Marty standing off to the side with Bernie, who'd gone back to Android Land. There's Carly, near the door. Don't see Sergeant Morton.

I walked to the front of the stage. A couple of men in the rear looked my way, then went back to their conversation.

I said, "Good evening."

Some guy in the back finished a joke. The group around him guffawed. One of them said, "Clarence, that's a real piss-cutter!"

I spoke louder. "I'm Harvey Kendall. When I was a young boy—"

An overweight man said to another hulking guy, "Billy? Is that Billy Swenson? I don't believe it!" The men grabbed each other in a bear hug.

I yelled, "When I was a young boy, I liked to play with fire." I grabbed the silver urn from my magic table and said, "Who's got a twenty-dollar bill?"

The few that heard me looked away, making sure they wouldn't catch my gaze. I asked again. After a moment, a skinny guy in a striped shirt came to the front of the stage and waved a bill at me.

"Thank you, sir," I said loudly. No one besides Skinny seemed to hear. I handed him a felt marker and asked him to write his name on the bill. A couple of men started to watch.

When he finished, I held up the bill and squinted at it. "Josh Stevens. Is that right?"

"Yup."

"Josh, did you know you can get three to five years for defacing federal property?"

A few men laughed. They came a little closer.

I tossed the twenty into the silver urn. It exploded in a blast of fire. That shut up the drunks. I said, "Ooops."

Laughter. Except for Josh, who was staring at the urn.

I put on this forced grin, dumped the ashes on the stage, squatted down, and rapidly pawed through the pieces. After a moment, I looked up. "Anyone else got a twenty?"

That got a laugh. More men moved toward the stage. A couple of them sat down in the folding chairs.

"Well," I said. "For my next trick . . ." I stood up. "I need someone up onstage. Any nude women here?" I shielded my eyes and scanned the hall. "How about a fatso who's showing a little butt crack?"

Some guys pushed a huge man forward. He had curly black hair, a high forehead, and biceps almost the size of my thigh. The big man shook his head, backed up, got pushed again, shook his head, then ambled forward with an "Oh, what the hell" expression. His buddies cheered.

When Sasquatch got on the stage, I saw he had a good six inches over me. Not to mention a hundred pounds.

I looked up at him. "What's your name, sir?"

"Dave."

I noticed he wasn't wearing a wedding ring. "Dave, you have a girlfriend?"

He nodded.

"Would you like to read her mind?"

He half-smiled.

I said, "Take a seat." I walked to the wings, grabbed a folding chair, opened it up, and put it at the front of the stage. When Dave sat down, I showed him a black velvet bag and turned it inside out to prove it was empty.

I said, "I'm getting vibrations about your girlfriend. Yes, definite vibrations. She's sending me her thoughts."

I stepped around behind Dave. "Signals getting stronger. She wants something you've never given her. It's materializing right here." I stayed behind Dave so he couldn't see me, and reached into the bag. "Vibrations getting stronger!" I came out with a twelve-inch rubber dildo, which I shook hard enough to flap around.

The audience howled, then cheered. As Dave spun in a circle, I changed the dildo into a bouquet of paper flowers. "Here you go, Dave. Take these home to her."

He squinted at me, then took the flowers in his oversize paw.

"Oh," I said. "It looks like there's something stuck in the bouquet."

Dave looked through the flowers and held up an egg. I produced a glass tumbler and told him to crack the egg into it. When he broke the shell, the insides slopped into the glass. Along with the yolk was a rolled-up twenty-dollar bill that had been inside the egg. I fished it out and told Dave to unroll it.

He read the name on the wet bill. "Josh Stevens."

Applause, whistles.

I saw Carly in the back, leaning against the wall, applauding.

Where's the Vegas guy?

Is that Sergeant Morton? No. Is it?

I went on to make Lisa appear in a flash of flames, then put her on her perch next to the magic table. I stuck a foot-long needle through my arm, which is a gross-looking trick that always goes over with a testosterone crowd. I did a giant cups-and-balls routine, an homage to the magician I'd seen at the Renaissance Fair when I was little. Except in this one, I kept making the balls larger, ending up with a bowling ball.

I raised my arms to quiet the audience.

"It is said that the magicians of ancient India were able to dematerialize and pass through solid objects. This was dismissed by historians as myth, but I've discovered it was true. After years of research, and more years of disciplined practice, I have mastered their art. Watch."

I wheeled out a six-foot-tall pane of glass, about the width of a door, and turned the thin edge toward the audience. Then I brought out two Chinese folding screens and stood them on the stage, one against each side of the glass.

The place went quiet. I walked behind one of the Chinese screens and waved a red handkerchief above the screen, so that the audience could see my hand.

I said, "One."

I lowered the handkerchief.

"Two."

"Three!" I raised the handkerchief on the other side of the glass. The audience gasped. *Yes!* I know I got it right when they gasp.

I kicked over the screen.

The men leapt to their feet, whistling, cheering. Off to the side, the squat hall manager gave me a thumbs-up. I went to Lisa's perch, set her on my shoulder, stepped forward, and took a few bows.

They kept clapping. Someone yelled, "More!" Then a bunch of them did.

Guys, it's not like being a rock star, who can just whip out his guitar and strum another tune. Magicians can't do encores unless the tricks are set up in advance.

Well . . . better to leave 'em wanting more.

The audience kept cheering. I backed up a few steps, bowed again. Wish I had another trick.

I said, "Thank you," not sure they could hear me over the noise.

I backed up farther and glanced to the side. The stage manager raised his eyebrows and threw his head toward the rope, asking if I wanted to end it. I nodded. He closed the curtain.

As soon as the curtains shut, I grabbed the dish towel that I keep under the magic table and mopped my face. I could still hear the muffled applause. Grinning, I pulled loose my shooting-star tie and walked offstage. The armpits of my shirt clung to my skin.

I grabbed the handle of my metal trunk, rolled it onstage next to the magic table, and unlatched the top. My pulse was still pumping hard in my neck. I fit my wooden duck Joanne into the cutout foam-rubber padding, then tossed in the deck of oversize playing cards from which Joanne picks the selected card.

Marty came rushing up with Bernie, the Vegas promoter. Marty pumped my hand, saying, "Harvey, that's the best I've ever seen you." As he spoke, he kept glancing at Bernie.

Bernie stuck out his hand. "Great job, kid. And I don't impress easily. You really got something."

I shook his hand. Couldn't help grinning.

Bernie said, "So you want to do Vegas, huh?"

"Yes, sir."

He screwed his mouth to the side. "You call me 'sir' one more time and you're back doing kiddies' birthday parties."

"Yes, si—Bernie."

He laughed, slapped my shoulder. "I like this kid. Look, I

can probably get you a small gig. Maybe a grand a week to start. Then work you up."

A grand a week? I almost laughed. Marty, standing behind Bernie, was vigorously shaking his head, mouthing *No.*

Bernie said, "Whaddaya say?"

"I'd love to do Vegas. You gotta talk to Marty about the deal."

Behind Bernie's back, Marty made an exaggerated sigh of relief and gave me the okay sign.

Carly came up and took hold of my arm. "That was awesome!"

"Thanks." I introduced her to the men.

Behind Carly, Marty gave me a raised-eyebrows-and-downturned-mouth-slow-head-bob that meant, This is a hot one; I didn't think you had it in you.

Off to the side, I heard a man clapping. All of us turned to see Sergeant Morton walking our way. His skinny partner trailed behind.

Shit.

My heart sped up again.

At least his badge isn't showing.

As he got closer, I took a step back.

Morton said, "Nice show, Mr. Kendall."

Marty looked at me, puzzled. He grabbed Bernie and pulled him away, glancing back over his shoulder. Carly held on to me.

Morton said, "Could we talk privately?"

I said, "Now?"

"It's important."

"I'm pretty busy."

He smiled. "I'm afraid I have to insist."

Carly said, "I'll wait over there." She walked to the side of the stage and stood by the curtain rope, watching us.

Morton rubbed his chin. "You've been a busy man, Mr. Kendall. Let's see. Breaking and entering the victim's apartment. By the way, thanks for letting us know the manager had seen you before."

I shook my head. "I'd never seen the manager before I went to Sherry's apartment and found the thumb drive."

"So why'd he think you looked familiar?"

"Same as Sherry's father. He probably recognized me from the pictures of suspects that you showed him."

"One little problem. We never showed him your picture. We talked to the manager before we got the DNA match from Virginia."

My voice rose. "He's lying. I've never seen him before."

In my peripheral vision, I saw Carly take a step toward us, looking worried.

Morton said, "I appreciate your finding the thumb drive. We'd have gotten to her boyfriend sooner or later, but your burglary skills moved that along nicely. Kevin was real helpful. We got a motive now. Someone walked in on them having sex. Jealousy's been one of the top three motives since biblical times."

I narrowed my eyes at Morton. "I never met Sherry Allen."

"This morning, you harassed her father. He also told us he'd seen you before." Morton shook his head. "You sure keep turning up like a bad penny."

I took a step toward him. "Her father said he recognized me from the photo you showed him. Look, I've been cooperating fully with you. Aren't you investigating the father of her child?"

"Abner moved to Florida and kept up his hobby of banging vulnerable young women. The last one was underage, so he's now cooling off in one of their state facilities. That's where he was when Sherry was strangled."

I felt my chest tighten.

My eyes stung. *Don't cry.*

I said, "I didn't do it. I never met this girl."

I looked over at Carly. She crossed her arms over her chest and fidgeted her fingers against her biceps. Her eyes were asking if I wanted her to come to me. I looked back at Morton.

Morton said, "Mr. Kendall, you're under arrest for the murder of Sherry Allen. You have the right to remain silent. Anything you say can and will be used—"

My hands began to shake. "You're arresting me? Now?"

"—against you in a court of law."

"My lawyer wrote a letter offering to surrender so this wouldn't happen."

"She did indeed. Then we found out you're being evicted. Today you left your apartment with several large trunks."

I forced a laugh. "Those were my stage props. They're right there." I pointed at the road cases.

Morton said, "You have the right to an attorney. If you can't afford one . . ." He finished reading my rights.

I said, "Fine. Let me finish packing up my tricks."

"You'll have to get someone else to do that."

"There is no one else."

"We'll give you a few minutes to find someone."

"These tricks are my profession. I can't earn a living without them. Besides, I have to get my bird home."

"Unless you find someone else to take care of the bird, we'll have to call animal control."

"Animal Control? No way. You'll really upset her. She's highly trained. She's part of my act. My livelihood."

"Then I suggest you make some calls."

I clenched my teeth, took out my cell phone, and keyed in Marty's number. Why is it so hard to hit the right numbers?

Carly looked at me, her expression hovering between worry and panic. I turned away from her.

When Marty answered, I said, "Where are you?"

"Negotiating your deal with Bernie."

"Where?"

"Outside the back door. Why?"

"Thank God." I let out a breath. "I need you to pack up my tricks and take my bird home."

"What?"

"Marty, please."

"Why?"

"I'll explain when you get here. Come back inside."

"Okay. I'm coming." I heard a metallic rattle. "Shit. The door's locked. Let me in."

"Stay there." I hung up and said to Morton, "I have to open the back door for him."

"You can do it on the way out." Morton took a pair of handcuffs from a leather pouch on his belt.

The sonofabitch is going to walk me out in handcuffs? Did Carly see that? I didn't want to look at her.

I said, "You don't need those."

"Then you need to walk out very nicely." Morton kept cuffs in his hand as he and his partner got on either side of me. They took hold of my arms.

I pulled free and said, "I'll walk out by myself."

Morton grabbed my elbow with a grip that shot an electric pain through my arm. I winced. *Don't yelp.*

Carly hurried over. "Harvey, what's going on?"

Morton forced me to start walking.

I said, "It's just a mistake."

She hurried alongside of us. "What kind of mistake?"

"I'm being . . . arrested."

She sucked in a mouthful of air.

I said to her, "Do me a favor? Call the attorney I work for? Tell her what's happened."

As we walked, I gave her all of Hannah's phone numbers. Carly punched them into her phone.

Morton said to Carly, "Tell the lawyer we're taking him to L.A. County jail, downtown."

We got to the back door. Morton pushed the bar and the door sprang open. Marty was standing on the concrete landing with Bernie, who was reading something on his Android.

As the cops walked me past them, Bernie looked up. He noticed Morton's grip on me, then looked at Marty with a "What the hell?" expression.

Marty hustled to catch up with us. He said, "What's going on?"

I whispered, "I'm being arrested."

"Arrested?!"

Bernie's head shot up from his Android.

I said, "Shhh. Take my keys." I looked at Morton. "Okay if I go into my pocket?"

Morton said, "Which pocket?"

"Front left."

He stuck his hand in my pocket, pulled out my key ring, and gave it to Marty. Marty took it, staring at me with his mouth slightly open.

I said, "Put Lisa in her cage. There's birdseed in the kitchen, and she needs water. The U-Haul goes back to a place on Sepulveda. The car—"

One of the conventioneers, a big man with a thick black beard, lumbered up. He said to me, "Great show, man."

"Um, thanks."

"You do birthday parties?"

Morton tightened his grip on my elbow, forcing me forward.

I motioned my head toward Marty and told Black Beard, "Talk to my agent here."

Morton said, "Let's go, Mr. Kendall." He forced me to walk faster.

I turned my head and called back, "Marty. Be careful with the bird."

Carly, falling behind, said, "What can I do?"

"Call Hannah. Right away."

CHAPTER TWENTY-NINE

At the downtown jail, Morton and Dupont walked me through a thick metal door, into a small area with a locked door in front of us. To the side, a uniformed woman stared at us through glass thick enough for a whale aquarium. She sat behind a console of TV monitors that showed different parts of the facility.

The door behind us clanked shut. The small space went dead quiet.

The door in front buzzed. Morton shoved it open and I heard a babbling crowd. He led me into a large, brightly lit room that was jammed with people. Off to the side, an officer wearing latex gloves was patting down a man in greasy clothes. Another cop steered a handcuffed kid with hollow red eyes. A smiling woman, missing patches of bleached hair, was chatting with a policeman like they were pals. No one even glanced at my sequined jacket.

Morton said, "Hands behind your neck. Feet apart."

I spread my legs and clasped my hands behind my neck. Dupont walked away while Morton squatted down and grabbled my ankle hard enough to make me take a step. He ran his hands up and down my legs.

Did Carly reach Hannah? Is Lisa okay? What's Hannah going to tell Carly about the murder charges?

While Morton groped my torso, Dupont came back, holding a clipboard. The printed form clamped to it read *Booking Sheet.*

Dupont clicked his ballpoint pen. "Full name."

"Harvey Allen Kendall." My voice cracked.

"Emergency contact?"

We went through my date of birth, citizenship, and similar crap. When we finished, he kept writing on his own. I looked at the sheet. Under the section titled "Charge Number 1," he'd written "Murder."

Holy shit.

Murder.

These guys really think I did it.

Well, obviously they think you did it, dumb-ass, or you wouldn't be down here at the jail. I bit my cuticle, drawing blood.

This will be on my record for the rest of my life? Anytime I try to get a job? Anytime someone Googles me?

My shirt was wet. It suddenly felt like there was no oxygen. The room was getting tighter and I had an almost overwhelming urge to run. Where the hell am I going to run in a locked room with fourteen thousand cops?

Holy fucking shit.

I felt something jab hard into my ribs. I yelped and grabbed Morton to keep from falling. He pushed me away. I turned and saw I'd been hit by a grizzled man who was weaving to keep his balance. The smell of alcohol seeped from his body. A cop pulled the drunk away from me. He stumbled a few steps, then collapsed.

I touched my ribs where he'd hit me. *Ow.* It felt bruised and was already throbbing.

Morton said, "This way."

I rubbed my ribs as I followed him to a wall phone. He gestured for me to make a call.

I dialed Hannah's cell.

C'mon.

Answer, damn it.

Shit. Voice mail.

I said, "I hope you got the message. I'm in L.A. County jail. Please. Get me out of here."

I tried her apartment. Left the same message.

Should I call my mother? No. She'll come down here and sit all night. Then I'll have that on my head in addition to the other heaps of shit.

Hannah, where the fuck are you?

Morton led me to another large room, where a cluster of people were pressing against a long counter with a black metal grate along the front edge. Behind the counter, two harried men were dealing with the masses.

Morton took me to the back of the crowd and said, "Wait your turn." He walked off to the side and took out his cell phone.

I looked at the swarm of people in front of me. My cuticle was still bleeding, so I stuck it in my mouth. It tasted like salty blood.

Why are the men behind the counter so slow? Is this line even moving? A mass of people pushed in behind me. It felt like I was getting digested inside the belly of some foul-smelling creature.

Someone shoved my back, throwing me into the man in front of me. The guy in front elbowed me. I started to shove him. Maybe not a good idea. I stuck my hands in my pockets. My breathing got so heavy that I was close to whooping.

It took almost an hour to get to the front. A man behind the counter, with a shaved head and thick black eyebrows, looked at me with tired eyes. "Where's your arresting officer?"

Morton elbowed his way in and handed the man my booking sheet. The bald guy started reading. Without looking up, he said, "Put everything but your clothes on the counter. Take out any body piercings."

Beside me, an African-American man started sobbing. I turned to see a cop twist the man's arm behind his back and lead him away.

The man behind the counter said, "You got hearing problems?"

"No."

"Dump your things on the counter."

I took off my watch, then emptied my pockets. Keys, cell phone, wallet, coins. I held on to the four Walking Liberty fifty-cent pieces I always carry. The guy behind the counter said, "Everything."

I looked at the coins in my palm. It had taken me almost a year to collect them. They were all dated 1945 and had the same patina. That way, the audience couldn't tell them apart.

He said, "C'mon, kid."

I slowly laid the coins on the counter.

The bald guy wrote an inventory, handed me the paper to sign, then shoveled all my stuff into a yellow vinyl pouch. I watched to make sure the vintage coins went in. He sealed the pouch with a numbered metal tab and wrote the numbers on my booking sheet.

The man said, "Let's have your shoes."

It was hard to bend down in the press of people. My knee hit some woman, who yelled, "Watch it, asshole." I lifted one foot, seesawed off a black leather shoe, then did the other. I handed them over the counter. Through my socks, I could feel the cold of the concrete floor. Are people going to step on my feet?

The bald man put my shoes in a brown paper bag, reached under the counter, and handed me a pair of red rubber sandals. I dropped them on the floor and stepped into them. Morton grabbed my arm and steered me back through the noisy crowd. My ribs throbbed. My elbow stung from his grip. My feet sloshed around in the oversize sandals. Where the hell is Hannah? She must have my message by now. I felt like I was going to start crying.

Morton took me down a long cinder-block hall, which had blue, red, and yellow stripes painted on the floor. The air smelled like antiseptic. It got quieter as we moved farther from the big room. Am I hearing echos of the yelling, or is that just in my ears?

Morton led me into a windowless room with floor-to-ceiling wooden shelves along two walls. Most of the shelves were stacked with folded orange jumpsuits. The rest had stacks of gray blankets. The only thing on the bare concrete floor was a locker-room bench.

A short man with the wiry build of a jockey looked me up and down with steel gray eyes. He pulled a jumpsuit from the pile marked "L" and said, "Strip down nekkid, then put this on." He held out the jumpsuit.

I looked around. The door was wide open. I'm supposed to strip right here? There're people walking by in the hall. The man circled his hand in the air, meaning, Hurry up.

I slowly took off my sequined jacket.

He handed me a large brown paper bag and said, "Put your clothes in this."

I took off my shirt, then my undershirt. My skin bristled with goose bumps. I undid my belt, unzipped my pants, and stepped out of them. I looked over at the door, shivering. I could hear Morton outside, talking on his cell phone. He said something I couldn't understand, then laughed.

I folded my clothes and put them in the paper bag. *Where the hell are you, Hannah?*

The man said, "Ain't got all night, kid."

I started to get into the jumpsuit. He said, "Drop your panties first."

"I don't keep my underwear on?"

"What was the first thing I said to you?"

Yeah, yeah. Strip nekkid.

I turned my back to the little man, slipped off my boxers, and quickly stepped into the jumpsuit. I missed a leg and had to jump a couple of steps to keep my balance. I banged my shin on the bench. Shit. Is the jockey laughing at me? I tried again. Finally got my legs in the damn thing. I pulled the top over my shoulders. The nylon was already chafing my bare crotch. I pulled the open sides of the zipper away from my body, then carefully zipped up.

The little man wrote my name and a number on the paper bag that held my clothes, folded the top over, then sealed it with plastic tape. He grabbed a gray blanket off one of the shelves and shoved it at me. I draped the scratchy fabric over my arm.

The jockey pointed at the open door. "On your way."

When I walked into the hall, Morton told his cell phone, "Gotta go." He stuck it in his pocket.

We followed a blue stripe on the floor to a small cinder-block room. Morton sat me in an old barber's chair whose red Naugahyde was patched with duct tape. A man whose face I couldn't see took mug shots of me, using a camera that was bolted inside a wire cage. Morton then led me to the next room, where he took my fingerprints with an electronic scanner.

We left the room and followed the blue floor stripe to a long hall with riveted metal walls that looked like the inside of a battleship. The blanket draped over my arm was starting to itch. I moved it to the other arm.

A guard in a short-sleeved uniform, sitting behind a small desk, stood up as we got there. He had wisps of a blond mustache and hairless arms.

Morton said, "Good night, Mr. Kendall. See you in court."

He pulled out his cell phone and walked away.

The guard opened a narrow metal door in the wall, reached inside, and pulled a lever that looked like a railroad switch. I heard a metallic clunk. A few feet down the hall, a barred door swung open.

He said, "This way." I followed the guard through the barred door into a wide hallway that was lined with rows of solid metal doors. Each one had a small square opening about five feet from the ground, with a black letter and a number stenciled above it. We stopped in front of the door marked C3.

The guard unclipped a large key ring from his belt. The keys were flat metal, about six inches long, cut with rectangular teeth. In all my years of locksmithing, I'd never seen keys like this. Must be custom-made for jails. How would the lock work?

The guard stuck a key in the cell's lock and turned it with a thunk. He grabbed the pull handle and leaned back as he jerked open the heavy door.

"Here you go." He gestured for me to go in.

I looked at him, then looked back up the hall. "Will my lawyer be able to see me as soon as she gets here?"

"We'll let you know."

"You'll let me know right away?"

He blew out a sarcastic breath. "Oh, sure. We got nothing to do besides get messages to the prisoners."

Prisoners?

Holy shit.

The guard said, "Inside."

I took a small step, just inside the door, then turned back to him so quickly that my foot came out of the sandal. I said, "How fast can I get bailed out?"

"There's no bail for murder."

I froze. "What?"

"You want that in sign language?"

I tried to get my foot back in the sandal. "No bail for murder? What's that mean?"

"It means you're gonna be here awhile."

He shoved the door shut.

CHAPTER THIRTY

I stood inside the cell, staring at the locked door, holding the scratchy blanket. The tiny room smelled like bleach, which didn't completely cover the smell of piss.

No bail for murder? How's that possible? I felt my chest tighten. Is he just razzing me?

I turned around, without going farther in. There were upper and lower metal bunks bolted to the gray concrete wall. On top of each bed was a thin blue vinyl mattress and a blue vinyl pillow. The only other thing in the cell was a stainless-steel pedestal sink, which had a seatless steel toilet jutting out from its base. The damn toilet was only about three feet from the bed. You're supposed to take a crap with some other guy watching you? You're supposed to sleep while some guy pisses right next to your head?

I realized I was gripping the blanket so hard that my fingers were shaking. I took a few steps, threw the blanket on the lower bunk, then sat down. I could feel the cold metal through the thin vinyl mattress. I looked up. The ceiling was a dusty metal grate with fluorescent lights buzzing above it.

Could I be in a place like this for the rest of my life? Or maybe get out when I'm an old man with an oversize asshole?

I looked at my wrist. Shit. They took my watch. Hannah, you goddam bitch, where are you? Get me the fuck outta here.

It's gotta be one in the morning by now. Why are the lights still on? Are they on all night? Whatever Hannah's doing, she must have gotten my message by now. Unless she's spending the night with Prince Mercedes. Wouldn't she check her cell phone?

No bail for murder? Does that mean I'll be in jail for months before I even go to trial? Years? That can't be right.

Can it?

My breathing was near a full-on whooping.

Can other people hear me? I felt my eyes flood. I started to cry with heaving sobs.

Stop it!

Get yourself together, for God's sake.

I laid down on the bunk and felt my chest heave. My feet stuck off the end. I unfolded the blanket and spread it around until it covered most of me. My chest was still heaving. How am I supposed to sleep with the lights on? I wiped at the corners of my eyes.

I sucked in a deep breath, held it, then blew it out. My breathing slowed a bit. The whoops wound down into whimpers.

I opened and closed my fists. My ribs still hurt from where that guy fell into me. Try to relax.

Yeah, right.

I let out a breath.

What kind of germs are on this mattress?

I closed my eyes. Could still see light through my lids.

How could my DNA match the DNA at the murder scene? It's impossible.

Well, obviously not impossible. How? Why?

I turned on my side, pulled the blanket around my shoulder.

Can you fake DNA? Am I being framed? Why me? I can't even grip a basketball, much less strangle someone. When I was a kid, while everyone was out playing football, I was inside doing magic tricks.

I rolled onto my back. The blanket came off my feet.

Hell, if I was looking at the evidence, even I'd think I was guilty. How can I defend myself? All I've got is David Hu's testimony that I was with him at the Magic Castle. Is that enough?

How am I going to pay for this? I can't work if I'm in jail. My rent is overdue. I've got no place to live.

Fuck. I have to sell my trick. No other choice.

I shook my head.

That trick is genius. Even Copperfield thought so. You only get a genius inspiration once in a lifetime. If I let it go, I'm back to working plumber conventions. . . .

I turned onto my side and curled up. There has to be an explanation for this fuckup. How did my DNA wind up in the dead girl? Think. How would I do it? How would I make everyone think it was real?

I heard the door lock turn. Hannah?

I sat up so fast that I banged my head on the lip of the upper bunk. *Ow.* Shit. I rubbed the Throb-spot.

The cell door swung open. A large Samoan man, bulging in his orange jumpsuit, walked in holding a blanket. I ran toward the door and called after the guard, saying, "Excuse me." Maybe he can find out something about Hannah.

The door closed. I called him through the small window. Yelled for him.

Asshole.

I turned around and saw the Samoan step on my bed, then climb to the upper bunk. When he laid down, the metal creaked. I got back in bed and stared at the bottom of the bunk over me.

How strong are those rivets? How strong is the concrete holding the bolts? I heard the Samoan breathing heavily.

I closed my eyes. Still saw the fucking light through my lids.

I laid there for a few hours, not sure if I was sleeping or not, until the door clunked open. A voice yelled, "Kendall."

Rubbing my dry eyes, I sat up on the metal bed, hunching to avoid hitting my head. "Yeah?"

"Your lawyer's here."

Yes! I sprang from the bed and hurried to the door.

The guard held up his hand. "Easy, tiger. Walk real slow."

He led me through a series of halls to a small room, where Hannah sat behind a gray metal table. The only other furnishing was a chair, which I noticed was bolted to the floor.

She half-smiled at me. Her eyes were red. She had no makeup on. Strands of loose hair dangled across her face. Never seen her look better.

The guard left and closed the door.

She said, "I can't believe those assholes arrested you after I wrote a letter offering to surrender. I am seriously pissed off."

"*You're* pissed off?"

Hannah tilted her head. "You okay?"

"Yeah, it's lovely here at Che Hoosegow. I got a mattress thinner than a Pop-Tart, and I'm three rivets away from being the meat in a Samoan sandwich."

"Huh?"

"Never mind. Just get me the hell out of here."

She stuck the tip of her tongue out the corner of her mouth. "Not so simple."

My breathing accelerated toward *whoop*. "What's that mean?"

"Well . . ."

I said, "The guard told me there's no bail for murder. Is that true?"

"Not exactly. The cops don't set bail for murder. It's up to a judge."

"Up to a judge? Does that mean the judge decides how much the bail is? Or that he decides whether there's any bail at all?"

"Both."

I swallowed. "You mean the judge doesn't have to set bail?"

"I'm pushing for an arraignment first thing in the morning. The only purpose of an arraignment is to enter a plea. You say 'Not Guilty'; then I ask the judge to set bail. I need to show you're a good person who—"

"Bring me some decent clothes. They took my—"

"No. I want you looking pathetic in your orange jumpsuit. It makes the judge more sympathetic to springing you loose."

I ran my fingers through my tangled hair. "Pathetic should be easy."

Hannah took a pack of gum from her purse, pulled out a stick, and folded it into her mouth. She held out the pack to me. I waved it off.

She said, "Don't get discouraged. I need some of your friends and family to sit there looking like sad puppies, showing their support. I may want some of them to tell the judge what a fine person you are." She chewed hard on the gum.

I shook my head. "Don't use my mother."

"Why not?"

"I don't want to upset her."

Hannah leaned back in her chair. "She'll be more upset when she notices you haven't shown up for six months."

Shit. I stood, paced. "Fine. Call her. Wait until morning. Otherwise, she'll come down here and sit all night."

"Who else you got?"

I gave her David Hu and my agent, Marty.

Probably not Carly.

I couldn't think of anyone else. Talk about pathetic . . .

Hannah stood. "I gotta get up early and push for the arraignment. Hang in there."

I nodded. "Thanks for coming down in the middle of the night."

She gave me one of those smiles that you give someone who's in the hospital when you say "I'll see you soon," but you really think they'll be dead in a week.

CHAPTER THIRTY-ONE

Next morning, they took me to court with my hands cuffed behind my back. A guard led me into a wood-paneled courtroom, where the elevated judge's podium was flanked by a U.S. flag on the left and a California flag with the silhouette of a bear on the right. Behind the podium was an empty high-backed black leather chair. In front were two wooden tables. Hannah sat behind one, wearing a crisp brown business dress. At the other was a thin man in a black suit and rep tie, studying an open file. He looked like he was in his forties, and he had a crescent scar at the corner of his eye that resembled a dried teardrop. With his tight mouth and scrunched eyes, it sure didn't look like he had a sense of humor. Gotta be the district attorney.

Behind the lawyer tables was a short wooden barrier, separating the court from several rows of wooden benches. My mother sat in the front row, biting her lip. Her eyes jittered. She saw me and forced a smile. Next to her, my agent, Marty, was yawning with a hand over his mouth. When he noticed me looking at him, his cheeks trembled as he stifled the yawn and gave me a wink. Guess David Hu couldn't make it.

The guard steered me to a chair next to Hannah. He told me to turn my back, then unfastened one handcuff and locked it to the chair arm. I sat down.

Hannah, wearing a forced smile, gave me a quick nod. I tried to smile back. It felt like there were a few thousand critters creeping over my scalp. Do I smell?

I looked at the handcuffs. I hadn't been able to see them behind my back. Good-quality cuffs: York 103's. With my picks, I could be out in thirty seconds.

Behind me, I heard the courtroom door open. I turned and saw David run in, clutching a briefcase. He slid onto a wooden bench in the back, breathing heavily, and gave me a thumbs-up.

I leaned over to Hannah and whispered, "What happens next?"

She whispered back. "We wait for the judge."

"What do I do?"

"Sit there and look like a waif."

A door behind the podium opened. Off to the side, a bailiff boomed, "All rise."

I heard the creak of butts leaving seats. As I stood, the handcuff cut into my wrist, jerking me to a halt before I could straighten. I leaned awkwardly to the side.

The bailiff said, "Los Angeles Superior Court is now in session, the honorable Benjamin Bowers presiding."

An African-American man with tightly coiled white hair came through the door behind the podium, moving fast enough to swirl his black robes. He nodded at the courtroom and sat.

The bailiff said, "Be seated."

I sat down and looked at the judge. This guy has the power to change the rest of my life. If he had a fight with his wife this morning, I could go down for twenty years. My locked hand shook hard enough to rattle the handcuff chain against the wooden chair. I grabbed the chair arm to steady myself.

The clerk said, "*People versus Kendall.*"

The judge put on half-glasses, sifted through some papers, then looked up over the glasses. "Are both sides ready?"

The black suit at the next table said, "Ken Warren for the people."

"Hannah Fisher for the defendant."

The judge looked at me. "Mr. Kendall?"

I whispered to Hannah, "Do I stand?"

She whispered, "No."

The judge said, "Mr. Kendall?"

I said, "Yes, sir." *Did my voice quaver?*

He stared into me and said, "The purpose of this proceeding is to advise you of your rights and the charges against you. It is also to consider bond and set conditions for such a bond, if one is appropriate in your case. This is not a trial. Do you understand?"

"Yes, sir."

"You have the right to remain silent. Anything you say will be used against you. You understand that?"

I nodded.

He said, "Answer audibly for the record, please."

"Yes, sir."

The judge wrote something, then looked at me. "Mr. Kendall, are you under the influence of drugs or alcohol?"

"No, sir."

"Have you had any drugs or alcohol in the last twenty-four hours?"

"No, sir."

Hannah stood. "Your Honor, the defendant waives formal reading of the charges."

"All right." The judge took off his reading glasses. "Mr. Kendall, you are accused of the murder of Sherry Allen. How do you plead?"

As I opened my mouth, Hannah said, "Not guilty."

I closed my mouth.

The DA stood, placed his hands on the table, and leaned forward, dangling his tie. "Your Honor, the people do not believe bail is appropriate in this case."

The judge looked at him. "Why is that, Mr. Warren?"

Is it a good sign that he's asking why? I looked at Hannah. She was studying the prosecutor.

Warren said, "This is a single man with no children and no appreciable assets. He lives in an apartment. His rent is overdue and his landlord has started eviction proceedings. Mr. Kendall is facing life in prison. There's a high risk that he will run."

Hannah stood. "Your Honor, Mr. Kendall has no criminal history. He's a well-respected member of the community. He's a substitute teacher with an exemplary record and an integral part of the professional magicians' community in Los Angeles. His mother is a forty-year resident of Los Angeles and she is here to vouch for him. So are two of his professional colleagues. Would the people supporting Mr. Kendall please stand?"

I twisted around to look. Mom, Marty, and David stood up.

The judge said, "You may be seated."

Hannah took three pieces of paper from her briefcase and held them out. "These are letters attesting to Mr. Kendall's character. I sent them to Sergeant Morton several weeks ago, along with a letter that offered to surrender Mr. Kendall. He is a responsible citizen, Your Honor. He is not a flight risk."

A court clerk came over to Hannah, took the papers, and delivered them to the judge. He studied the top page, pulled it off, then read the next. After reading the last page, he set it down and looked up.

Warren said, "The surrender letter was written before Mr. Kendall was facing eviction. He moved two trunks out of his apartment last night."

Hannah said, "Those trunks contained his magic tricks, which he used in a performance last night. Your Honor, may I approach the bench?"

The judge nodded. As she walked to the podium, Warren scrambled to get there at the same time. They spoke quietly.

I leaned forward, craning my ear, but couldn't hear anything.

Hannah gestured back toward the courtroom. Warren shook his head and pointed at the ground, as if he were saying, Right here. I heard Warren say "flight risk." I heard Hannah say "responsible."

After a few minutes of mumbling, they walked away. Warren looked like he had something sour in his mouth. Hannah was smiling.

The judge said, "Bail is set for one million dollars."

I jolted so hard that it rattled my handcuff chain. *One million dollars?* Why the hell is Hannah smiling?

One . . . *million* . . . dollars? Why not a billion, you asshole?

Hannah started gathering up her papers, grinning. I spoke louder than I intended. "Did he say one *million*?"

"A million is very good for a murder case. You only have to pay ten percent of that for a bond."

I feigned relief. "That's fabulous news. I'll just write a hundred-thousand-dollar check out of petty cash."

She tapped her papers against the table to square them. "It's already worked out."

"What do you mean?"

Hannah stuffed the papers in her briefcase. "They're calling the next case. I'll explain later."

"Later? When later?" The bailiff came over and unlocked the handcuff on the chair arm.

She picked up her briefcase. "As soon as they get us an attorney room."

The bailiff said, "Stand up."

When I stood, he positioned my hands behind my back. The bailiff racheted the loose cuff onto my free wrist. I looked back at Mom. Her eyes were red. She forced a smile.

Mom said, "It's going to be all right. I love you."

CHAPTER THIRTY-TWO

The guard put me in a tiny room down the hall from the courtroom. The only furnishings were two chairs and a small table. Since my hands were still cuffed behind my back, I figured it'd be awkward to maneuver into a seat, so I stood.

The guard said, "Your lawyer will be here in a few minutes. I'll wait outside." He closed the door behind him.

Will he be able to hear us?

A few minutes later, Hannah came in, holding her briefcase. She closed the door, sat down, realized I wasn't going to sit, then stood. She said, "I'm not supposed to tell you this."

"Tell me what?"

She blinked rapidly. "What I'm about to tell you. But you're the client, so you're entitled to know." She fidgeted with the handle of her briefcase.

"Okay. Tell me."

She tightened her lips. "The only way we got bail was because your mother put up her house as collateral."

I jolted back like I'd been hit with a blast of wind. "She . . . what?"

"The judge was going to deny bail. He thought you were a flight risk."

My scalp suddenly itched. I went to scratch it. The cuffs stopped me. I said, "So that's what happened when you walked up to the judge?"

"I said your mother was putting up her house as collateral for the bond. I said you'd never leave her homeless. That's why he agreed to bail. Barely."

I lowered myself awkwardly into one of the chairs. It pinned my arms against my back.

Hannah said, "Your mother insisted I not tell you. I don't feel right hiding it from you. You need to know before she actually pays the bail bond."

"She's paying the hundred thousand?"

"Yes. And giving the bondsman her house as collateral."

"Does she get her money back when I show up for trial?"

"She gets her house back. The bondsman keeps the hundred grand as the cost of the bond. Of course, if you don't show up for trial, she's on the hook for the full million. Which means she loses her house."

I wrenched myself into a standing position. The cuffs cut my wrists. I spoke sternly. "Why did you let her do that?"

She narrowed her gaze at me. "Don't use that tone with me. She told me to get you out and not tell you about the house. I'm the one who's letting you know before she actually does it."

I closed my eyes, let out a breath.

Can I let Mom do something like that? Part of me wishes I'd found this out after I was free, so I wouldn't have the dilemma. Can't say I love that part of myself.

I opened my eyes. "How long would I be in jail if we don't put up bail?"

"Hard to say. You're entitled to a speedy trial, but we have to prepare your case properly. Figure four to six months."

Six months?!

I bit my lower lip. "When do I have to decide?"

"In the next few hours. I have to stop her if you don't want this. She'll be pissed at me, but that has to be settled between the two of you."

When I got back to my cell, the Samoan was gone.

I sat on the bunk, let out a breath, and rubbed my wrists where the cuffs had been.

I swiveled my butt around, threw my legs on the bed, and lay back.

With the heel of my fist, I thumped the gray concrete wall. Hit it again. And again.

Can I spend months here? *Months?* I'm this freaked out after just one night. . . .

I pictured Mom scraping the last bits of tuna out of a can. I saw her standing in an art-supply store, digging through her purse, then looking sheepishly at the clerk. "Could you hold these brushes for a few days?"

What happens if I stay in jail? It'll kill my career. I finally got some momentum with that Vegas promoter. He offered me a thousand a week. Marty probably got him higher. With that kind of dough, I could start paying Mom back.

Assuming the Vegas gig wasn't derailed because I got arrested in front of the promoter.

I rolled off the bed and paced the cell. The length was exactly four paces. What's that, maybe twelve feet? I turned around and paced back.

I peed in the steel toilet. The stream hitting the stainless steel rang loudly. How're you supposed to sleep through that?

Can I let Mom risk her house?

On the other hand, she wanted to pay Nadler that kind of money. If I'd gone with Nadler, she'd have paid his fees *and* paid the bond on top. Look how much I saved her by using Hannah.

Would Nadler have gotten me off without bail? He's certainly a better-connected lawyer. Way more experienced.

Nah. Even Clarence Darrow couldn't have gotten it cheaper. Not with the DNA evidence.

A couple of hours later, lunch came in a brown paper bag. I sat on the bunk and crinkled it open. Bologna sandwich on white bread. Bag of corn chips.

I peeled up the top slice of bread to look inside. The mayonnaise puckered against the meat. I leaned down and smelled the bologna.

Without eating, I put the food aside and started pacing. I looked at the door. Through the open-grate ceiling, I heard two men yelling at each other in Spanish.

How'd I get into this? How did someone get my DNA to the crime scene? How would I do it as a magician?

I paced faster. I have a trick where someone signs a card with a felt marker; then I make it vanish and reappear, taped to the outside of a window. Since it's signed, I obviously have to use the same card. Did someone plant my DNA at the scene? How could anyone have gotten it? Maybe I left some saliva somewhere. Even blood. But semen?

Can you duplicate someone's DNA? That sounds impossible. Even if you could, why me? Why not go for some obvious criminal type?

I kept pacing. How would the great magicians of the past have done it? The ones who did the big tricks? Houdini's were mostly escapes. What about the illusionists?

Harry Blackstone. The wiry man with flailing hair. One of the greatest in the vaudeville era. He has a room dedicated to him at the Magic Castle. Blackstone once told an audience he was going to perform a trick so enormous that they had to go outdoors to see it. He guided them out, row by row. When they got to the street, they saw that the theater was on fire. His spiel—something we magicians call "patter"—had gotten them out safely.

Blackstone did spectacular stage tricks. The Dancing Handkerchief that darted through the air, and still danced after being plugged inside a glass bottle. The Electric Cabinet, where he locked his assistant inside and speared her with lighted fluorescent bulbs. His signature trick: pretending to hypnotize a woman in a flowing gown, placing her on a table, without hiding her inside a box, and running a huge buzz saw through her midsection.

Blackstone also did a trick where he made a woman disappear onstage, then had her instantly run down the aisle from the back of the theater. It stunned the audiences of the day. That trick's still good for a few gasps. Yet it was one of his simplest. Because . . .

I stopped pacing.

Hang on. . . .

Could that be it?

Blackstone used twins. He made one twin vanish onstage, then had the other run down the aisle.

Twins have identical DNA.

In our first meeting, Hannah asked if I had a twin. I said no, but could I? Could I have been adopted? Separated from a twin brother?

Mom's always taking in foster kids. . . .

Impossible. She wouldn't lie to me all these years. No way.

Would she?

There's no way she'd let me get arrested without telling me about a twin.

Maybe she doesn't know. Maybe I was adopted and separated from my brother at birth.

A twin would explain everything. How my DNA got there. Why I looked familiar to the apartment manager.

I walked over to the cell door and put my palms against the cold metal.

I can't stay in here. I gotta work on my defense.

I'll pay every penny back to Mom. I swear.

Even if I have to sell my trick to Copperfield.

CHAPTER THIRTY-THREE

They sprang me in the afternoon. When I walked out the door of the granite building, I stopped at the top of the concrete steps and squinted in the bright sun. Shielding my eyes with my hand, I watched people hurrying along the sidewalk. Do you people have any idea how incredible it is to just go wherever you want? I took a deep breath of the fresh air, let it out slowly.

I felt someone touch my arm and jumped.

Hannah said, "Sorry. I didn't mean to scare you."

I took her hand and shook it. "Thank you."

She held on to my hand for a moment. "C'mon. I'll give you a ride home."

We walked a few blocks to an open parking lot, then drove off in her blue hybrid.

I said, "Would you take me to my mother's house?"

She nodded.

After a few blocks, Hannah cleared her throat. She spoke with her eyes fixed on the road. "So. The woman who called me after you were arrested. Is that your girlfriend?"

"How's your boyfriend with the Mercedes?"

She tightened her grip on the wheel. "He's just a friend."

Hannah pressed the button to lower her window. A chilly wind rushed through the car.

I said, "I think I figured out how my DNA might have gotten in . . . um, ended up at the crime scene."

Hannah looked over at me. "Oh?"

"Maybe I have a twin."

"You told me you don't."

"I know. I thought about it more in jail. Mom's always taking in foster kids. Maybe I'm adopted."

Hannah screwed her mouth to the side. "You think she'd keep something like that from you?"

"She didn't tell me that she put up her house for bond money."

We pulled up to the curb in front of Mom's house. I opened the car door. Hannah kept the motor running.

I got out of the car and said, "You want to come in?"

"I have to get to the office. Obviously, you should take the day off."

She reached over, pulled the car door shut, and drove off.

As I walked up the sidewalk, the family of plaster baby ducks stared at me. At least those babies know who their mother is.

I felt my heart in my neck as I rang Mom's bell. Ed, the seven-year-old foster kid, opened the front door. "Hi, Uncle Harvey."

I said, "Where's Mom?"

"In the backyard. Show me a trick."

"Later, okay?"

"C'mon."

"Sorry. I really gotta talk to Mom."

I hurried through the house, then out the back door. Mom was on her knees in the garden. She was daubing black paste on a twig that was tied to the gnarled branch of a bare-limbed shrub.

I said, "Mom?"

She looked up, sprang to her feet, ran to me, and grabbed me under my arms in a bear hug. Mom squeezed my ribs so hard that my hands involuntarily went out to the sides.

I closed my arms around her and hugged.

Has she always been this short?

I said, "You shouldn't have put up your house."

She looked up with shiny eyes. "That woman told you?"

Yikes! "No, no." *Think, think. . . .* "The, uh, bail bondsman told me."

Mom went back to squeezing my chest. "You weren't supposed to know."

"And you weren't supposed to do that. But thank you. I'll pay back every penny."

"Shut up." Mom's chest heaved against mine. I could feel my shirt getting wet against her face.

I looked over my shoulder. The three foster kids were in the back doorway, spying on us. When they saw me looking, they giggled and disappeared.

I said, "Mom . . ."

She let go and stepped back, wiping her eyes. "Yes?"

"I want to . . . I mean . . ." Maybe I'd better ease into this twin thing.

I gestured toward the twig she'd been daubing. "What were you doing down there?"

She looked at the shrub, then back at me. "Grafting a plum tree. You cut a notch in the bark of a root stock, then slant-cut the branch from a young tree, tie them together, and paint the joint with a grafting sealant. They'll grow together and I'll get a strong plant. You hungry?"

"No."

She bent down to pick up her knife and the bottle of dark paste she'd been daubing. When she straightened up, she said, "What's eating you? I mean, besides the arrest."

"Isn't that enough?"

She tightened the cap on the paste bottle. "Yes. But it's not all that's on your mind."

"Why do you say that?"

"Because I'm your mother, and mothers know these things. Spit it out."

I shifted my weight. I glanced at the back door. The kids' heads disappeared.

I stared at the branch she'd been grafting and said, "I got to thinking about my DNA at the crime scene. I mean, how it could have gotten there."

She put the knife in the pocket of her jeans. "And . . ."

"See, magicians sometimes use twins in their act. So I thought, well, maybe I might have a twin. That would explain the DNA."

She screwed her mouth to the side, like she wasn't sure if I was joking. "A twin?"

"Yeah."

"Let's see. . . ." She squinted her eyes and put the tip of her index finger against her lips, in a mock thinking gesture. "I'm sure I would've remembered a second kid coming out."

"Mom, I'm serious."

She furrowed her forehead. "No, Harvey. You don't have a twin."

I cleared my throat. "Am I adopted?"

Her head jerked back. "What did you say?"

"Am I—"

"You think I wouldn't have told you something like that?"

"Well, I . . . I dunno. I mean, yes, of course I'm sure you'd have told me, but maybe you were worried about my feelings or something?"

Mom shook her head.

I said, "It doesn't matter if I am. I love you. But if I was separated from a twin—"

"It's been two generations since they separated twins for adoption." Her eyes teared. "You think I lied to you all these years?" The bottle of paste fell out of her hand.

"No, no, of course not." I retrieved the paste bottle and handed it to her. "It's just . . . just that I'm getting desperate."

Mom snatched the bottle from me. Still frowning, she said, "It took me two years to get pregnant with you. Two years."

"Mom, I'm—"

"Come with me."

She stomped into the house, scattering the foster kids like frightened geese. I followed behind. When we got to the kitchen, Mom motioned her head toward the table. "Sit."

She left the kitchen.

I sat down slowly.

From her bedroom, I heard some clanking. A few moments later, Mom came back with a gray metal lockbox and clunked it hard on the table. She stuck a key in the lock and turned.

Mom opened the lid with a squeal. The insides smelled like old paper. She pawed through, took out a few photos, and shoved them at me.

I looked at the top picture. Mom, with her legs in hospital stirrups, her face beaded with sweat. A doctor was pulling a mucus-covered baby's head out of her. She said, "Harvey Allen Kendall, age ten seconds."

I dropped the picture. "Eeeew. Yuck. Mom, that's gross."

"You believe me now?"

I pushed the photo away. "I believed you before."

Mom threw the pictures into the box and slammed the lid.

CHAPTER THIRTY-FOUR

After Mom dropped me off at my apartment house, I trudged up the stairs. Were the steps always this hard to climb?

In my mind, I still had a vivid image of my gross birth photo.

Do those things fade with time?

Who shows something like that to their kid?

As I walked down the hall to my apartment, I wondered if I'd find a sheriff's lock on the door. Don't they, like, have to take you to court before they can evict you? Is there an excuse for being in jail?

I unlocked the door, shoved it open, and started to walk in.

I stopped in the doorway.

The living room floor was covered with open books, CDs, clothes, and couch pillows. Looking through the bedroom door, I saw that my bed had been stripped and the linens were in a messy pile on the floor. My dresser drawers were pulled out.

Guess the cops finally got around to searching my apartment.

Shit.

I let out a sigh and took a step inside. My magic trunks were open. The tricks were strewn on the carpet. Did you figure out the secrets, you assholes? If you damaged one single trick, I'll sue the shit out of you. I took a few steps toward the kitchen. The cabinet doors were ajar. The shelves were empty. Dishes, silverware, and cereal boxes were scattered on the counter.

I turned and walked slowly through the living room. Is this what a battlefield feels like after a war?

I went into my bedroom and saw Lisa standing on the dresser. When she saw me, her eyes went red. She screeched and tried to fly to me, flapping off feathers as she fluttered to the carpet. I picked her up and stroked her chest. Her expression was a mixture of *Thank God you're back* and *Where the hell have you been, you sonofabitch?*

I put Lisa on my shoulder. She sidestepped close to my neck. I sat on the bare mattress and looked around. The open dresser drawers were empty. Everything had been dumped on the floor.

They poked through my most private things? Even the ancient condoms? Did you get a good laugh when you saw they hadn't been used for years? My head throbbed.

I really ought to clean this up.

I put Lisa on my finger, laid back on the bed, and closed my eyes. I'll just rest for a few minutes. . . .

I dreamed I was swimming in dark water. In the distance, something was chirping. It grew louder. I tried to swim toward it. Can't see. Am I moving? Am I going backward?

I opened my eyes. The chirping was my phone's electronic ring. Lisa was standing on the mattress near my head, pecking at the ticking. I picked up the bird, groaned off the bed, and answered the phone.

Hannah said, "How are you doing?"

"Fabulous. Best day of my life."

Silence.

I said, "When I got home, I found my apartment had been redecorated by the Los Angeles Society of Interior Cops."

She blew out a breath. "I've seen their work." I heard Hannah shuffling papers. "I'm meeting your friend David Hu as soon as he gets back in town. We need his alibi to have any shot at reasonable doubt. I want to make sure he's solid."

"He will be." *I sincerely hope.*

Hannah said, "I hate to bring this up now, but I got a call from the DNA lab. They said your bill hasn't been paid."

I grimaced. "I know. I'm a little short." I started pacing.

Hannah let out a breath. "I'm willing to ride with you on my fees, but we can't put on much of a defense if we can't pay the lab. They may not tell me the results if there's an outstanding bill. And if they find a glitch in the DNA, we'll need someone from the lab to testify, which won't be a small number."

"I'll take care of it."

"How?"

I raised my voice. "I'll take care of it."

She hung up.

I looked at the dead phone.

Called Hannah back.

Got her voice mail.

After slamming down the phone, I checked my answering machine.

No messages.

Over two days?

My agent, Marty, knew where I was, so I guess he wouldn't have called. Wouldn't Carly call to see how I'm doing? She probably doesn't know I'm out of jail. Why didn't she leave a message, you know, for when I was back?

I checked my cell phone. No voice mails. No missed calls.

I dialed Carly's number. When the voice mail answered, I said, "I just wanted to say thanks for calling my lawyer. I'm so sorry you had to see that. It was all a mistake and I'm at home now. Please call me."

I called Marty's cell. He answered right away.

I said, "What's up with the Vegas gig?"

I heard the sound of traffic in the background.

I said, "Marty?"

He spoke evenly. "Do you, by any slight chance, remember that you got arrested while Bernie was watching?"

"Hang on. Lemme see. . . . Oh yeah. I *did* get arrested, you flaming asshole."

"Getting hauled off by the cops didn't exactly inspire his confidence."

I shook my head. "It was just a misunderstanding. Besides, what's that got to do with the Vegas gig? Bernie said he loved me."

"He did. He's just a teensy bit concerned that if he books you into one of his rooms, you could become, shall we say, 'indisposed'?"

"That's ridiculous."

"No, it's not. How'd you like to run a theater and wonder if your headliner is going to the slammer?"

I shifted the phone to my other ear. "It's not like I'd just disappear overnight. Even if I got jail time, which is highly unlikely, he'd have plenty of notice." *I think.*

"Yeah, well, that's nice. Unfortunately, there's a shitload of magicians who aren't involved with the criminal justice system. Harvey, the Vegas gig is dead until this thing is settled."

I sat down so fast that Lisa dug her claws into my shoulder. "Marty, I need the money."

"And I could use the ten percent. Sorry. I tried. I really did."

I slammed down the phone.

I felt my heartbeat in my ears.

All right. Think.

I rubbed my eyes.

How do I beat this thing?

Shit.

Even I'm starting to wonder if maybe I sleepwalked and killed her. . . .

I stopped rubbing my eyes and saw flashing pinpoints. I blinked them away and looked around my messy apartment. Man. They even dumped out my overdue bills. Next to that pile was the crumpled eviction notice.

The Vegas gig is on hold. The school system obviously has me on their *Ten Most Un-Wanted* list. I can't take any more money from Mom. It'll take me years to pay back the hundred grand.

I blew out a ruffled breath through my lips. Only one way to raise the money.

I stepped carefully through the crap on my living room floor, got down on my knees, and dug out my address book. I stood up and opened it to the *G*'s. Stared at the page. Can I do this?

I punched in the first six digits of the phone number.

Put my finger on the last one.

Started to push it.

Hung up.

I looked at Lisa and said, "You got any ideas?" She cocked her head.

I dialed the number.

One ring.

Should I hang up?

Second ring.

Maybe he won't answer.

Herb Gold picked up. "Yeah?"

"Herb, it's Harvey. Tell Copperfield I'll sell my crystal trunk."

I heard a band saw in the background. "Sorry, kid. I know that's tough."

"Tell him I want a hundred grand for it."

Herb laughed. "Just a hundred? Why don't you go for half a mil?"

I sat on the arm of my couch. "I'm serious."

"Sorry, this is Herb Gold. Did you mean to call the nut ward at L.A. County Hospital?"

I stood up. "I need a hundred grand."

"And I could use a nine-inch dick."

I scrunched the phone between my shoulder and my ear. "Herb, I'm not just selling the trick. I'm selling my shot at the big leagues."

"Kid, he offered twenty-five. That was a stretch."

"You said thirty."

"I said I'd *try* for thirty. He offered twenty-five."

"Well, the price is a hundred."

"So in other words, you don't really want to sell."

"Tell him that's the offer."

I hung up.

CHAPTER THIRTY-FIVE

Throughout the evening, I tried Carly every couple of hours.

Next morning, I called her as soon as I woke up. No answer.

Maybe she's out of town. I'm sure she'll call as soon as she gets the messages.

Wouldn't she have her cell with her?

Maybe she left her cell at home. Maybe it's got a dead battery.

When I got to Hannah's office the next morning, she was typing on her computer. I started filing.

We didn't talk during the day.

Late in the afternoon, she left the office for a meeting with a potential client. I took the liberty of leaving a little early and drove toward Carly's apartment. *She's obviously avoiding me, so I'll just show up and have a little discussion.* Since we met for coffee at five thirty, and that was pretty close to her apartment, she should be home around that time.

I got to her building just before six and buzzed the intercom. She answered right away. "Yes?"

I said, "Carly, it's Harvey. I need to talk to you."

I listened to the static of the intercom.

She said, "This is really awkward."

"Give me five minutes. Then I'll never bother you again."

More static.

She said, "I don't . . ."

"Four minutes."

"Harvey . . ."

"Three minutes. Final offer."

The static went silent.

The door buzzed.

I pulled it open and ran quickly to her unit. Before I could knock, she opened her door about twelve inches. Her hand gripped the door edge so tightly that her fingers blanched.

I said, "Can I come in?"

"I think it's better if we talk here."

"Okay. Start the stopwatch. So, I'm guessing you didn't return my calls because most of your dates don't end with the man getting arrested. Am I warm?"

Her face stayed somber.

I said, "Well, we have something in common. It's never happened to me before, either."

Carly closed the door slightly. "I don't think there's anything funny about this."

I lowered my head. "Sorry. Look, I understand you barely know me. I can't blame you for being cautious."

"*Cautious?*" Her voice rose. "Harvey, you know I have a deep moral conviction about the sanctity of life. Your lawyer told me you were arrested for murder."

Thanks, Hannah.

I leaned my hand against the doorjamb. Carly backed up half a step.

She said, "On top of that, I got blindsided by this whole thing. You might have at least had the decency to tell me yourself."

"Well, it's not exactly the kind of thing you rush to tell someone you've just met. Besides, it's all a mistake. I thought it would go away."

"When we first met, you lied about why you were at the lab."

"I told you the truth. I said I was dropping off evidence for a criminal lawyer. I just didn't mention—"

"It's not like you got a speeding ticket. Even if you put aside my views on human life, how would you feel if someone you dated was accused of murder?"

Whoa. How would I feel?

What if I'd just met her, and the cops thought she'd murdered her last boyfriend?

I said, "Carly, I really like you. It would have been nice to have your support right now, but I can't blame you. We hardly know each other."

She blinked a few times.

I stepped back from her door and said, "I guess we'll both have to see how we feel when this is over."

I turned and walked slowly down the hall.

I didn't hear the door closing behind me.

I didn't look back.

CHAPTER THIRTY-SIX

Next morning, when I got to Hannah's office, I saw her father sitting at her desk. Hannah was standing beside him.

Her father looked at me with that intense stare. "Morning, Harvey."

"Mr. Fisher."

"Please. Call me Bruce."

Well, aren't we all touchy-feely. "Morning, Bruce. You look like you're feeling a lot better."

"Yes." He turned back to Hannah, as if I had just ceased to exist. Bruce said, "I think you're going to lose the motion to suppress evidence in the Desmond case."

Hannah shifted her weight. "I'm not so sure."

"You already got the bounce from the publicity. Sure, you'll get some more if you win, but that'll be down the road. And most likely you'll lose. The jury will hate your client and love the celebrity father of the victim. Take the plea bargain and move on."

She put her hands on her hips. "If I take a long shot and bring it home, then I'll have really done something."

Bruce slowly shook his head. He tightened his lip on one side, as if to say, How can I possibly explain this to someone so naïve? "Well, if you're not going to take my advice, that's your prerogative."

Hannah spoke louder. "Something about this case stinks. I'm going to find it."

Bruce turned up his palms. "Then go right ahead. Experience holds a dear school."

"The rest of that expression is, 'And fools can learn no other way.'" Hannah reddened. "Are you calling me a fool?"

He smiled, as if to say, If the shoe fits . . .

Hannah sputtered, "You don't respect my judgment, do you?"

"You're a very bright young woman. On the other hand, I've got thirty-plus years of experience, which gives me an excellent gut instinct."

"Well, I have a gut instinct that I can win this case, so I'm going to follow it."

Bruce held up his hands, still grinning. "I'm just trying to be helpful."

She jerked her thumb toward the door. "Well, be helpful by letting me have my desk."

He looked startled. Bruce quickly recovered, then stared at her. He didn't get out of the chair.

She crossed her arms over her chest. "Dad?"

He put his hands on the desk and used it to hoist himself out of the chair. Bruce grimaced as he straightened up. Is he really in pain?

Her father cleared his throat, then strode out of her office, leaving the door open.

Hannah started to run after him, then stopped short. She slammed the door.

When she turned around toward me, I said, "Bravo. You stood up to the old man."

Hannah's stoic expression dissolved into pain. Her eyes got wet. "He was only trying to help me."

Actually, he was trying to control you, but I see absolutely no upside in getting between you and your father.

She turned toward the closed door, her back to me. Her head stooped forward. A quick shiver went through her body.

I took a step toward Hannah.

Should I touch her? I reached out, then stopped my hand in midair, a couple of inches above her shoulder.

I said, "Hannah?"

Keeping her back to me, she shook her head. Hannah took a few steps forward, grabbed the door, flung it open, and ran out of the office.

She got back about a half hour later. Her posture was ramrod-straight, her face serious. In other words, full-blast attorney mode.

Hannah walked past me to her desk, with an expression that said, You are not to mention my father. As she dove into her computer, I could feel the force field walling her off.

Hannah left the office for her mysterious meeting a little before one. While she was out, and mostly because I thought her father was an arrogant asshole, I pulled out the Desmond file and started looking through it. Maybe I can find something she missed and she'll give me a gold sticky star. Right after she gives me a lecture about slacking off my filing.

Desmond's police report said that LAPD officer Beeks saw Desmond driving a late-model red Mercedes sports coupe on

Wilshire Boulevard near Bundy, at one A.M. on March 18. Two hours after Jason Hedges was shot in the parking lot of Silver Shadows, a nightclub in Echo Park. Because Desmond's vehicle headlights weren't turned on, the officer made a routine stop and noticed blood on Desmond's clothes. He then searched the car and found a handgun in the glove compartment.

I flipped the page and read that a ballistic test confirmed the gun was used to shoot Hedges.

Holy Shit.

How the hell is Hannah going to get around this one?

Why would she put a nasty punk like this back on the streets?

As I turned to the next page, I heard the office door start to open. I quickly dropped the file, grabbed some papers, and acted like I was sorting them. Hannah walked in, looking at me suspiciously.

Late in the afternoon, Hannah's fax machine screeched to life, then spit out a piece of paper. She picked it up, read it, then looked at me, narrowing her eyes.

Why do I suddenly feel like a kid whose mother just got his report card?

Still holding the fax, Hannah sat down in her desk chair.

She said, "Harvey?"

"Yeah . . ."

"Pull up a chair."

I cleared my throat. "What's up?"

"Have a seat." She gestured at the chair.

I picked up the guest chair, carried it over to her desk, spun it around backward, and sat with my legs astride the seat. I crossed my forearms over the back. "What?"

Hannah held the fax out for me. I took it and read the blurry print.

My arrest report from Virginia, back when I was in college.

I said, "This is the DUI. Where they took my DNA. I told you about it."

"You didn't mention that you got violent when they arrested you."

I dropped the hand holding my paper to the side. "That's because I have a fear of needles. I told you about that phobia, remember?"

"You're saying, because you have a phobia, you . . ." She held out her hand for the paper. I gave it to her. Hannah read, "'. . . attempted to flee, then attacked Officer Daniels, bruising Daniels's face and neck.'"

I tightened my lips. "I had cancer when I was seven. I needed a bunch of painful injections. You know what chemotherapy is like? My hair came out in chunks. I puked up the insides of my lungs. My bones felt like they were under a blowtorch."

Her eyes softened.

I said, "One time, the chemo nurse made a mistake with the needle. She had to stick me five or six times. I have this vivid memory that my arm was spurting blood. My mother says I imagined it. I was just bleeding badly. Whatever happened, my arm swelled up twice as big, and the skin turned purple-black. It hurt so much that I could barely touch it for weeks."

"I'm sorry."

"Anyway, before I could take any more chemo shots, they had to first give me a tranquilizer. By mouth."

"But taking DNA is just a matter of a mouth swab."

"Not in Virginia. Not back in those days."

"Even then, they would have done swabs as well as using needles. At least in California, they'd only use a needle if someone was really an asshole."

I grimaced. "Well, I mighta suggested something about the cop having carnal desires for his mother."

She nodded. "That would probably do it." Hannah let out a sigh. "Look, I certainly understand the childhood trauma. But you were an adult when this happened. Why would you hit a cop?"

"First of all, I was drunk, which, I've discovered, makes me paranoid. Second, phobias aren't rational. How do you feel about slithering snakes?"

Hannah shifted in her seat. "Okay. Still, violence doesn't look good in this context."

I stood, straddling the seat, gripping the chair back. "I'm sure my doctor can testify this is a long-standing phobia."

Hannah shrugged. "Well, it is what it is." She dropped the paper on her desk.

"Is there something I should do about it?"

"There's nothing we can do at this point."

"When do we hear from the lab about the DNA sample?"

"Should be anytime now. If they'll tell me without being paid."

I felt my face flush.

Hannah said, "I need to meet with David Hu. To verify your alibi."

"You haven't met him yet?"

"I can't pin him down. First he was traveling; now he says he's tied up in meetings."

I pulled the chair from between my legs and set it to the side. "I'll fix that."

I grabbed the phone and called David's office. His assistant said he was in a meeting. I said, "Get him. It's urgent."

A few minutes later, David came on the line. "Your house better be on fire. I just left two CEOs, three investment bankers, and four lawyers in a conference room."

I said, "How come you're not meeting with Hannah?"

"We're merging two tech companies. I've been in nonstop meetings since I got back. Including the one you just pulled me out of."

"This is, like, really important."

"Okay, okay."

"When?"

"I'm in the closing. Probably an all-nighter."

"Tomorrow?"

"You're busting my ass."

"See how you feel when you're facing jail time."

He let out an *Aaaargh.* "All right. Tomorrow night. Soon as I can get off work. At the Magic Castle?"

"Done."

He hung up.

That night, I called David's home and left a message on his machine. "Just reminding you. We're meeting Hannah tomorrow night. Also, remember we were together all night on February twenty-second."

CHAPTER THIRTY-SEVEN

The next night, I pulled up in front of the Magic Castle a little after seven. I walked up to Hannah, who was standing by the door. In my back pocket, I had the schedule of magicians performing on the night Sherry was killed. Just in case David's memory needed a little refreshing.

We went inside to the front desk and I gave Tillie my membership card. She swiped it through the slot in the reader.

As Tillie gave back my card, Hannah said to her, "Does your computer keep a log of member sign-ins?"

"Yes. But just for the last couple of years, since we installed it."

"Can you take a look at February twenty-second of this year?"

Good one, Hannah! I smiled.

Tillie said, "I think that's confidential."

I said, "It's important. All we need to do is verify that I was here, and what time I signed in."

"Well . . . Okay, Harvey."

Tillie punched a few keys. "Yep. You got here at six forty."

Oh yeah!

Hannah said, "What time did he leave?"

Tillie shook her head. "Sorry, honey, we don't keep track of that."

Oh shit.

I took Hannah to the bookshelf, where she said "Open Sesame" to let us inside. We walked past a full-size suit of armor as we entered the Victorian mansion. I watched her looking at the hand-carved wooden staircase, the red velvet furniture, and the gold-framed oil paintings of famous magicians. Is she impressed? In a corner, I saw my pal Lenny at a small table covered with green felt. He was surrounded by half a dozen people who were watching him do impromptu card tricks. As he fanned out the deck, Lenny gave me a wink. I waved back.

We walked past a number of regulars, who all said hi to me.

I said, "Come see Irma."

I took Hannah to a room behind the bar, decorated with stained-glass panels, red velvet curtains with gold fringe, and a baby grand piano that was playing "Feelings" by itself. In front of the keyboard was an empty chair. Gold-braided ropes hung between the chair arms and the piano to keep people from sitting there. Next to the piano, on a pedestal table, was a round gilded birdcage with dollar bills stuck between the bars.

I said, "Irma's the ghost that plays the piano."

Hannah gave me a smirk. "I've seen player pianos before."

"It's not a player piano."

She snorted. "Yeah, right."

When the song finished, a man and woman clapped. The man stuck a dollar bill into the birdcage, and the invisible bird chirped. A little swing inside the cage moved back and forth. Irma played "We're in the Money." The couple laughed.

When the song finished, I said, "Very nice, Irma."

The piano hit two notes that sounded like *Thank you.*

Hannah cocked her head.

I said, "How old are you, Irma?" She played "Rock of Ages."

I turned to Hannah. "You have a request?"

"Yeah. Let's find your alibi and get out of here."

I put on a half grin. "Well, aren't you Mary Sunshine."

"I'm probably going to lose the Desmond case, I just got my period, and I ran out of Midol. Find David."

Maybe a little too much information . . . I said, "I don't think he's here yet."

She rolled her eyes.

I said, "Come have a drink."

We sat at the bar where David usually sits. When Jordan, the bartender, brought my fizzy water and Hannah's Diet Coke, he said, "Harvey, you know where I can find a used prediction slate?"

"I've got an extra." I may have a lot more than that for sale pretty soon.

"I can only swing twenty bucks."

"That's cool."

He gave me a two-handed thumbs-up. "Thanks."

When Jordan walked off, Hannah said, "You obviously come here a lot."

"Under any other circumstances, that'd be a great opening line."

She smiled at me, then sipped her Diet Coke. "The other magicians look at you like they admire you."

Am I blushing? "It's a nice community." I stirred my bubbly water with my straw. "We're all very friendly. We show each other new tricks. Exchange techniques."

"You tell each other your secrets?"

"Sure. Except the ones we use to fool other magicians."

She turned a little toward me on the stool. "What do you mean?"

I leaned in. "It's no big deal to fool laymen. Once magicians reach a certain level, the challenge is to fool other magicians. That means doing a standard trick in a completely different way. You'd never notice the difference. Only a magician would."

"Like what?"

I took a sip of water. "It's a little hard to explain. For example, one way to keep track of a selected card is to keep a little break in the deck. If you did a card trick for a magician, you might hold up the deck and show all the sides, so he could see there's no break."

"Show me something."

I can hardly think of a worse audience than someone who's lost their Midol. "Well . . ."

"C'mon."

"All right. Put out your left hand."

She held out her arm.

"Open your hand."

She turned her palm up and spread her fingers. I took a fifty-cent piece out of my pocket, placed it on her palm, and said, "Hold this tight."

She closed her fingers around the coin.

I took hold of her wrist. I said, "I'm going to get the coin out of your hand no matter how hard you hold on." I felt her muscles tighten.

I said, "You gotta look away." She turned her head, still gripping hard.

After a moment, I said, "Okay, you can look now."

She turned her head back. "I've still got the coin."

"Let me see."

She opened her hand. I grabbed the coin and said, "There. I got it."

She gave a sarcastic *Phhhh.* "That's the stupidest trick I've ever seen."

"Possibly." I smiled. "But see how you like this one." I held up the watch I'd taken off her wrist. She looked at her naked wrist, back at the watch, and said, "How . . ."

I gave her my *Ta-Da* smile.

I felt a hand clap me on the shoulder.

I turned to see David Hu. He said, "Sorry I'm late. Hi, Hannah. Long time. You look . . . great."

Hannah smiled politely. From her expression, she had no clue that she'd ever seen him before.

David walked around and took the stool on the other side of Hannah. When he got behind her, he pointed at her, stuck out his tongue, and panted, pantomiming that he thought she was hot. I picked up my glass and rattled the ice.

Without David's ordering, the bartender clunked down a whiskey in front of him. David took a swallow and let out an *Ahhhh.*

He said to Hannah, "I heard you went to Harvard Law."

"Yes. Harvey really appreciates your taking the time to meet with us. It's an essential element of his case."

"No problem." David took another sip of whiskey.

Hannah said, "Tell me what you remember about February twenty-second."

"I was here with Harvey."

"What time?"

David shot his eyes at me.

I said, "From around seven until—"

Hannah spun around and glowered at me. "Please keep quiet. I need David's recollection." She turned back to him.

David finished his whiskey and motioned for another one.

Hannah said, "What time were you here?"

David ran his tongue over his lips. "From seven thirty to, I dunno, maybe eleven or so?" He looked at me. I nodded.

Hannah said, "How do you know it was February twenty-second?"

"Well, Harvey and I are here most every night."

"Don't you occasionally miss nights?"

"Yes."

"So how can you be sure you were here on the twenty-second?"

I took the show schedule out of my pocket, held it up, and pointed at it.

David raised his head as if to say, *Right!* "I remember which magician we saw that night."

"Who was that?"

"Um, I'm not sure right now. When Harvey first asked me, he showed me the schedule and that jogged my memory."

Hannah spun around, saw the schedule in my hand.

She said, "I assume that's the schedule?"

"Uh, yeah." I handed it to her. Behind Hannah, the bartender gave David a new whiskey. He quickly took a drink.

Hannah looked at the schedule, then slid it across the bar to David. He picked it up, read it, and tapped a name printed there. David said, "Andy Valentine. I remember we saw Andy Valentine."

I smiled at him, nodding broadly. He winked.

Hannah said, "This schedule says that Valentine was in the Close-up Gallery for a week. How do you know you saw him on the twenty-second and not the twenty-third? Or the twenty-first?"

"I, well . . . Harvey told me it was the twenty-second."

"That's the only way you know?"

"Well . . ." David drained the whiskey glass. "I trust him."

After David's interrogation, I walked Hannah to the front door of the Castle. As soon as we got outside, she said, "That guy is useless."

The attendant saw me and started for my car. I motioned for him to stop and gave him Hannah's ticket.

I said, "You were pretty hard on him."

"Hard? I was a pussycat compared to how the district attorney would fricassee his ass."

"He's a credible guy. Investment banker with a major firm."

"First off, he doesn't remember anything. Second, he's an alcoholic, in case you didn't notice. Most people think that impairs your memory."

Hannah's car pulled up. The attendant got out and stood there with the door open.

She walked to her car, saying, "In short, David is worse than no alibi at all. He'd just look like a clumsy attempt to fool the jurors."

She got in and drove off.

CHAPTER THIRTY-EIGHT

Son of a fucking bitch.

I stomped down the hall toward my apartment. Every goddam strand of hope I had was unraveling.

Son of a fucking bitch. How can this be happening to me? I bit off a chunk of cuticle.

As I passed the manager's apartment, her door opened.

Mrs. Talia said, "Harvey?"

I snapped out, "What?" Her face blanched as she took a half step back.

I stopped and faced her and spoke through my teeth. "What?"

"I'm really sorry. The landlord filed an eviction proceeding because you didn't pay within the three days." The small gray-haired woman extended a trembling arm, holding out a packet of papers like she was feeding a vicious animal.

I snatched the papers out of her hand. "Great, perfect. Have a wonderful night."

She quickly backed into her apartment and slammed the door.

I went to my apartment and threw open the door hard enough to bang it into the cheap fucking plaster wall. I tossed the eviction papers in the general direction of my living room and turned on the lights. Well, at least I still have electricity.

From the living room, I heard Lisa shrieking in her cage, like she always does when I come home. I looked around at the jumble of books, clothes, and papers.

Fuck it. The landlord can clean it up.

I sat down on the couch, leaned forward at the waist, and scratched my head with the fingernails of both hands. I could feel the dandruff fluttering off. I scratched harder.

Shit. I got no work. Even if I had a job, it'd take me ten years to pay Mom what I owe her. Not to mention the expense of the DNA expert. And God only knows what other bills are in that pile over there.

I stopped scratching. My scalp throbbed.

Shit. Only one choice.

I kicked through the living room mess, grabbed the phone from under a pile of clothes, and called Herb Gold.

When he answered, I said, "Did you talk to Copperfield about my trick?"

"He wanted to know if you were serious about that price."

"You told him I was?"

"Yeah."

"And . . ."

"His exact words were: 'I wouldn't pay a hundred grand for a trick if Houdini came back and offered it to me.'"

I started pacing. "What's the best he'll do?"

"He originally said twenty-five g's. I don't even know if that's still good."

Shit.

I let out a breath.

Well, twenty-five would pay off my rent, back bills, the DNA expert, and the rest of Hannah's fees. I'd even have a few bucks toward Mom's hundred grand.

Can I really sell? You get an inspiration like this once in a lifetime. Without it, I'm just another hack magician.

Assuming I don't go down for Sherry Allen's murder. Then, of course, it doesn't much matter what I owe. . . .

I let out a breath. "All right. Tell him it's a deal."

CHAPTER THIRTY-NINE

Next morning, as I walked into Hannah's office, she said, "You're late."

"Sorry." I rubbed my eyes. "I was up most of the night. My star witness is a lush. Every other suspect has an alibi. I owe my mother more than I can pay back in the next decade. I owe you, I owe the DNA expert, and I have a stack of bills from creditors whose names I can't even pronounce. Oh, and I'm getting evicted."

Hannah stood up. "Well, there's a little good news. The cops haven't been able to confirm that Sherry's father was in Seattle like he says. I'll take any reasonable doubt at this point."

"Yeah. Sure."

She looked at me sympathetically. "I can help with your eviction. Bring me the papers. I'll stall it for a couple of months."

"How much will that cost?"

"Just start showing up to work on time. We'll figure out the finances later."

I let out a sigh. "I can't ask you to wait any longer for your dough. I'm going to sell one of my tricks."

She wrinkled her forehead. "Sell what?"

I explained how I'd conceived my Crystal Fantasy trick, been working on it for six months, couldn't afford to finish it, and decided to take Copperfield's offer. I also explained how it would set back my career.

Her eyes softened. "I'm sorry."

I shrugged.

Hannah twisted her mouth to the side. "Didn't that Vegas guy hire you on the basis of the show you did the other night?"

"Yeah."

"You didn't have your new trick in that show, did you?"

"No. But he's only hiring me for small-time gigs. To make the big leap, I need something spectacular."

She sat down at her desk. "You're a clever man. You'll invent other tricks."

"I appreciate your confidence. Unfortunately, that's a little like telling Paul McCartney to just go write another Sgt. Pepper album."

Hannah looked down at her desk.

I left for lunch a little before one o'clock and saw Hannah get in her car for her daily meeting.

What is this daily meeting of hers? Why's she so mysterious about it?

As she drove out of the parking lot, I glanced over at my car.

Hmm.

I climbed in and drove after her.

A few blocks away, I spotted her stopped at a light. I stayed back a couple of car lengths and followed her down Lankershim to Moorpark, and onto the 101 freeway. A tractor-trailer, painted with a yellow "Have a nice day" face, cut me off.

Shit. Where'd she go?

Shit.

I got off at Coldwater Canyon and drove back to the office.

Whatever. She'll be going again tomorrow.

When I got back from lunch, the phone was ringing. I rushed to grab it.

A familiar man's voice said, "May I speak to Ms. Fisher, please?"

"She's not in."

"Mr. Kendall?"

I swallowed. "Hello, Sergeant Morton."

He said, "I suppose this message is more for you than her anyway. We verified that Sherry Allen's father was in Seattle on the night of the murder. That leaves you as the last man standing, Mr. Kendall. Why don't you just tell me what happened and save everyone a lot of trouble?"

"My lawyer says I shouldn't talk to the police."

I clunked down the phone.

I sat in the chair behind Hannah's desk and scratched my scalp with my fingernails.

My alibi, David Hu—gone.

Sherry's father as a suspect—gone.

Father of her kid—in jail in Florida.

Boyfriend—three witnesses put him at work.

Her apartment manager will testify that I look familiar.

My DNA at the crime scene.

Hell, if I was a juror, I'd fry my ass.

How can this be? There has to be a mistake with the DNA. Has to be.

If we exclude the DNA, there's only the apartment manager. After what Hannah did to David, I'm sure she can destroy that guy.

So without the DNA, nothing really connects me to the crime.

Without his having been seen by the entire audience, there was nothing to connect John Wilkes Booth to Lincoln's assassination.

The DNA expert has to come through.

No other choice.

What's taking them so long? Are they deliberately slowing down because they haven't been paid?

Shit.

That night, I sat home watching television with Lisa on my shoulder. I pointed the remote at the screen and flipped from a shot of an audience laughing to a wildlife documentary that showed a bunch of crocodiles splashing in a river.

I looked around my living room. I really should clean up the mess that the cops left in my apartment.

Tomorrow maybe.

I flipped the channel. A bunch of people in suits, sitting around an oval table, yelling at each other.

Should I call Carly? It'd be great to . . .

Why would I subject myself to another rejection?

Because the thought of her . . .

Am I an idiot to think about calling her? If she even answers, she'll probably hang up on me. This is a woman who worries about the lives of fetuses. She thinks I'm a murderer of grown-ups.

Still . . . I'd really like to see her. . . .

I am a sick puppy.

I flipped to a program about old locomotives and grabbed the phone. I dialed all but the last digit of Carly's home number. Can't call the cell. She'll see my number. Does her home phone have caller ID? The handset shrieked at me for not dialing. I hung up, dialed all but the last digit, and put my finger on the final button.

I hung up, sank back on the couch, and flipped through more channels.

I stopped on a bombastic preacher. He was a round man, dressed in a pinstripe navy suit and matching vest, pacing in front of a clear-glass podium with a huge bouquet of flowers on the floor in front of it. A scrolling message at the bottom of the screen invited me to send money to Reverend Jim.

Jim's cheeks flushed as he spoke into a wireless microphone, pronouncing *God* as if the word had two syllables.

The preacher said, "How many miracles do we see on a daily basis? How many? Hundreds, perhaps? Yet we take them all for granted. Isn't it a miracle that the sun comes up each morning?"

Yeah, well, it also goes down.

"Isn't it a miracle that we awaken each day with pure sweet air to breathe?"

You clearly don't live in Los Angeles.

The phone rang. I fumbled it off the hook.

"Harvey, it's Marty. How you doin'?"

"Never been better. What's up?"

"I got you a gig."

I sat up so fast that Lisa flapped her wings in a "What the hell?"

I said, "Excellent!"

"Convention of bank officers."

"Bank officers?" That'll be a million yuks.

"It pays two hundred bucks."

Yes! "Thanks, Marty. I can't tell you how much this means to me. Especially right now."

"Just remember who takes care of you, baby."

I hung up the phone and stared at Reverend Jim, who was still talking about miracles.

I looked at the phone.

No . . . It's just a coincidence that Marty called now. . . .

Next evening, I went to the Magic Castle to meet Herb Gold. I walked downstairs to the basement, past caricatures of magicians that lined the walls, and went into the Hat and Hare Pub, a small bar designed to look like an English pub. It had a pressed-tin ceiling, walls painted to look like a stone dungeon, and a dartboard inside a shallow wooden cabinet. I wanted a drink, but the bartender had spread a velvet cloth on the bar and was doing a coin trick for the people sitting on stools.

I took a seat at one of the cocktail tables, whose top was an old manhole cover covered with glass. Herb came in a few minutes later, holding a beer. He plopped down, took a sip that left a blotch of foam on his upper lip, then set the beer on the table. Herb stuck his large paw into his plaid sports jacket and came out with some folded papers.

He said, "Here's the Copperfield contract." He opened the papers and laid them on the table in front of me. The folded sides stood up from the manhole cover. He said, "Twenty-five grand. I tried to get him up, but that's all there was. Less my commission, of course."

I sat up. "Commission?"

"Yeah. I get ten percent for brokering these deals."

"Twenty-five hundred dollars?"

"Guess you got an A in math." He picked up his glass and sucked in a slug of beer.

"You didn't tell me you were taking a commission."

"Thought I did. I always get a commission. You think I'm doing this for my health?" He set down his beer glass with a clunk.

"So, you mean, I only get twenty-two five?"

"No, you get twenty-five. The commission is a cost of doing business."

"You know I need this money. That twenty-five hundred makes a big difference to me."

"You got it backward. I'm bringing you twenty-two five that's gonna save your ass, when nobody else is steppin' up."

I rubbed the back of my neck. "How could you spring something like this on me at the last minute?"

"Sorry, I thought you knew how these things work. Look, I gotta make a living, too." He picked up his beer and gulped down another couple of swallows. "Why're you bustin' my balls, kid? I'm tryin' to help you."

I looked at him, then picked up the contract and tried to read in the low light. "Seller"—I guess that's me—"hereby grants all rights of every nature or sort . . ." I skimmed the page and flipped to the next one. "Seller agrees not to divulge the secret of the trick to any third party. . . ."

Farther down the page, it read: "Seller agrees not to perform the trick."

I looked at Herb. "I can't ever do the trick?"

"Whaddaya think you're selling, chopped liver? He wants it exclusive. That's standard."

I came to the end and put down the contract.

Herb took a pen from his jacket and held it out.

I didn't take the pen. "I have to show it to my lawyer."

He laughed. "Lemme see if I got this right. You don't want to pay me for bringing you money, but you wanna throw away money on a lawyer?"

"I'm not signing it tonight."

Herb put his pen away. "Fine. Do what you want. No telling how long Copperfield will sit around waiting."

He picked up his beer, drained the glass down to a slithering trail of foam, then lumbered off.

Next morning at the office, I was sitting on the floor filing while Hannah typed at warp speed.

I stood up and said, "You remember how I said I was selling my magic trick?"

She kept typing. "Yeah."

"I got the contract. You think you could take a look?"

She stopped typing, stared at the computer screen, and wrinkled her forehead. "Sure."

"The guy who brought me the deal wants ten percent. Is that fair?"

"No clue." Still staring at the screen, she hit one typewriter key a number of times.

I set the folded contract on her desk. She didn't look up at it.

I went back to filing.

Just before one, Hannah left for her meeting. I walked outside, keeping my distance, then got in my car just as she drove off.

I followed her onto the freeway, then off onto Reseda Boulevard, where she headed north. I stayed back a few car lengths and kept in a different lane.

A few miles up, she turned right on a side street just before Sherman Way.

There's not much traffic on the side street. Better hold back so she doesn't see me.

I got into the right lane and slowed down. Someone behind me honked. I waved them around. They gunned past me.

I turned off Reseda just in time to see her make a left turn on the next street. I slowed down and rounded the corner. Hannah drove into an open parking lot behind a bank. I stopped on the street. She parked her car and walked toward a beige two-story building, where a cluster of about twenty people were standing around outside. The crowd was mostly women, a lot of them on the heavy side. When Hannah walked up, she hugged a few of them, then stood there talking.

Just before one o'clock, they all went inside. The door closed.

I got out of my car and walked toward the building. If I stand against the wall beside the window, will I be able to hear through the glass? Will she see me?

A man rushing toward the building saw me, turned, and came over. He said, "Can I help you?"

"I, well . . ."

"You going to the meeting?"

"Maybe."

He smiled. "You a newcomer?"

"Um, sort of."

"Welcome. I'm Michael."

"I'm Kyle. Which meeting is this?"

"Overeaters Anonymous."

CHAPTER FORTY

I drove away from the Overeaters Anonymous building.

Why do I feel like I need a shower? What kind of creep noses into the most private part of someone's life?

Shit. No wonder she didn't want me to know. It *really* is none of my business.

I'm such an asshole.

Back at the office, I dove into the filing. Nothing works off guilt like burying yourself in work.

I realized I was actually making progress, I might even catch up in the next few days.

I wiped my forehead with the back of my hand, then squared up a pile of papers.

What am I missing about my case? I know there's something.

An hour later, when Hannah got back, she went straight to her computer without looking at me.

Does she know I followed her? Did she see me walking toward the building? Did that guy Michael rat me out?

Not likely, or she'd be taking my head off.

I avoided looking in her direction as I clipped some blue-backed court papers into a file.

Later in the afternoon, Hannah said, "I read that contract for the sale of your trick."

I stopped my punch halfway through a stack of papers. "And?"

She held up the contract. "It looks fine. I mean, I don't know anything about magic deals, but there's nothing unusual in it."

"Thanks."

Hannah set the papers on her desk. She softened her voice. "You sure you want to sell your trick?"

I walked over, took the contract off her desk, folded it up, and stuck it in my back pocket.

When I got home that night, my answering machine was blinking. I hit the PLAY button.

Carly's voice. "Uh, hello, Harvey. I feel I owe you an apology. You can call, if you want to. I'll understand if you don't."

The words were nice enough. Her tone was robotic, like she didn't mean a word she was saying.

I don't need any more humiliation, thank you very much.

I erased the message and turned on the TV for background noise while I prepped for the magic gig that Marty booked for me.

Am I gonna be okay performing with a murder case over my head?

Murder. The word sounds so . . .

Shake it off.

Those bankers are paying you to perform. You owe them your best.

I opened the lid of one of my magic trunks, looked inside, and scrunched my forehead in thought.

Okay. Which tricks work best for a convention of bank officers?

Money tricks, of course. The Miser's Dream, where I pull coins out of the air and drop them in a bucket. The signed twenty-dollar bill in the egg. What else? I pawed through the trunk. I can fill in with generics. Mismade Flag. Dice box. Haven't done the linking rings in a while. Nah. They're pretty trite.

Should I call Carly? Did she really want to apologize? She did make a gesture. I mean, she didn't have to call.

Can I expect more than just an apology? I mean, maybe a Close Encounter of the Fourth Kind? I'd sure love to release some of the poisons in my system.

If I got that far, would I limp out again? All those thoughts about fertile eggs sure took the joy out of humping.

Can you put a second condom over the first one? Would I feel anything if I did?

What's the strongest condom made? Could I trust anything short of a threaded endcap for an iron pipe?

I threw the oversize deck of cards into my trunk, grabbed the phone, and dialed Carly's number before I had a chance to overthink it.

She answered right away.

I stood up, holding the phone. "Hi. It's Harvey. I got your message."

"Yes. Thank you for calling."

On my TV, the audience laughed.

Carly said, "I wanted to say I'm sorry for the way I acted."

I started pacing. "Apology accepted. Do you—"

"Wait. I need to say something."

I stopped pacing. "All right . . ."

I heard her breathing. She said, "I haven't been totally honest with you."

On the television, I heard a woman tell a dog to sit.

She said, "I . . . well, the truth is, I was in a relationship with someone who'd been in New York for a few months, and he just got back, and, well, you know, we had that kind of awkward reunion after you've been apart and you feel like strangers but you don't want to feel that way. Anyway, I feel like I have to give it a chance with him."

"I see." Sounds like your relationship's got a really great chance, with you falling into bed with me on the first date.

She said, "I was attracted to you. I guess I got a little carried away. I never do that. Then I was embarrassed, so I shut you down without telling you the whole story. I had no right to play with your emotions like that. I'm sorry."

The woman on TV told her dog to roll over.

I said, "Okay . . ."

"Can you forgive me?" Her voice sounded like she was bracing for a barrage. "I mean, it'd be nice to be friends."

I sighed. "Carly. I'll tell it to you straight. I find you incredibly attractive. I'm lousy at being friends when I'm that attracted to someone. So let's leave it like this. If things don't work out with your New Yorker, give me a call."

It sounded like her breath caught. "You hate me."

I softened my voice. "No. Just the opposite. I don't want to make things difficult for you." *Actually,* I wouldn't mind making it a little difficult.

"Harvey . . ."

"I appreciate your apologizing to me. Not everyone would do that. I hope your relationship works out." *About as much as I'd like to walk over broken glass on my lips.*

She said, "Maybe I'll see you again."

"Maybe so. Bye, Carly."

I hung up the phone and stared at it. Shook my head.

As I sat on the couch, I heard the crumple of Copperfield's contract in my back pocket.

I pulled out the papers, looked at them.

Can I really sign this thing?

What choice do I have?

Clenching the contract in my fist, I got up and dug through the crap on my floor, found a pen, then sat on the couch. I folded the paper creases backward so I could lay the contract flat on my coffee table.

I opened it to the signature page.

I looked around my apartment. How could I have left this mess for so long? How can I live like this?

Ah . . . what difference does it make anyway?

I picked up the pen.

CHAPTER FORTY-ONE

Next morning, I parked at Hannah's office, then walked over to a corner mailbox on Lankershim. I opened the metal door of the mailbox, reached into my pocket, and grabbed the sealed envelope with the signed Copperfield contract. The smell of exhaust from cars idling at the corner stung my lungs. Isn't there some kind of smog law that cuts down on those fumes?

I put the envelope on the metal door but didn't close it. The traffic light changed. The cars accelerated. Did those assholes ever hear of mufflers?

I looked at the envelope lying there on the bare metal. I started to release the door handle. The metal groaned. I tightened my grip on the handle.

A woman's voice behind me said, "Can you hurry it up?"

I grabbed the envelope, let the metal door clunk shut, and stepped aside. The woman glared at me. I clutched the envelope tight in my hand. She dropped in two envelopes, let the mailbox door slam, then walked away.

I tightened my lips, looked down the street. The gutters were strewn with crumpled papers. The sidewalk was smeared with dirt.

I sighed, opened the mailbox again, and laid down the envelope. I closed my eyes. I heard a motorcycle chutter past.

Keeping my eyes closed, I let go of the handle.

When I got to work, I went through the motions of filing. Throughout the morning, if Hannah spoke to me, she got one-word answers.

Just before lunch, she said, "What's eating you?"

"Nothing."

She raised her eyebrows, as if to say, Gimme a break.

"I sold my magic trick."

Her face looked pained. "I'm sorry. I know what that meant to you."

"Yeah, well . . . what am I gonna do?"

"I hope it wasn't because of my fees. I said I'd work with you."

"Unfortunately, you're not the only wolf snapping at the door."

Hannah said, "Is it *sold* sold?"

I turned toward her. "What do you mean?"

"Have you signed the deal and gotten the money?"

"I signed and mailed it this morning."

"Did they sign first?"

"No."

She brightened. "You could call them and say you're revoking the offer. You're free to do that before it's accepted."

I shook my head. "Much as I'd love to, I need the money. I've got overdue rent, I owe you and the lab, and I'm sure there'll be trial expenses. Not to mention the hundred grand my mother put up."

Hannah took a couple of steps toward me. "Have you thought about a BK?"

"A what?"

"A bankruptcy."

"Oh. I thought you meant Burger King. Doesn't a bankruptcy, like, totally screw up your credit?"

"I won't say it's good for your credit rating. But it's a legitimate protection for people who get overwhelmed by debts."

I took a fifty-cent piece out of my pocket and ran it over my knuckles. "If I do that, won't my mother end up holding the bag for my bail?"

"Technically, yes. But you could use the bankruptcy to get rid of your other debts, then pay your mother voluntarily."

I ran the coin over my hand a few more times. Her eyes followed it.

I said, "It'll take me years to pay Mom if I don't sell the trick. I mean, it'll take me years anyway, but at least I can get her a decent chunk right away."

I put the coin back in my pocket.

CHAPTER FORTY-TWO

At three A.M., I was lying in bed on my back, staring at the ceiling. I pulled a pillow over my face. It was hard to breathe with the pillow on my nose. I pushed it harder against my face.

Can still breathe.

I threw off the pillow and turned on my side, pulled my knees up toward my chest.

Shit. I got up and turned on the television. Obscure cable channels are awesome at that hour of the morning, at least if your taste is as weird as mine. There're infomercials for shit I'd never consider during the day, but somehow I find those products riveting when I'm sleep-deprived.

First came some gizmo that vacuum-seals your food into plastic pouches. Hmm . . . I could really save some money. . . .

Next channel had people sitting on a beach in Hawaiian shirts, talking about how much money they made from this real estate course.

I clicked around the dial, yawning, until I settled on a black-and-white rerun of a 1950s show. It was called *Candid Camera* and they hid a camera to film practical jokes. Wow, people actually did that before the Internet.

This blond woman drove a 1954 Packard downhill into a gas station. She got out of the car and told the attendant that her car didn't work right. He opened the hood, did a double take, and said, "You ain't got no engine!"

I found myself laughing out loud. In the background, I heard Lisa kick up birdseed in her cage.

The station went to a commercial for dog food.

I leaned back, closed my eyes, then suddenly sat up straight.

Wait a minute. . . .

A hidden camera. Maybe . . .

I deflated. No way there was any kind of security camera at Sherry Allen's apartment. First, the owners were obviously too cheap, and second, the cops would've found it right away.

But . . . hang on. . . .

Maybe there's another place. . . .

I didn't get to sleep that night because I got hooked on *Casablanca* for the eighteenth time and couldn't stop watching until the two men walked off in their beautiful friendship.

Around seven in the morning, I took a shower, then drove over the hill to Wilshire Boulevard. I parked on the street, sat in the car, and scanned the stores while I waited for them to open. Dry cleaner's, restaurant, supermarket, fast food, and . . .

Morris's Jewelry Store.

That's the best bet.

Just before nine, I saw a short old man, hunched at the shoulders, walk up to the jewelry store and take out his keys. I waited until he was inside, so he wouldn't think I was trying to jump him, then walked in.

He looked up from behind the counter. "Good morning, young man. How may I help you?"

"Does your store have a surveillance camera?"

The old man stiffened. I saw his hand go under the counter. "Why would you ask such a thing?"

Later that morning, groggy but pumped with adrenaline, I walked into Hannah's office.

She was yelling before I was halfway through the door. "I told you I would not tolerate any more tardiness and I meant it. You're fired. I resign as your lawyer. Get out." She stuck her arm out stiffly, pointing at the door like she was giving some low-level Nazi salute.

I held up my hand like a traffic cop. "Before you froth over, let me tell you where I've been."

"I don't give a good goddam where you've been. You're ten times over your screwup limit. Out!" Her face was reddening, her stiffened arm trembling.

"Fine. Fire me. Then I won't bother telling you how I just saved your ass on the Desmond case."

Her face screwed up in puzzlement. "Your cutesy little tricks won't work this time. Just get out."

"So I should take this with me?" I held up a DVD.

"Yes. Go."

She was actually kinda hot-looking when she got all red-faced and sweaty. I said, "I don't think you mean that."

"You bet your ass I mean it. OUT!"

"You really ought to see this."

Her eyes shot to the DVD. I could see she was curious despite herself. "What is that thing?"

"It's a DVD."

"I can see that, smart-ass. I've got no time for games."

"Sorry, it's the performer in me. You know, building up to the big moment."

"Performers should know how to read their audience. Make your point in the next ten seconds or get out."

I held up the DVD and turned it so it sparkled in the light. "This is a surveillance video from a supermarket on Wilshire Boulevard. Taken on March eighteenth, at one eighteen A.M."

Her eyebrows lowered. "The time Oliver Desmond was stopped by the police?"

"Precisely."

Hannah took a step closer, lowering her weapon arm. Her face was draining toward neutral. She said, "It's a video of the street?"

"Yes. And guess what? It's a full-on view of a cop stopping Desmond's car. A car whose headlights were turned on."

Hannah's mouth fell open. She shook her head. "Really?"

"No, April Fool's." I smirked, nodding my head. "Yes, for real. Watch it."

She took the DVD and cradled it like it was some fragile flower. Hannah ran over to her computer, stuck it in the drive, and clicked PLAY.

She watched the video intently, then looked up at me. "Harvey, you're . . . brilliant."

I felt myself blush. "Actually, I'm more of a late-night TV fan, but I'll take 'brilliant.'"

That afternoon, I felt someone shaking me. As I sat up with a start, I realized I'd been sleeping. Shit. I'd fallen asleep on Hannah's desk. She was still shaking me.

I blinked away the fog and I noticed I'd drooled a spit blot on her desk pad. I put my arm over the wet spot.

I looked up at Hannah, who was grinning. She said, "Guess what?"

I swallowed the foul taste in my mouth. "I give up."

Hannah said, "I showed the district attorney your DVD and he's dropping the Desmond case. They don't want to embarrass the cops, and I suspect they're also hoping we don't sue the city for harassment."

I stood up. "Congratulations!"

Hannah made a pumping motion with her hand. "Yes! I won the case that my father told me to plead out."

"Excellent!"

She nodded rapidly. "On the way back from downtown, I phoned Desmond's parents. They were so grateful that they gave me a huge bonus!" Beaming, she bobbed her head from side to side.

"Awesome."

Suddenly, I felt the burden of my case slam into me like some party-crashing thug. My case wasn't going away so easily. My shoulders sagged and I slumped into a nosedive depression.

She said, "Harvey."

"Yeah?"

The tip of her tongue came through her lips. "Because you found the video, I'm going to give you a five-thousand-dollar bonus."

I felt my head snap up. "Uh . . . thanks." Not sure I sounded very enthusiastic.

She said, "I'll also have enough to loan you some money. You won't have to sell your trick."

I felt my breath catch and turned fully toward her. I looked her in the eyes and blinked hard, to make sure my eyes stayed clear.

I said, "I can't tell you how much that means to me, but I

can't go any further in debt. It'll take me years to get above water, even after I sell the trick."

She looked at me with an "Are you sure?" expression.

I picked up to the metal punch, stuck in some papers, and jammed the lever down hard.

Hannah clapped her hands, startling me. She said, "Well, I'm buying dinner tonight. To celebrate."

"I don't need charity."

"Why do you have to say an asshole thing like that to someone who's trying to be nice?"

"Sorry."

She took a step forward. "Is that a yes?"

Well, I don't exactly feel like celebrating, but I guess it beats sitting home and moping. "Sure."

Considering the state of my pocketbook, I'd have been thrilled with McDonald's. Hannah chose Tommaso's, an Italian place on Ventura Boulevard.

We walked into the dark restaurant, which was almost empty. Through the low lights, I saw brick walls with oozing mortar, hung with tattered Italian wine posters. There was also a poster for the Italian version of *Rambo,* and the obligatory map of Italy.

We sat in a dark red booth in the back. The lights were so atmospheric that I could barely read the damn menu. The waiter brought a basket of breadsticks. Hannah's eyes shot to them. I took one and snapped off a piece. I offered the basket to Hannah and got the same vigorous headshake I'd gotten when I'd offered her peanuts at the bar.

I said, "You don't eat bread?"

"If you're that curious about how I keep my weight off, why

didn't you come into the Overeaters Anonymous meeting after you followed me?"

Oh shit. I felt my face flush up like a gas burner. "Uh, well, umm—"

Can she see me redden in this light?

"You are possibly the worst tail I've ever seen. I saw you the second you came after me. I easily lost you on the freeway the first time, and I'd have ditched you the second time, except I was running late."

Why is my back suddenly itching? "I guess I owe you an apology."

"Yes. You do."

"I'm sorry. How come you didn't say anything before now?"

"I was going to skewer your ass when I got back from the meeting, but you have so much trouble in your life that I felt guilty coming down on you."

"So now I get the skewering?"

"That was a slap on the wrist. If you were being skewered, your guts would be hanging out on the table."

I closed the menu. "Well, now I'm really hungry."

She laughed. Had I seen her laugh before?

I said, "It's an occupational hazard of magicians that we have to look behind the curtains. I can't watch a magic show without figuring out how it's done. Secrets drive me nuts. So when you made your meetings a mystery, I couldn't help myself."

A waiter appeared. "*Signora e signore,* what will we be having this evening?"

Hannah looked up at the waiter. "I'll have broiled fish, steamed vegetables, and a green salad. You have low-fat dressing?"

He didn't look up from scribbling on a pad. "No, signora."

"Okay, just bring oil and vinegar."

The waiter kept writing. "And you, signore?"

I said to Hannah, "Would it, like, bother you if I have pasta?"

She waved her hand. "Have whatever."

I ordered a Caesar salad and spaghetti with sausage.

Why do I feel like I should oink?

When the waiter left, I said, "So, were you inviting me to ask about your meeting, or not? I can't really read you."

"Good. I like being unreadable."

"That's nice, because you just did it again."

She repositioned her knife, fork, and spoon. "I'll tell you a little about OA; then the subject is closed."

"Fair enough."

"It's basically Alcoholics Anonymous applied to food. I can't describe what it's like to have an addiction, since you don't have one. How would you tell a person who was blind from birth what the color orange looks like?"

"I guess I couldn't."

"Right. There's no common vocabulary. Why would someone get drunk and lose his family, his house, and his business? Not rational. Yet he's compelled to do it. Same thing with food. Why would someone overeat when they know it's unhealthy? Knowing how to lose weight is easy. Just eat less, right?"

"Sounds right to me."

"Knowing and doing are very different things. I can't do it without the support of the organization."

"So, it's like a diet club, where you weigh in?"

"No weighing. Nothing like that. It's based on the Twelve Steps."

"Wasn't that an old Hitchcock movie?"

"Close. That was *The Thirty-Nine Steps*."

The waiter showed up with the salads. Hannah dribbled some of the oil and vinegar on hers.

I took a forkful of Caesar and said, "You don't feel deprived, knowing there's things you can't eat?"

"Not really. I feel so much better living a healthy life. Besides, there's nothing I *can't* eat. Just things I choose not to eat."

"You can go the rest of your life without eating bread or nuts?"

"I don't know. But I can do it for twenty-four hours. That's all I have to worry about."

"How do you—"

Hannah held up her fork. "That's enough about OA. If you're really curious, there's tons of information on the Internet." She took a bite of salad and chewed.

I tried to get a crouton on my fork. It split in half.

Hannah said, "My father called right before we left the office."

"Oh?"

"I told him how I resolved the Desmond case. He was surprised."

Surprised that anyone did something well without him?

Hannah grinned. "I told him I was going to dinner to celebrate, and he asked for the name of the restaurant. He said he was sending something over."

I leaned closer. "That's intriguing. What do you think it is?"

She shrugged. "No idea."

"Let's guess." I scrunched my forehead. "Hmm." I raised my index finger as if to say, Aha. "I got it. A chorus of belly-button whistlers."

She laughed. Her eyes twinkled.

Hannah shook her head. "Too trite. I think"—she twisted her mouth to the side—"a troupe of dancing dogs."

I chuckled. Not bad for someone who probably tells jokes by numbering the paragraphs, like she's writing a legal brief. I said, "Maybe a snake charmer, complete with flute, wicker basket, and cobra."

The waiter walked up to the table, picked up the salad plates, and left.

I said, "Whatever your father does, it's very thoughtful of him."

"Yeah. If he doesn't forget."

Hannah rearranged the position of her knife, fork, and spoon again. She pulled her water glass a little closer, then gave it a small turn in place. She said, "Are you close to your father?"

"He passed away when I was fifteen."

Her eyes softened. "I'm sorry. I should have remembered. You told that to Sherry's father."

"It was really hard on my mom."

Hannah said, "He must have been pretty young."

"Forty-eight. Heart attack. I came home from school and the police were there. A deliveryman had seen him through the front window and called the cops. One of the officers phoned Mom. He said there'd been a burglary at the house and asked her to please come home." I felt my voice catch. "They were nice enough to wait and tell her in person."

She patted my hand, then left hers on top of mine. Hannah said, "I guess your father issues trump mine."

I shook my head. "It's not a contest."

A woman's voice said, "Well. Hello, you two."

Hannah pulled back her hand. We looked up at Hannah's sister, Susan, who had materialized next to our table. Susan had a sly smile, like she'd caught us making out. She was clutching a gold handbag against her skinny blue silk dress, which was cut low to show off her tits-standing-at-attention.

Hannah cleared her throat. "Hi."

I said, "Nice to see you again."

Susan looked at me. She smiled, almost sexily, like she was debating whether it might be fun to take me away from Hannah. I smiled back. I might be had for a night. . . .

Susan turned her attention back to Hannah. She said, "Daddy asked me to bring this by." Susan opened her purse, pulled out an envelope, and gave it to Hannah.

Hannah took it and laid it on the table.

Susan stood there. "Aren't you going to open it?"

Hannah glanced at her. "Later. Thanks for bringing it."

Susan closed her purse with a snap.

Hannah toyed with her fork.

Guess we're not inviting Susan to join us.

Susan smiled stiffly. "Well, have a nice evening." She shot a quick glance at the envelope on the table, then turned and walked off.

As soon as Susan's back was to us, Hannah relaxed her posture.

I said, "How much older is Susan?" I'd learned that trick a long time ago. Always assume the other woman is older, even if her hair's in pigtails.

"Actually, I'm four months older."

"You don't look . . ." My mouth dropped a bit. I shook my head, like I was trying to rattle something loose. "Did you say *four* months?"

Hannah nodded.

"How could . . ."

The waiter showed up with our dinners. "Okay. Which of you had the fish?"

Hannah held up her hand. He slid the plate in front of her, then dropped the spaghetti in front of me.

He said, "Need anything else?"

My friend here would like a sisterectomy. "No, we're fine."

As soon as the waiter left, I scrunched a little closer to Hannah. "How can your sister be four months younger?"

She sighed. "When I was fourteen, my mother found out that my father had a second family."

I felt my eyebrows jolt up. Well, Bruceie Baby.

Guess that explains Susan's anorexic gene.

Not to mention the divorce . . .

I forced my brows back down.

Hannah cut a piece of fish, speared it with the fork, then set the fork on her plate without eating. "Dad never married Susan's mother. He later left Mom for his Pilates instructor. And no, she's not the current wife. Gillian is number three."

I looked at Hannah. "I think you just pulled ahead in the father derby."

"As someone once said, 'It's not a contest.'" She picked up her fork and ate the bite of fish, then cut off a chunk of broccoli.

I clapped my hands, startling her. "You know, you've successfully gotten me out of my funk, so let's make tonight a *real* celebration. Let's do something exotic after dinner."

Hannah drew back. "'Exotic'?"

"Yeah. Let's go . . . to a gay disco. Or let's ride the bumper cars at the Santa Monica pier. Or find a karaoke bar and sing some oldies."

Her expression looked as if she were rapidly sinking in quicksand. "You're kidding, right?"

"C'mon. Loosen up. It'll be good for you."

She shook her head. "I haven't got the energy for any of those things."

"Okay. What do you suggest?"

Hannah scrunched her brow. "Huh?"

"What do you do for fun?"

"Well . . . I read. I like word puzzles. I watch some television."

I twisted another forkful of spaghetti. "What kind of television?"

"News, mostly. A few PBS shows."

Aren't you a ball of fire? "You like music?" I stuffed the spaghetti in my mouth and chewed quickly.

"I don't hear much. When I'm in the car, I listen to NPR news and a few of the talk shows. But I like music."

"Lemme see . . . You're probably not a heavy-metal freak."

"Good guess."

I speared a slice of sausage. "Okay. I got it. I know where we're going."

"Who said we're going anywhere?"

"I did. It'll be fun." I popped the sausage in my mouth.

"I have to get up early tomorrow."

"I'll have you home before your curfew." I went for more spaghetti.

"Where are you thinking of going?"

"Not thinking. Doing. And it's a surprise."

"I don't like surprises."

Imagine that. A control freak who doesn't like surprises. "Trust me."

"I don't trust you."

"You're very smart."

We negotiated a deal. She'd follow me to our surprise destination. That way, she'd have her own car and could leave if she wasn't happy.

When we finished eating, Hannah waved at the waiter for the check. He didn't see her. She slowly lowered her hand behind her neck, then acted like she was scratching the back of her head. Why do people do that?

I said, "Before we head for our surprise, aren't you going to open your father's envelope?"

Her mouth opened and her eyebrows went up in an "Oh yeah, I forgot." She picked up the envelope and said, "It looks pretty small for dancing dogs."

"Yeah. It's probably the snake charmer."

Hannah tore the flap and took out a note. I could see it was handwritten, but I couldn't get a good enough look to read it.

Her eyes went over the page, then got teary. Her mouth formed a broad smile.

She shook her head and said, "Wow."

" 'Wow' what? C'mon. Give it up."

Hannah picked up her napkin and dabbed at the corner of her eye. "This is the nicest thing I've ever gotten from my father."

I held out my hand for the paper.

She reread the note, then handed it to me.

Hannah—
I'm so proud of you.
The check's taken care of.
Dad.

CHAPTER FORTY-THREE

After leaving Tommaso's, Hannah followed me as I drove toward *Lune Bleue,* a fancy name for a dive on Ventura Boulevard in Studio City. I hadn't been there since I needed a phony ID. Sure hope it's still open.

There it is. The sign's lit up. Good indication that the club's still there.

I stuck my hand out the window, signaling Hannah to park with the valet, then drove a couple of blocks farther, turned onto a residential street, and found a free parking space. By the time I hiked back to the club, Hannah was standing in front.

She said, "This place is a dump."

"I knew you'd like it." I touched her elbow and led her inside. We heard soft jazz behind a black velvet curtain. As we came around it, I saw a quartet playing on a small riser. Sax, piano, stand-up bass, and a drummer swishing wire brushes on the drumheads. A number of small round tables surrounded the crowded dance floor. The walls were painted with caricatures of Miles Davis, Thelonious Monk, John Coltrane, Count Basie, Dave Brubeck, and a number of other jazz greats.

When the music ended, the audience clapped softly. The people on the dance floor went to their tables.

I spotted an empty table in the back and threw my head toward it, signaling Hannah to follow me. We wove through the people and sat down. No wonder this table's empty. There's a post that blocks the view of the musicians.

She said, "How'd you know I like jazz?"

"Simple. I eliminated every other kind of music known to man."

She laughed. Second real laugh tonight. Her eyes sparkled.

A waitress appeared. "What'll it be?"

I said, "I'll just have ice water for now."

She pointed to a laminated card, folded into a triangle on the table that read: *Two drink minimum per person.*

I said, "Sparkling water."

Hannah ordered a Diet Coke. There goes twenty bucks. Screw it. I won't get that many nights out.

The group started another song. With the post in our line of sight, I coulda saved the drink money and put on the radio.

I said, "Mind if we stand a minute? I'd like to watch these guys."

"Okay."

We got up and moved a few steps away. The stand-up bass player picked the strings with his index and middle fingers, like his fingers were imitating a walking man. The drummer bobbed his head in time to the music.

These guys are good. Watching a good jazz ensemble is like hearing a conversation. First they play together. Then they play off each other.

The sax player closed his eyes and held up his horn. I closed my eyes. What was it I once read about a great jazz saxophonist? Something like, "He wove his notes like whirls of smoke."

I opened my eyes. Hannah was almost imperceptibly moving

her body in rhythm to the music. Wow. That's the equivalent of my swinging from the rafters.

I said, "You want to dance?"

She stopped moving. "No."

"Why not?"

"I can think of several hundred reasons."

"Give me one."

"I'm a shitty dancer."

"So am I. Try another one."

"I haven't danced since college."

"That means you know how. So far, no prize."

"I'd be self-conscious."

"In front of all your close friends here?"

"I'll look foolish."

"I hate to break it to you, but these people are far more interested in themselves than in watching you."

"You don't understand. When you're a fat kid, people make fun of you while you're dancing. It leaves scars."

"Unfortunately for your excuse factory, you're now a normal-size adult." I grabbed her hand and pulled her toward the dance floor.

"Harvey, stop."

From the tone of her voice, I could tell it wasn't a real "Stop." It was a Pull me so it's not my fault that we're out here "Stop."

I got her to the dance floor, took her right hand in my left, and put my right hand on her waist. Hannah gave an exasperated sigh, then started dancing.

We had enough space between us to satisfy a high school chaperone. With each step, I closed a little of it.

I said, "Where do you want to be in ten years?"

"What?"

"I mean, what do you want to accomplish in life?"

"I want to be the biggest criminal lawyer in Los Angeles."

"That's it?"

"Well, I want to get married and have children. I doubt I'll have time for that until I'm further along in my career. Or until my biological clock ticks me into it."

"How many kids?"

"I don't know. One at a time. At least two, though. Only kids don't do so well in life."

"I'm an only kid."

She pulled back to look at me. "Oh. I didn't mean it like that."

I drew her back in, a little closer this time. "No big deal. Besides, it's only partially true. After Dad died, my mother took in a stream of foster children. She loved kids, and it helped pay the bills."

"How was it, with all those kids coming and going?"

"I hated it at first. You know, sharing Mom. Some of them were pretty seriously troubled. A six-year-old once set the living room curtains on fire."

The music stopped. Everyone on the dance floor applauded. Hannah started for the table. I grabbed her hand. Another song started. I pulled her back onto the dance floor. She resisted for a second, then started moving with the music.

Hannah said, "So what do you want out of life? I mean, besides being Houdini?"

"There'll never be another Houdini. He captured a unique time in history. Houdini became a metaphor for immigrants escaping the chains of poverty."

"We were talking about your goals."

"Right. I want to be big enough that they'll build me a theater in Vegas. That's the ultimate goal for magicians. I also want to get married and have kids."

"How many?"

"More than one."

She smiled. We were close enough that I could feel her breath against my chest. I pulled her against me. She's not pulling away. Can she feel my heart thumping? Can she feel the lower part of my body getting anxious to thump?

The song ended. Hannah got away before I could grab her. I hustled back to the table. Our twenty-dollar drinks were sitting there.

As I sat down, I said, "That wasn't so bad, was it?"

"I guess I'm not humiliated, if that's what you mean."

"You sure know how to make a guy feel appreciated."

She smirked at me.

I said, "C'mon. It was fun. Let's dance some more." I grabbed her hand.

She took her hand back. "I think that's enough."

"Something wrong?"

She looked at me. "We have a lot of work to do on your case. I think we need to keep things professional."

I grabbed the plastic straw in my drink and pinched it.

Hannah said, "You're facing serious charges. I need to be one hundred percent objective."

I turned up my hands in surrender. "Okay, okay. We'll postpone this discussion until my case is over." *Assuming I'm not doing twenty to life on a chain gang.*

She looked at her watch and grabbed her purse. "I didn't realize it was so late. Thanks for this. It was really fun." She reached into her wallet and pulled out two twenties. "That's for the drinks."

"I'll take care of it."

"I insist."

She pushed the bills into my palm and closed her hand around mine to keep them there.

"Hannah . . ."

She let go of my hand and hurried off.

CHAPTER FORTY-FOUR

Monday morning, I got to work before Hannah and started filing. When she walked in, she looked at me, then quickly looked away.

I said, "I'm pleased to be able to say something you've never heard before."

She glanced at me. "What's that?"

I gave a little bow. "Your filing is completely up-to-date."

"Really?" She looked around the office for her piles of paper. *You won't see any.* She looked back at me. "Well done. Thank you."

"You're welcome. By the way, I'm doing a magic show tonight, if you'd like to come."

"I . . . well, I'll see if I can make it."

I rubbed my palms together. "Now, what can I do until you create another tidal wave of documents?"

Hannah put her purse on her desk. "I've thought it over, and I've decided you can consider your legal fees fully paid."

"You mean . . . I'm finished working?"

"Yes. You can leave now, if you like."

Not that I've got anywhere to go . . . I cocked my head. "You're not kicking me out because I made you feel awkward at the jazz club, are you?"

She tightened her lips. "You sure know how to deflate someone who's making a nice gesture."

I did an exaggerated grimace. "Let me rephrase that. How incredibly generous. I can't thank you enough."

The phone rang. Hannah quickly grabbed it. "Oh. Hi, Chris." She put her hand over the phone. "It's the DNA lab," she whispered. "I paid them off."

I whispered, "Thank you" as I hurried over next to her.

Hannah sat down at her desk and jotted notes while she listened. I strained my ear to pick up the conversation but couldn't hear anything.

Hannah said, "Uh-huh." Scribble, scribble. "I see." Scribble. "Okay, well thanks." She hung up.

I said, "Well?"

"Have a seat."

"Oh shit."

She motioned for me to sit.

I grabbed a chair, pulled it close to her desk, and sat. "Hit me."

She took a deep breath, then let it out slowly. "The DNA sample at the crime scene matches your database DNA. We can't use it to create reasonable doubt."

I crossed my arms over my chest and let out a long breath. "So." I uncrossed my arms. Clenched my fists. "Where's this leave us?"

"Your DNA is at the crime scene. The apartment manager says you look familiar. Her father was in Seattle. The father of her child was in jail. Three people will testify that her boyfriend Kevin was working at the time of the murder. Your alibi at the Magic Castle is useless. How do you think it looks?"

My head throbbed. I rubbed my mouth with my fingertips. Is it hot in here?

I said, "It looks like I am royally fu—screwed." I jumped up and started pacing. "Goddammit! It's NOT my DNA! All these fucking experts are wrong. There is an explanation. We're just missing it."

Hannah let me keep pacing for quite a while before she said, "The DA offered a deal."

I sat down in the chair, hooked my feet around its legs, and grabbed the seat with my hands. "What kind of deal?"

"A plea bargain. You agree to serve time, they agree not to have a trial."

"I've seen enough TV to know what a plea bargain is. How much time?"

Hannah cleared her throat. "Fifteen years."

I jumped up. "Fifteen years!"

"With good behavior, you're out in eleven or twelve."

I rolled my eyes. "Oh, that makes me feel so much better." I got up and started pacing, clenching my teeth. It really is hot in here.

Hannah's eyes followed me. She said, "I'm sure it's negotiable. But for any kind of deal, you're looking at years in prison."

I kept pacing. "The alternative?"

"If we go to trial, you're facing an L-WOPP. That's Life without Possibility of Parole. We can probably argue it wasn't premeditated, so you wouldn't get life, but any way you slice it, it's a lot more years than what they're offering."

I ran my fingers through my hair.

I looked at Hannah. Her eyebrows were steepled sympathetically.

I said, "What do you think I should do?" I bit off a chunk of what little cuticle I had left.

She shook her head. "Only you can make that decision."

"Do you think I'm guilty?"

She glanced away, then looked at me. "What I think doesn't matter. It's the opinion of twelve people in a jury box that's important."

I stopped pacing and stood in front of her. "Spoken like a true lawyer. Now answer me. Do you think I did this?"

She held my gaze. "No. I don't."

"Thank you."

"Unfortunately, my opinion is totally irrelevant. The evidence against you is bad. You won't say 'I had sex with her but didn't kill her,' so there's no way to explain the DNA. Frankly, I don't even know what defense we'd use."

"Put me on the stand. I'll tell the truth. I didn't have sex with her. I never even knew her."

"Murder defendants never go on the stand. Besides, they'd be asking you questions like 'How did your semen end up in a woman you never met?' "

I went back to pacing.

Hannah spoke softly. "Why don't you take some time and think about it?"

I walked out of her office.

I strode to my car, jerked the door open, started to get in, then slammed it. Better not drive when I'm this upset. Better not spend the money on gas.

How can this be happening?

I walked hard down Magnolia, moving fast enough to turn people's heads. Fuck 'em.

I decided to jog around North Hollywood Park, a few acres of scrubby trees just up the road.

Why me? Why would some conspiracy pick me as the victim? I'm nobody.

Maybe that's why. Because I'm nobody and can't fight back.

Makes no sense.

I walked faster. My wet armpits squished with each stride. The air smelled like car exhaust.

How can I win this case? I can't explain the DNA. Even Hannah doesn't see a defense.

There has to be one. What?

I got to the park and jogged over the brittle grass, weaving around the sparse pine trees. My chest heaved. I could hear my breath wheezing in my ears.

If I'm really going down for this, am I better off taking a deal? At least there's certainty. No chance of an LWOPP.

Do time for a crime I didn't commit? Spend years in a place like that cell downtown? With its bleached urine smell? Someone crapping two feet from my face? Some big guy bending me over in the shower?

If I take the deal, I'll be over forty when I get out. My magic career? Dead. Chance of marriage and family? Zippo. Unless I meet one of those freaks who propose to convicted felons while they're doing time.

I came to a chain-link fence at the end of the park. They call this puny little space a park? I stuck my fingers through the fence wires, grabbed hold, and stared through it at a dry concrete creek bed. My labored breathing sawed through my lungs. I shook the fence as hard as I could rattling it in waves.

Shoulders slumped, I turned around and shambled off, with no idea where I was headed.

CHAPTER FORTY-FIVE

I spent the rest of the morning walking through the streets of North Hollywood, hoping for a brilliant insight.

None came.

By early afternoon, I went home to prepare for my magic show that night. Can't say I felt much like performing, but I needed every goddam penny.

I stuck Lisa on my shoulder and finished organizing the tricks for the bankers' convention. Is the bird keeping closer to my neck than usual?

Just as I was locking my magic trunk, the phone rang.

Hannah said, "How are you doing?"

"Peachy."

I heard her breathing.

She said, "I'm sorry."

"Yeah."

The bird pecked at my ear.

I said, "Are you going to make my magic show tonight?"

"Oh. Well, I . . . it turns out I have another commitment. I'm sorry. I would really have liked to."

Big surprise.

I drove to the Sportsmen's Lodge, a faux alpine chalet on the corner of Ventura Boulevard and Coldwater Canyon in Studio City. After pulling under the parking canopy in the rear, I got out with Lisa on my shoulder and unlocked the U-Haul. I rolled my first case along the sidewalk toward the building, then pushed it over a footbridge that arched over a small pond. A couple of black swans paddled through the water, looking very pissed off about being penned in. I'm gaining a whole new sympathy for you, boys.

Shake it off. Got a show to do.

When I got the second case inside, I put Lisa on her perch and started unloading the tricks.

Keep your mind on the show. These people are paying you. They deserve your best.

I shoulda brought one of my escape routines. Might be the last time I get to use it.

I unfolded my black velvet table and set up the coins for Miser's Dream. I put the Dice Box on the table, then arranged the cards for Joanne the Duck. I unpacked my silver urn for the signed twenty-dollar bill, then took out the red, white, and blue silks for my Mismade Flag. That's the trick where I blend the silks into an American flag but "accidentally" drop the blue one, so the flag comes out with just red and white. Then I put the blue silk in with the mismade flag, and produce . . .

My body jerked, as if I'd been stung by a bee. Lisa dug her claws into my shoulder to keep her balance.

Wait a minute. . . .

Blending.

Is it possible?

I thought about Mom grafting that shrub in the backyard. What did she say? The little branch becomes part of the root stock?

I've been thinking someone duplicated my DNA. What if . . .

Could that be how my DNA ended up at the crime scene?

Could it . . .

Long shot, but . . .

I know who can tell me.

I pulled out my cell phone and dialed Carly's apartment. Got her voice mail. "Carly. It's Harvey. Call as soon as you get this. It's urgent."

I left the same message on her cell, then shoved the phone into my pocket.

Did I piss her off so badly that she won't call back? If I have to, I'll call her every half hour. Forever.

This could be the explanation. It's so simple. The most brilliant magic secrets are often simple. Could this case be the same?

Carly will know.

I heard a thunk and my head shot up. Is Sergeant Morton coming to haul me off, like the last time I did a show?

I don't see anything. Probably something fell in the next room.

No. Morton won't show. The court's got a million bucks of some bail bondsman's money that says he can't touch me.

For now anyway.

I went on setting up the tricks. I took out my cell phone and made sure it was on vibrate and loud ring. I checked to see if I'd missed a call.

Why isn't she calling back?

In the foyer, I heard the muffled sound of bankers chatting it up.

I looked at my watch. Twenty minutes to showtime. C'mon Carly.

I finished setting up the tricks and looked at my cell phone again. No calls.

Ten minutes to go.

What the hell . . .

I called her again. Got voice mail. "This is really, really urgent. Please. Please. Call me. Right away."

Maybe she's getting stoned and humping Mr. New York.

They gotta come up for air sooner or later.

The doors to the dining room swung open. The sound of the conversations grew louder.

The bankers started trickling inside. I gave my phone one last look.

Shit.

I turned it off.

The show went incredibly well. Two standing ovations from people who sit all day. Afterward, I got a lot of compliments, even a few requests for my card. *Better book me quickly.*

As soon as the last banker was gone, I turned on my cell. One voice mail.

"Harvey, this is Carly. I got your—"

Yes!

I hung up on the voice mail and called her back.

I heard the phone clunk. "Hullo?" Her voice was heavy with sleep.

"Did I wake you?"

She yawned. "It's okay."

"It's only ten o'clock."

"I'm in New York."

"Oh. Sorry."

Her voice got a little steadier. "You said it was an emergency."

I cleared my throat. "You used to do genetic research, right?"

She yawned. "Uh-huh."

"I need to ask you a question about DNA."

"Okay."

"Well. Here's the thing. I was watching my mother graft a branch onto a shrub, and I started wondering—is it possible to change someone's DNA?"

"Not without a radical procedure."

My heart thunked. *It is possible!* "What kind of procedure?"

"Like a bone-marrow transplant."

"What's that?"

"You take bone marrow from a donor's hip and inject it into the patient. The patient takes on the DNA of the donor."

I said, "Would this be done for someone who had cancer?" Like me, when I was seven?

"Not most cancers. It's a very specialized procedure."

"Which cancers is it used for?"

I heard the rustling of sheets, like she was sitting up. "Is this about your case?"

"Yeah."

Her voice cleared. "Explain please."

I told her about my DNA being at the crime scene, and how I'd had cancer as a child.

She said, "What kind of cancer did you have?"

"Leukemia."

Her sheets swished. "Bingo."

CHAPTER FORTY-SIX

As soon as I hung up with Carly, I called Hannah on her cell.

No answer. Left an urgent message.

Not at home, either. Shit.

Is she out . . .? tumbling around with her Mercedes Prince?

I packed my tricks and hurried home. Just as I came through my apartment door with Lisa on my shoulder, the phone rang.

Hannah said, "This better be important."

"Someone else has my DNA." Lisa pecked at my ear.

"Statistically, those chances are about one in a billion."

"Unless you had leukemia as a child."

"What?"

I told her what Carly said.

Silence.

I said, "Hannah?"

Hannah cleared her throat. "Is that true?"

"Yes." Lisa shuddered on my shoulder. I said, "Carly works at the DNA lab. Isn't this all we need for 'reasonable doubt'? Can you get the charges dismissed?"

It sounded like Hannah was shifting the phone around. She said, "Not so fast. First, I have to legally verify this is scientific fact. Second, if it is, we need to know who the other person is."

"Why? As long as there's someone out there, isn't that enough to throw doubt on me?"

"Not really. The apartment manager connected you to the scene."

I fell onto my couch.

Hannah said, "Finding this person may be difficult. Medical records are private."

"Hey. I'm the guy that found Sherry's thumb drive."

"If you're thinking of breaking and entering a hospital, I would remind you that's a crime. You probably don't need another one on your record. Also, there's an excellent chance that stolen records won't be admissible in court. Most judges won't let you profit from an illegal act."

Got it. In other words, you don't need to hear how I get those records. "Leave that to me."

Hannah said, "What if this other person is living in Africa? Or dead?"

"He wasn't in Africa when the murder happened. And he definitely wasn't dead."

"How can you be so sure?"

"Simple." I rubbed Lisa's chest. "I didn't do it. That means he did."

CHAPTER FORTY-SEVEN

Next morning, I drove to my mother's house. When the foster kids opened the door, I smelled baking brownies. In a chorus, they said, "Show us a trick, Uncle Harvey."

"Okay, okay." I did the one where I take a regular-size deck and turn it into a tiny one. That was good for an *Ooooh.*

I went into the kitchen and sat down at the table.

Mom said, "You hungry?"

Why does walking into her kitchen always make me hungry? "Do I smell warm brownies?"

She took a pan out of the oven, used a sifter to sprinkle powdered sugar on top, then cut me a gigantic piece. Mom put it on a plate, slid it in front of me, and licked the chocolate residue off her fingers. She sat down with an *Umph.*

I took a bite of the brownie, then chewed until I was able to talk. "Where was I treated for leukemia?"

She drew back. "Why?"

"I've figured out what happened in the criminal case. When you have a bone-marrow transplant, you take on the DNA of the donor."

Mom's eyes widened. "The killer was that nice young man?"

I bolted upright, sending a spray of powdered sugar off the brownie. "You know who he is?"

"You met him, too."

I set down the brownie. "I did? When?"

"When you were eight years old. About a year after your treatment. The hospital has an event every year for all their donors and recipients."

"Why haven't we been going?"

Mom leaned back. "Because of what happened when we went to the first event, one year after your transplant. As soon as we turned into the hospital driveway, you recognized the place and thought you were going to get more shots. You screamed so loud that people in the parking lot held their ears. You grabbed the car door and wouldn't let go. When I finally got you to the picnic area, you were sobbing. Then you ran away. I found you behind some bushes, dragged you back, and finally located your donor. You hid behind me and wouldn't talk to him."

"Really? I don't remember any of that."

"Well, I do." Mom reached over, picked up my brownie, and took a bite. "That's why we never went back." Her words were mushy from chewing.

"Tell me about the donor."

She set the brownie on my plate and dusted powdered sugar off her hands. "He was probably in his late twenties. Brown hair, bluish eyes. He told me his sister died of leukemia back in the days before they had bone-marrow transplants. So he put himself in a marrow registry when he was twenty. We were very lucky to find a match for you. It's not so easy."

"You know his name?"

She shook her head. "Honey, it's been over twenty years."

"You don't have it written down anywhere?"

She looked pained.

I toyed with the edge of the brownie plate. "Do you know if the hospital's records are sealed?"

"I would think so. We signed all kinds of papers that said we had no right to know the donor's name."

I stood up. "What's the name of the hospital?"

"City of Hope."

I went home and stuck my lockpicks in my pocket. Good chance the files are in a locked room, probably in a locked file cabinet. If they even have twenty-year-old files at the hospital. They might be in some warehouse. Or destroyed.

I took the 210 freeway to the city of Duarte, where City of Hope is located, and turned into the hospital's long driveway. I went past rolling lawns dotted with beige stucco cottages, past enormous redwood trees whose branches swayed in the wind. On my right, behind a hedge, I saw a rose garden.

This place looks more like a college campus than a hospital. There must be a hundred acres here.

As I got near the parking lot, I felt myself gripping the wheel. I slowed the car, then stopped. Looked in my rearview mirror.

I rolled down the window. Sucked in a deep breath. Let it out slowly.

I don't consciously remember this place. Why do I want to run?

Forcing my foot against the gas pedal, I chugged up to about 10 miles per hour, then turned into the parking lot.

I don't see any spaces. Should I come back?

C'mon. This is silly.

I opened the glove compartment, pulled a tissue from the plastic packet, and patted my forehead.

There's a space.

I pulled into it, killed the engine, and climbed out. As I walked down the sidewalk alongside the driveway, I jangled my keys. In the distance, I saw a courtyard with a huge water fountain. Behind it was a sprawling two-story concrete building whose facade was feathered with trees. To my right, the multicolored blooms of the rose garden caught my eye. Among the roses was a tall iron gate gilded in gold, with cut metal lettering: *There Is No Profit in Curing the Body if in the Process We Destroy the Soul.*

As I got closer to the main building, I saw that the large marble fountain sprayed arcs of water below a modernistic bronze statue of a mother and father with their arms stretched over their heads, holding up a child. I walked to the edge of the fountain and stood there, listening to the shush of the water, feeling the droplets spray my face.

Get on with it.

I forced myself to walk inside the hospital, where a round woman at the front desk said, "May I help you?"

I cleared my throat. "Um . . . Hi."

She nodded. "Hello."

"I was a bone-marrow-transplant patient here many years ago."

The woman broke into a broad grin. "Well, welcome back."

"Uh . . . thanks. I was wondering—how can I get information on my marrow donor?"

"Since you're asking, I assume it wasn't a relative?"

"Yes. I mean, no, it wasn't."

She picked up the phone, dialed an extension, explained that I was looking for my donor, then hung up. She turned around and called out, "Helen, can you take this gentleman down to MUD?"

I said, "MUD?"

She chuckled. "Sorry. Our code around here. It means Matched Unrelated Donors."

Helen led me down the hall and into an elevator. We went to the basement, then walked along a stark white corridor to a set of gray double doors, which Helen opened for me. I stepped into a large area with blue-green walls and an array of cubicles with gray fabric walls. I heard a whir overhead and looked up at a metal track hanging a couple of feet from the ceiling. A metal box about the size of a briefcase was moving along the track.

Helen noticed me watching and said, "That's our system of moving patient records around the hospital. What's your last name, dear?"

The metal box disappeared through a hole in the wall. I looked at Helen. "Kendall."

A woman's voice said, "That'd be me." A tall lady with wavy black hair stood up behind her cubicle wall. "We divide the alphabet. I've got *I* through *P*." She motioned me over.

I walked over to the tall woman, who stuck out her hand. "I'm Jill Buccholz. Have a seat."

We shook hands. Her hand was a lot warmer than mine.

I sat next to Jill's desk and looked around the room. In the back, I saw a door with a high-security lock. Would that be the file room? Pretty high-tech lock. Not sure I can pick it.

Jill said, "Mr. Kendall?"

I looked back at her. Did she catch me casing the place?

"How can I help you, Mr. Kendall?"

I explained that I was looking for my donor.

She said, "If the donor signed a consent form saying you could know his or her identity, then it's easy. If not, I have to send a request to the hospital where the person donated. They'll try to contact the donor. If they can, and if the person's willing to meet, we can put you in touch."

"That sounds like it could take a long time." I pulled my chair a little closer, trying to look at her computer screen. It was turned so I couldn't see. Guess she's done this before.

Jill said, "If the hospital can't find the donor, or if the person's not willing to meet, the only thing I can tell you is the person's gender and age at the time of donation."

"It's a he."

"You were already told?"

"I met him when I was little."

She raised her eyebrows in an "Ah!" expression. "If you met him, I'm sure he signed a consent. This should be easy. Spell your name, please?"

Jill punched my name into the computer. "Here we go. Your donor was James Caldwell. Age twenty-eight at the time of donation."

Why does that name sound familiar? I said, "Do you have his contact information?"

"I have an address and phone from the date of his registration. That was thirty years ago."

"I'll take it."

She tapped the computer keys. A printer on her desk hummed, then chugged out a page. She handed it to me.

James Caldwell
10527 Lucerne Drive
Simi Valley, CA
805-555-8121

I stared at the page, furrowing my forehead.

Caldwell . . .

Why does that name sound familiar? It's not that common a name.

I slowly shook my head. Can't think of it.

Maybe I'm just getting desperate.

I said, "Thanks," folded the paper in half, and stood up.

As soon as I got outside, I opened my cell phone and dialed Caldwell's number.

A woman answered. *"¿Bueno?"*

"Is James Caldwell there?"

"¿Mande?"

"Caldwell. You speak English? *¿Inglés?"*

I got a barrage in Spanish.

I hung up and walked toward my car. The soles of my shoes scraped the concrete sidewalk.

Caldwell. I know that name. . . .

How?

I called Hannah. "Does the name James Caldwell sound familiar to you?"

"No. Should it?"

I twisted my mouth to the side. "Can you look him up on your computer?"

"What's this about?"

"I'll explain later. It's urgent."

"I'm in the middle of—"

"C'mon, Hannah."

Sounded like she was banging the keyboard hard.

"Got it."

I felt my pulse spike. "Excellent. Give me his info."

"He died in the Boston Massacre of 1770."

"Probably not the same guy." A little lady in a walker cut in front of me. "Give it another try."

"Will you please explain what's going on?"

I hurried around Grandma Walker. "Caldwell is . . ."

Of course!

I stopped suddenly, almost tripping the old lady, who said, "Watch it, sonny."

Hannah said, "Harvey?"

I suddenly remembered and broke into a wide grin.

That's how I know the name Caldwell.

It all fits.

Holy Shit.

CHAPTER FORTY-EIGHT

Hannah and I walked into the district attorney's cramped downtown office. The thin man, who had a crescent scar at the corner of his eye, was on the phone. He stood behind a desk piled with legal files, empty Styrofoam cups, and a ceramic coffee mug jammed with ballpoint pens. A worn brass nameplate on the desk said *Ken Warren.*

Warren was wearing a white shirt, buttoned tight to his neck. As he leaned over the desk and opened a file, his black tie swung like a pendulum. He said to the phone, "Tell him six years. Period. Otherwise, we start trial Monday."

A young woman rushed in and shoved a paper in front of him. He crooked the phone between his shoulder and ear, grabbed a pen from the mug, and slashed a few strokes at the bottom of a page. She took the paper and scurried off.

Warren said to the phone, "Fine. Done." He hung up and looked at me, squinting like he couldn't quite place me, then looked at Hannah. "What's up?"

"Can we sit?"

He glanced at the door. "Yeah, sure."

Hannah took the open chair. I moved some files off the other one and sat. Warren stood behind his desk.

She said, "This is Harvey Kendall."

He raised his eyebrows and opened his mouth in an *Ah,* like it all came back to him. "Right. Murder suspect."

Hannah said, "You have to dismiss his case."

His mouth formed a half smile. "And why would I do that?"

"The evidence is based on his DNA, correct?"

"I've got fourteen murder cases. I can't keep all the details in my head."

"Well, without this 'detail,' you've only got thirteen cases."

He looked at his watch. "Will you please get to the point?"

"Mr. Kendall had leukemia as a child. It turns out that the treatment for leukemia is a bone-marrow transplant, which changes your DNA. He and the donor have the same DNA."

Warren looked at her, then at me. "I've never heard of such a thing."

"It's true. Look it up on the Internet. I found several articles about it this morning."

"Thanks, but I'll ask one of my forensic scientists. Assuming it's true, how do I know this other person was even in the city?"

Hannah stood. "Because the bone-marrow donor was James Caldwell, the victim's apartment manager."

CHAPTER FORTY-NINE

Hannah said to the district attorney, "When the victim broke up with her boyfriend, Kevin, she said she was dating an older man. Kevin said, while they were having sex, someone came in and yelled, 'Slut.' There was no forced entry, so he had to have a key to her building and her apartment. The boyfriend said her dog barked, then shut up. The dog would have gone quiet because it knew the manager."

I said, "The manager left in a jealous rage, then came back the next night, had rough sex with her, and strangled her. You found his semen and thought it was mine because of the DNA."

Hannah said, "The City of Hope will verify that the manager was the marrow donor."

I said, "The apartment manager said I looked familiar. It's not because I knew Sherry. It's because we met when I was a child, a year after my transplant."

Hannah stood. "There's nothing other than DNA to connect my client to the crime. He never met the victim. Besides, if two people have the same DNA, there's more than reasonable doubt which one of them did it. You've got to dismiss."

Warren sat, then pushed on his temples with his fingertips. "I will, of course, have to verify all of this."

When we left the DA's office, I bounced down the hall. Couldn't help grinning. Hannah had a pretty big smile herself.

I said, "What happens next?"

"Warren has to go through his due diligence to verify our story. That'll take a few days, but essentially it's over."

I walked a little faster. "Will they take a DNA sample from the apartment manager?"

"Yes. But he probably won't go down for this."

I stopped. "Why not?"

Hannah turned to face me. "Because of you. There's no way to prove which one of you did it."

"Really?"

She nodded. "Really. There's no way for the prosecution to show guilt beyond a reasonable doubt."

I let out a sigh. "That's . . . shitty."

"Well, sometimes in life, things don't tie up in neat little packages."

We started walking slowly.

Shit.

This guy literally gets away with murder? Why do I feel guilty about that?

Guess there's nothing I can do.

I wrinkled my forehead.

On the other hand . . .

The apartment manager doesn't know any of this yet.

Maybe there's a whole other angle. . . .

CHAPTER FIFTY

I walked up to the security gate at Sherry Allen's apartment building and buzzed the manager.

Caldwell's voice came through the intercom. "Yes?"

I held down the metal pushpin with the tip of my index finger. "It's Harvey Kendall."

"Who?"

"Kendall. We met a few weeks ago, when I was asking about Sherry Allen." The metal pin felt like it was denting my finger.

I heard a clunk. The line went dead.

I buzzed again.

The manager said, "You got a lotta nerve coming around here."

I tried to sound pleasant. "Can I come in for a minute?"

He hung up.

I let go of the metal pin. My finger throbbed at the indentation point. I used my middle finger to buzz him again.

Then again.

Caldwell's voice came on. "Do I have to call the cops again?"

"You don't want to do that. I have something here that's important to you."

"What are you talking about?"

"I'll tell you in person. Give me five minutes."

After a moment of static, the speaker went dead.

The gate lock buzzed.

I quickly pulled the handle, then squatted down, took the wooden wedge from my back pocket, and placed it so the gate would stay open. I hustled up the sidewalk, yanked open the front door, propped it open the same way, and hurried into the dim hallway. The air smelled like mildew.

I blinked my eyes, trying to adjust to the low light. Down the hall, Caldwell stepped out of his apartment, leaned against the doorjamb, and studied me. As I got near him, he planted his feet shoulder-length apart and folded his arms over his chest, straining the buttons of his Hawaiian shirt.

He said, "What is this about?"

"We need to talk privately."

Not moving, he stared into me. "You got four more minutes."

"I think you'd prefer to do this privately."

Keeping his eyes on me, he backed into his apartment. I stepped inside and closed the door.

Caldwell said, "Three and a half minutes."

I reached into my pocket and took out a clear plastic package with a spoon that said *Burbank*. "Here. This is for your collection." I nodded toward the rack of city spoons on his living room wall.

He looked at the spoon, then up at me. "This your idea of a joke?"

I went into his living room and put the spoon on his coffee table. "It seemed right to bring you something, since I'm about to ask you for something."

"What do you want?"

"I figured out why you think I look familiar."

His mouth twisted into a smirk. "Me, too. You came around here to see Sherry; then you killed her."

"You know I didn't."

Caldwell's eyes narrowed. His left eye twithed. "You saying I'm a—"

"I look familiar because we met when I was seven years old, Mr. Caldwell. You were my bone-marrow donor."

Caldwell took a half step back. His eyes widened.

I said, "We met at City of Hope's annual donor picnic when I was a kid."

He stared hard at me.

I said, "See, when you gave me your bone marrow, you also gave me something else. Because of the transplant, we have identical DNA."

"That's ridiculous."

"It's a scientific fact. The cops found your semen in Sherry Allen and thought it was mine."

He shook his head. "I never slept with Sherry Allen."

"The police have e-mails saying she was involved with an older man. Right before she was killed, you found her in bed with her boyfriend, Kevin. Sherry's dog barked a couple of times, then stopped. That's because the dog knew you. You called Sherry a slut, stormed out, then came back the next night and strangled her."

Caldwell's chest rose and fell in deep breaths. His hands formed into fists.

I forced myself to hold my ground.

He suddenly leapt forward, grabbed me, and groped my chest and back. "You wearing a wire?"

"No, no. Search all you want. When you hear the rest of what I have to say, you'll know why I'm not wearing a wire."

He shoved me backward. I scrambled in awkward steps to keep from falling.

Caldwell said, "Face the wall. Hands up, feet apart."

I went to the wall and put my palms against it. He methodically patted me down.

Caldwell backed up and said, "Now strip."

I turned around. "What?"

"In case you're wearing some fancy new device. Strip."

"You just searched me."

He went into the kitchen, opened a drawer, and took out a shiny butcher knife that flashed as it caught the light. As Caldwell came toward me, it looked like a six-foot scimitar. "Strip."

"Okay, okay."

Keeping my eyes on the knife, I unbuttoned my shirt and took it off. Caldwell, still clutching the knife, held out his free hand and wriggled his fingers in a "Hand it over" gesture. I gave him the shirt.

As I took off my undershirt, he felt all through the shirt's fabric, then dropped it on the floor.

I said, "I told you I'm not wearing a wire." My bare skin bristled in the humming blast of the air-conditioning vent.

Caldwell took my undershirt, checked it, and threw it on the floor. "Keep going."

"Keep going?"

He held up the knife.

I undid my belt, let my pants drop, stepped out, and handed them over. He emptied the pockets, then felt all through the fabric. "Drop your shorts."

"C'mon . . ."

"Drop 'em and turn around in place."

Memories of stripping in the jailhouse flashed back. My hands shook as I hooked my thumbs in the elastic band of my undershorts, dropped them to my ankles, turned around in small steps, then pulled them back up.

Caldwell said, "All right. Now what's this about?"

"I want to get dressed first."

He looked at me, then nodded.

I picked up the pile of clothes and stepped back from him. I grabbed my undershirt from the tangle and pulled it quickly over my head so I could keep my eyes on him. I then picked up the shirt, stuck my arms through the sleeves, and started buttoning. Why is it so difficult to work a goddam shirt button?

Caldwell said, "Talk." He twisted the knife in his hand.

I let out a breath, still feeling humiliated from the strip search, and spoke as I kept buttoning the shirt. "I can get you out of all this."

Caldwell narrowed his eyes. "What's that mean?"

"When Sherry was killed, I wasn't in Los Angeles. I told that to the cops, but they didn't believe me, because of the DNA."

I grabbed my pants and stepped into them, missed one leg, and did a couple of jumps as I worked my foot through the pant leg. "When I found out that you and I have the same DNA, I was on my way to tell the cops. Since I can prove I wasn't in Los Angeles, that leaves you holding the bag."

He shifted his weight.

I zipped up my pants and fastened the belt buckle. "But I haven't gone to the cops yet. I had a better idea. See, I need some money. So I don't have to sell this magic trick that I've spent years developing."

"Huh?"

"I'm a professional magician. My career depends on having an original trick. Anyway, I thought to myself, maybe you and I can make a business deal."

He squinted at me.

I said, "If you play ball with me, I'd be willing to say I was in Los Angeles after all. Then, with both of us having DNA at the crime scene, they can't convict either of us."

Caldwell wrinkled his forehead. "That's what would happen?"

"Yeah. I checked it with a lawyer."

He slightly loosened his grip on the knife. Didn't he?

Caldwell furrowed his forehead. "So you're saying, if I give you money, you'll tell the cops you were here and neither of us gets convicted?"

"Exactly."

"How much money?"

"Twenty-five thousand dollars."

He staggered back a step, like he'd been shoved in the chest. "I don't have that kind of money."

"You can pay me over time. Say a few thousand now, then a thousand a month."

Caldwell shook his head. "This sounds like blackmail."

"That's because it is. Look, either way, I'm skating the murder charge. I can either leave you to the wolves or give you a pass. Your choice."

He stared at me. "I can think of something else. Maybe you came here and threatened me, trying to get me to cover up your murder. When I refused, you attacked me and I slit your throat in self-defense."

My heart thudded in my neck. I swallowed.

I said, "I suppose you could try that. And since you're better at these things than I am, you might kill me. But then you've got two murders on your hands. This one will be right in your apartment, 'cause I'm not going out to some remote location with you. Think about it, Mr. Caldwell. Killing me doesn't exactly make you look like a pacifist, now does it? Besides, why would you want to take that kind of chance? I'm offering you a risk-free Get Out of Jail card."

Caldwell started pacing.

The air conditioner hummed.

Still pacing, he said, "How . . . how would I know you'd keep your word?"

"Once I tell the cops I was in town, I can't go back on it. I'm more worried about you keeping yours. I'm thinking I want something in writing."

He stopped pacing. "NO. Nothing in writing."

I shrugged. "Then I need more money up front."

"I haven't got it."

"Borrow it."

He dropped the knife on the coffee table with a clunk, then fell back on his couch, as if he was out of breath. "I need to think about all this."

"Twenty-four hours. Then I'm getting my ass outta this mess. Come along or don't. Up to you."

I started for the door.

Caldwell said, "How much would you need up front?"

I turned around. "How much you got?"

"Maybe five grand."

"Borrow another five. Ten now, a thousand a month, and we got a deal."

Caldwell pulled himself up to a standing position. His face looked weary. "Maybe I could do seventy-five hundred now, then a grand a month."

I smiled. "All right. Done." I stuck out my hand.

He didn't take it.

I softened my voice. "You know, I'm not just doing this for the money. I wouldn't feel very good about letting a killer stay on the streets if I didn't think you were a decent guy who just got provoked."

He narrowed his eyes in a "What are you up to?" look. "You don't know anything about me."

Oh shit. Did I go too far?

I said, "I do know something about you. You donated bone marrow. That's a painful thing to do, especially for a total stranger."

He kept staring at me.

I said, "My mom told me it was because of your sister. She had leukemia, too, huh?"

His eyes teared. "Yeah. Poor little Angie. I felt so . . . hopeless. It was before they had bone-marrow transplants. Leukemia was a death sentence." As he looked away, his eyes reflected the light.

"I do know you. You've got a good heart."

He quickly wiped at one eye with his index finger.

I said, "On top of that, I met that kid Kevin. The one you caught her with. Hard to believe she'd fall for someone like that." I gave him a sympathetic look.

He turned his head back toward me.

I said, "I've certainly had times in my life that I wanted to strangle people, and just like you, I'm no killer. I can't imagine how you felt, walking in on the two of them."

He let out a sigh. "I didn't mean to k—" He looked up at me. "You're right. I've never done anything like that before. And never will again."

I nodded. "I appreciate your saying that. It makes me feel a lot better about all this."

"That'd make you the only one." His face was hardening again.

I walked to the door of his apartment and opened it, to reveal Morton, Dupont, and Hannah standing in the hall.

Morton, wearing a white plastic earpiece with a twisted wire that led into his shirt pocket, stepped inside. "Mr. Caldwell, you are under arrest for the murder of Sherry Allen. You have the right to remain silent—"

Caldwell's eyes shot to me. "What is this?"

Morton said, "We got a recording of your admission, Mr. Caldwell." He tapped the listening device in his ear.

Caldwell's eyes burned into me. "There was no wire. I . . . I checked you."

I went over to his coffee table, grabbed the packaged *Burbank* spoon, and held it up. "The basis of all good magic. Misdirection."

"You son of a bitch!" He started at me.

Morton grabbed him. Dupont came around behind and snapped handcuffs onto his wrists.

Morton finished reading Caldwell his rights.

Outside the building, I watched Morton put his hand on Caldwell's head as he guided him into the backseat of the police car. Morton shut the door with a metallic slam.

As soon as they drove off, Hannah and I walked down the street.

She said, "Good job in there."

"Thanks. I wasn't sure he'd buy the 'out of L.A.' bit. I guess he was desperate enough."

"You made him desperate enough. And you handled his death threat really well. I thought we'd have to crash in before you got the admission."

I felt my face flush. "Um, thanks."

A few steps later, I clapped my hands, startling her. "This deserves a celebration. I know another jazz club—"

She shook her head. "I don't think so. I—"

I hurried ahead, making a gesture for her to follow. "C'mon. Do something for fun besides a Mensa puzzle."

Hannah stepped in front of me, forcing me to stop. She said, "If you had shut up, you'd have heard me say, 'I don't want to go to a jazz club. I'd rather take one of your other suggestions.'"

She grabbed the handle of her car door and said, "Let's go ride the bumper cars at the Santa Monica pier."

AUTHOR'S NOTE

If you're standing in a bookstore, don't read this, because it will spoil the book. You should, however, buy the book, then read this at the end.

I come by magic legitimately. It's been my serious hobby (on and off) since I was six years old and watched Mark Wilson's magic show on local TV in Dallas, Texas. When I was little, my mother would leave me at Douglas Magicland, the local store, for hours at a time. I would talk to the staff and dream about tricks I couldn't afford. I was always appreciative that Mom let me hang out there for so much time. It didn't occur to me until years later that she was using the store as a free babysitter.

When I got older, I became a magician member of the very real Magic Castle that's described in the book. That meant I had to pass a performance test, which made me incredibly nervous.

Incidentally, all the tricks that Harvey does are real.

It is scientifically accurate that a bone-marrow transplant changes the recipient's DNA. If you don't believe me, look it up on the Internet. However, it only changes the DNA of the recipient's bloodstream. That's why Harvey's blood sample in the DNA database matched the donor's semen. Had they taken a cheek swab from Harvey, his DNA wouldn't have matched Caldwell's. That would have gotten Harvey off the hook, but it wouldn't have convicted Caldwell—he would have claimed that he'd had sex with Sherry but hadn't killed her. Thus, Harvey's getting him to confess was crucial to hanging Caldwell (though Mrs. Caldwell might have administered her own form of justice after learning about the other woman).

The City of Hope is a wonderful hospital, with one of the most successful bone-marrow-transplant programs in the world, and I'm grateful for the hospital's assistance. Its motto, which sums up the spirit of its environment, is quoted on the iron gate described in the text: There Is No Profit in Curing the Body if in the Process We Destroy the Soul.

Overeaters Anonymous is a real organization, and you can find information about it on the Internet. It consists of people who, without profit motive (it charges no dues or fees), help each other with food issues, whether the issue is overeating, anorexia, or bulimia. I'm thankful for the help of several OA members who, according to the traditions of the program, must remain anonymous. Their stories are truly inspiring, including that of a woman who lost over two hundred and fifty pounds and kept it off for more than thirty years.

By the way, the answer to the caterpillar problem on page 148 is, in fact, an average speed of four and a half. Assume the caterpillar goes nine inches in each direction. It takes one hour to get there but three hours to get back (it can only go three inches per hour on the return trip). So it traveled eighteen inches in four hours. Eighteen divided by four equals four and a half.

I first want to thank Barry Krost and Steve Troha for believing in Harvey, and Brendan Deneen for his incredible support and vision. I'm also grateful to the following folk who generously shared their expertise: Captain Ray Peavey (retired) of the Los Angeles Sheriff's Department for his help with homicide-investigation procedures; Blair Berk and Richard Hirsch for their help with criminal law issues; Dean Gialamas, Director, Orange County Sheriff, Coroner Forensic Services, and Bruce Houlihan, for their help with DNA tests and practices; Dr. Ed Ritvo for his help with autism and life in general; Dr. Eva Pressler for her help with pediatric medical issues; Dr. Steve Forman, Jill Kendall (no relation to Harvey), Sharon White, and Britta Buccholz of the City of Hope for their help with the bone-marrow-transplant program; Jack Palladino for his private detecting skills; and Brad Meltzer for his advice and support.

I especially want to thank Sol Stein, my writing coach and friend.

And most of all thanks to my wife Shana, my love and my soul mate, and our growing family: Danny, David, Rona, Josh, Lindsey, Jordan, Benjamin, Talia, Ollie, Tobey & Tina.

2/2014